Advance Praise

Until It's Over is a study in force and discovery that cultivates riveting moments, blending personal interaction, political struggle, and investigative processes to create a perfect storm of unexpected controversies with satisfying plot twists.

— D. Donovan, *Midwest Book Review*

Seeped in history and Native American tradition, Dorothy Van Soest's new novel, *Until It's Over*, draws the reader into a decades-old case involving a Senate candidate whose popular facade masks a sordid past. In a compelling, twisty, and often emotionally wrenching story, journalist J.B. Harrell and his friend Sylvia Jensen uncover what really happened all those years ago--and also come to terms with their own pasts. Definitely worth reading!

— Deborah Kalb, writer, editor, podcaster, book blogger, and author of *Everything She Most Admired, Off to Join the Circus*

Dorothy Van Soest's enthralling new addition to the Sylvia Jensen mysteries, *Until It's Over*, is a must-read. When a decades-old crime resurfaces, activist Sylvia Jensen and investigative reporter J.B. Harrell are thrust into a battle where troubling memories, buried secrets, and social injustice collide. This powerful novel of resilience and justice shows how confronting the past can open the way to healing and to change. *Until It's Over* is a mystery that is both plausible and haunting. You won't want to miss this one.

— Terry Korth Fischer, author of The *Rory Naysmith* Mysteries.

No one combines mystery fiction with social justice issues like Dorothy Van Soest. In *Until It's Over*, she wraps up the Sylvia Jensen/J.B. Harrell mysteries in grand style as they reach far back into the very heart of collective and personal trauma to uncover the unsavory past of a would-be U.S. senator. I was rivetted from beginning to end! Brava!

— Carol Mossman, PhD, author of *Writing with a Vengeance*

The powerful message of *Until It's Over* is both timely and timeless. Dorothy Van Soest brings warmth, intelligence, and deep compassion to protagonists who struggle, stumble, and ultimately find the strength to accomplish together what no one could do alone. The book>s themes of justice, resilience, and our fragile, essential human bonds resonate long after the last page is turned.

— Amanda Barusch, author of *Aging Angry: Making Peace with Rage.*

. . . a gripping and important tale about the enduring impact of both historical trauma and early trauma exposure and the remarkable resilience of the human spirit. This story is a powerful reminder that while the past shapes us, we have the agency to transform our pain into meaningful action that can lead to social justice.

— Angelique Day, PhD, MSW, Professor, School of Social work, University of Washington, and former senior policy adviser, Administration for Children, Youth and Families, U.S. Department of Health and Human Services

Until It's Over is a powerful testament to the enduring courage of those who find the right moment to confront injustice, regardless of the years that have passed, and holds sacred space until everyone finds their moment. This pivotal novel is a triumph—blending gripping suspense with a resounding call for justice—and a must-read for anyone who believes that nothing is truly over until the truth prevails.

— Noél Busch-Armendariz, PhD, Director of The University of Texas at Austin School of Social Work Institute on Domestic Violence & Sexual Assault (IDVSA) and author of *Human Trafficking: Applying Research, Theory, and Case Studies for Social Work and the Helping Professions (2nd edition)*

Until It's Over is Dorothy van Soest's latest installment in the Sylvia Jenson mysteries. From the first pages of Sylvia and J. B. Harrell's familiar bickering, to the exquisitely elegant, pitch perfect conclusion, this is the work of an author at the top of her craft! Wisely plan your time as to when you will begin reading it, because you will not want to put it down.

— Mary Swigonski, author of *Letters from Eleanor Roosevelt*, and blog, *JustAlchemy*.

When Sylvia Jensen refuses to be silenced by a politician with dark secrets, her investigation takes her deep into the past, to the secret springs of guilt, regret, fear and trauma. This exciting tale, full of compassion and psychological insight, gives voice to the victims of injustice.

— B. Morrison, author of the memoir *Innocent: Confessions of a Welfare Mother* and two poetry collections, *Terrarium* and *Here at Least*.

I always look forward to Dorothy Van Soest's next Sylvia Jensen mystery. Sylvia, a retired social worker, and J.B. Harrell, a journalist with a childhood tied to Sylvia, make an exceptional team. In her latest novel, *Until It's Over*, Van Soest reminds us that trauma experienced in our childhoods may remain dormant until ignited back into our present consciousness. This story rekindles the lessons of the "*personal is political*" and demonstrates how the collective voices of women can pursue justice and become a catalyst for resiliency.

— Fran Danis, author of *Origin Stories from the Movements to End Domestic Violence*

This engaging novel, *Until It's Over*, walks us through the way a community heals itself, individually and collectively, by calling out a sexual perpetrator. By fleshing out several characters, it beautifully deals how, despite trauma, dissociation and the effects of narcissism, people are able to survive and thrive.

— Robin Shapiro, LICSW, author of *EMDR Solutions, Easy Ego State Interventions, Doing Psychotherapy,* and *Trauma Treatment Protocols*

ALSO BY DOROTHY VAN SOEST

FICTION

Just Mercy

At the Center

Death, Unchartered

Nuclear Option

NON-FICTION

Social Work Practice for Social Justice: From Cultural Competence to Anti-Oppression (2nd edition)

Diversity Education for Social Justice: Mastering Teaching Skills

Social Work Practice for Social Justice: Cultural Competence in Action (1st edition)

The Global Crisis of Violence: Common Problems, Universal Causes,Shared Solutions

Challenges of Violence Worldwide: An Educational Resource

Challenges of Violence Worldwide: Curriculum Module

Incorporating Peace and Social Justice into the Social Work Curriculum

Empowerment of People for Peace

Until It’s Over

Until It's Over

A Novel

Dorothy Van Soest

First Edition

Library of Congress Control Number: 2025948863

Casebound ISBN: 978-1-62720-677-8
Paperback ISBN: 978-1-62720-678-5
Ebook ISBN: 978-1-62720-679-2

Printed in the United States of America

Internal Design by Chsrlie Quick
Cover design by Kai Conrath
Editorial Development by Samantha Vitale
Promotional Development by Grace Gilrane

Apprentice House Press
Loyola University Maryland
4501 N. Charles Street
Baltimore, MD 21210
410.617.5265
www.ApprenticeHouse.com
info@ApprenticeHouse.com

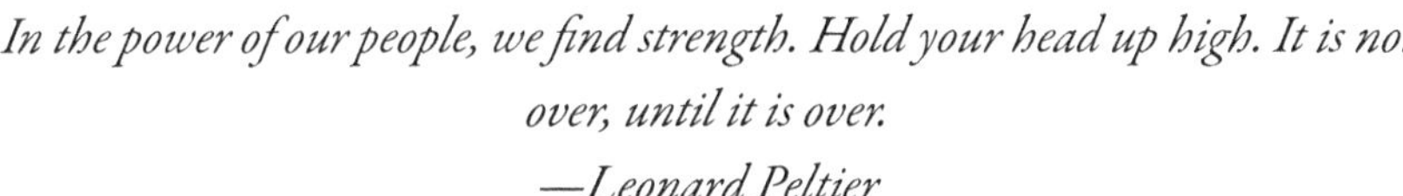

In the power of our people, we find strength. Hold your head up high. It is not over, until it is over.
—Leonard Peltier

Part One

When the Past Is Not the Past

Chapter One

"Well?" Sylvia Jensen squeezed J. B.'s arm as she shouted up at him over the din, her eyes flashing excitement.

"Well, what?" He gave her a blank look, as if he didn't already know what she was asking.

"You *are* covering this, aren't you?" It was clearly an order, not a request.

J. B., always amused by her bossiness, reached into the pocket of his suit jacket to pull out the little notepad and pen he always carried with him. Sylvia mistook the gesture for the answer she wanted and released her grip on his arm, turned her attention back to the action in the rotunda. Truth be told, J. B. Harrell the journalist had not decided whether to write an article about today's action or not, but out of habit, he had already crafted an opening paragraph in his head.

> *Even surrounded by etched marble that seems to fix their feet to the floor, thousands of crystal pieces that dangle from a chandelier over their heads, and a blinding white light that beams at them from every direction, the almost two hundred people gathered the morning of June 14 in the state capitol rotunda seemed not the least bit intimidated by such blatant displays of bureaucratic power. Their relentless drumming and reverberating chants bounced off every angle of the chamber with the force of a hurricane, their shouted demands reinforced by as many homemade signs as there were protesters:*
>
> *Keep it in the ground! No uranium mining!*

Protect sovereign land!
Clean up, not start up!
Radioactive Pollution Kills!
Drop the Charges!

The turnout was impressive, especially considering the demonstration had been hastily planned just the day before, right after word got around that Peter Minter had been arrested for trespassing at the corporate headquarters of the Midwest Mining Company. News traveled fast in Indian country and then was strategically passed on to Monrow City's many allied organizations, so the crowd was a nice mix of urban Indians and allies of all ages. As soon as Sylvia had got wind of the plans, she'd decided, without a moment's hesitation, that she would go. And when she called J. B. with the news, his response was immediate as well. "I'll take the red-eye out of LaGuardia tonight and pick you up in a taxi on my way to the capitol."

Both J. B. and Sylvia had the utmost respect for Peter Minter, having worked with him years ago, albeit in different ways and for differing lengths of time. That they would be there to support him was never a question. They looked forward to seeing each other as well. It had been way too long, over a year, since J. B. had been back in Monrow City, and because of the pandemic, it had been a couple of years before that.

The morning of the demonstration, as J. B. watched Sylvia make her way from her apartment building to the taxi, it had tugged at his heartstrings to see her walking so slowly, with a slight limp and using a cane. She was wearing the same clothes she had always worn to demonstrations, her decades-old stained and worn peasant blouse and ankle-length faded denim skirt, only now it looked like they were swallowing her up, a visual reminder that she was in her eighties now. She had declared, on her eightieth birthday, that from now on she was going to leave protesting to the young. And yet, here she was.

She slid into the back seat of the cab next to J. B., and they hugged each other with an ease and closeness that would have been impossible for either of them to predict—or even imagine—when he was seven-year-old Jamie Buckley and she was Mrs. Waters, the thirty-year-old social worker who had turned his life upside down forever. All in the past now, so much to be forgiven or forgotten or that was no longer important, so much that was too mind-boggling to even think about.

"You are the only person I know who wears a suit to a protest!"

J. B. heard and received her words with chuckled relief. No hello niceties, no beating around the bush, same old Sylvia.

"Not just *any* suit." He proudly patted the elastic-waisted drawstring trousers of his lightweight gray suit. "It's airy, it breathes, it's perfect for warm weather."

"Looks all *wrinkled* up to me . . . like some fool slept in it on a plane all night." She winked at him, clearly having the time of her life and wanting him to continue their banter.

"It's seersucker. It's *supposed* to be wrinkled." J. B. flashed his suit jacket open to expose the crewneck T-shirt underneath. She clapped her hands with glee and erupted into full-throated laughter.

When they walked into the state capitol rotunda, Sylvia was bombarded by people happy to see her, hugging her as if it might be their last chance, shouting hello to her over the echoing din in the chamber. In between greeting people, she chanted along with the crowd, stomping her feet and clapping her hands, clearly in her element, her creased cheeks rosy, her voice shaky but just as determined as in the old days. J. B. looked around, hoping to see some of the folks he'd interviewed for a feature article that was published last year in the *New York Times Magazine* about the high rates of cancer, birth defects, and spontaneous abortions resulting from uranium mining on or near Indian homelands.

About fifteen minutes after they arrived, the drumming stopped, and soon after that, the chanting as well. A small, wizened man with an Ojibwe rabbit-skin blanket protecting his shoulders from the cold AC shuffled to the center of the rotunda. A stocky man dressed in a casual light green shirt open at the neck cupped the Indigenous elder's elbow with one hand; with the other he held a megaphone. Peter Minter pushed his oversized black glasses up on his nose and lifted his white shoulder-length hair from under the edge of the blanket. "Oh my, how Peter has aged," Sylvia whispered, to which J. B. nodded his agreement while wisely refraining from sharing his observation that Peter seemed to have shrunk even more than she had.

The crowd welcomed Peter with cheers and whistles that shook the chamber to its core and continued for a very long time, quieting only when he raised his hands and then motioned for silence with a downward wave of his palms. With the other man holding the megaphone in front of him, Peter thanked them all for coming.

"Poor man is exhausted," Sylvia whispered to J. B. with a shake of her head. "He must have spent the night in jail."

"Dear friends," Peter said. "I have asked a friend to speak for me. Please welcome Tony, who will soon be our new U.S. senator."

With an exaggerated, almost theatrical movement, the man called Tony, in a pale blue shirt with a red tie, helped Peter sit down on a chair that had been placed behind him. Then he stepped forward with his legs in a wide stance like a wrestler and reached for the megaphone, bringing it up to his lips. He didn't say anything for a few seconds while he rotated his muscular body one smooth turn at a time, establishing eye contact with each person in the rotunda. J. B., who recognized him from photographs but had never seen him in person, was impressed at how athletic he looked for a man in his eighties, with a sureness and comfort in his demeanor that matched his youthful crew cut.

"Hello, everyone. I am grateful, as we all are, to Peter for his lifelong commitment and activism, and I am honored to be here with him today. My name is Anthony Jordane, but my friends call me Tony."

An audible gasp escaped Sylvia's lips, and she raised her hands in the air as if in a revival meeting. "Oh my God! What the hell is *he* doing here?"

A few folks shot questioning looks in her direction, but Anthony Jordane focused everyone's attention back to him by speaking louder into the megaphone.

"I grew up in this state and, as some of you know, have been successful in business." He paused and once again turned his body, slowly looking into each skeptical face, of which there were more than a few. Then he stopped, took a step back, and placed his hand on Peter Minter's shoulder. "My friend here knows my heart. He knows I am his humble servant."

Sylvia grasped at J. B.'s arm, tugged on his jacket sleeve, and hissed in his ear. "The *hell* he is."

Confused by such a snide remark, J. B. whispered back. "But Sylvia,

Peter invited Jordane to speak, and I wrote some positive things about him, too, not that long ago."

"Peter, we are here to honor you." Anthony Jordane stood back on his heels and smiled as the crowd chanted *Peter! Peter! Peter!*

"When Peter disrupted the Midwest Mining Company's board meeting yesterday," he continued, "he acted for all of us. He spoke truth to power about how Indian land in our state is radioactive. It is still not cleaned up after decades of open-pit mining. The health and lives of people near those mines have been and continue to be sacrificed." He cocked his head, nodding his approval when he heard a bubble of hisses and boos from the crowd. "That's right, folks. And now people are talking about using nuclear power to supposedly save our environment, which is why Peter is demanding, in a voice louder than ever, that the mines on our land be cleaned up and closed up. We all stand here with you today, Peter, to say that *never again* will we be exploited."

Anthony Jordane nodded and smiled at Peter while people chanted *Never again! Never again!*

"That's right, friends. *Never again!* I am honored to be here and to stand with you."

At that point, Peter Minter stood up and started clapping. Then Anthony Jordane held the megaphone close to Peter's lips and he said, "Thank you, miigwech, thank you." The crowd started clapping and chanting—*Thank you! Miigwech! Thank you! Miigwech!*—quieting only when Peter Minter sat down again.

"Thank *you*, dear friends. We are in this fight together. But enough talking. It's time to act." Anthony Jordane paused for effect and then, in a deep low voice and with his lips pressed against the megaphone, he said, "Now is the time to deliver the goods."

"NO! Liar! Bastard! No! NO! NO!"

J. B., like everyone else, had been so caught up in the enthusiasm and hope of the moment that he hadn't noticed Sylvia's growing agitation, hadn't heard her muttering angrily under her breath, not until he heard her shriek, saw her lunge toward Anthony Jordane with a wild look in her eyes, and then watched her collapse in a lifeless heap onto the hard marble floor.

Chapter Two

Sylvia was lucky. According to the admitting nurse at the Monrow City Hospital emergency room, the least busy time of day was six in the morning to noon. So when the ambulance arrived at eleven o'clock, Sylvia was the only patient, as all the night admissions having already been discharged or admitted to the hospital.

J. B. had persuaded the paramedics to let him ride along in the front seat of the ambulance, but it didn't work with the ER staff, which is why he found himself left to his own devices in an empty waiting room that reeked of chlorine and bleach cleaning products. After calling his wife, Mentayer, and promising to keep her updated, and fielding calls and texts from Sylvia's friends and neighbors who had somehow gotten ahold of his cell phone number, there was nothing left for him to do but wait.

He paced back and forth, from the vending machines at one end to the plastic chairs at the other, not so much remembering or re-living what had happened several hours earlier, but more like re-experiencing it, replaying the same movie reel in his head, as if in doing so he could somehow turn back the clock and do a retake of the scene. He could still feel the hard marble hit his knees as he dropped to the floor next to Sylvia, still feel the panic that blocked the airway in his throat as he held her thin, frail wrist and found no pulse, as he brought his ear to her nose and felt no breath. He could still hear the sounds, now blurred together—His own voice: *Sylvia, are you okay? Can you hear me?* Others shouting *Call 911* and *Make way, I know how to do CPR.* The rhythmic pushing of someone's hands on Sylvia's chest, the siren in the background getting louder, then *The ambulance is here. Make way, everyone step aside.* The beeping of a defibrillator.

Exhausted, he finally stopped pacing, made a quick stop at the hand sanitizer station, and then collapsed onto one of the plastic chairs, bending over with his head between his knees, arms dangling at his sides and palms pressed flat on the gray vinyl floor, holding on to that precious moment when he knew that Sylvia was alive, when he heard the EMT's radioed message *On our way with a female cardiac, stabilized*, the same wave of relief that had rushed over him then rushed over him again.

The automatic sliding glass door opened with a hum and J. B. sat up. He was so taken aback and pleased to see Peter Minter shuffling his way toward him that he drew him into a warm embrace, something he had never done before and that surprised each of them in equal measure.

"Is she?"

J. B. nodded and said, "As far as I know." Then he pointed to the row of plastic chairs. "They're hard and uncomfortable, but it's better than nothing."

Peter dropped onto a chair with a thud of visible relief. J. B. sat in the chair next to him, ran his fingers through his unkempt hair and then stroked the uncharacteristic stubble on his chin. He knew how disheveled he looked compared to Peter, whose thin white hair was pulled back into a neat ponytail that rested on the back of a crisp white shirt that matched creased white slacks. They sat side by side for a few seconds, each of them staring at the door to the ER, as if in silent agreement that, unless someone came through that door and told them otherwise, Sylvia was still alive.

"Have you seen her? Were you in there with her?"

J. B. shook his head. "Only family."

Peter placed his hand on J. B.'s shoulder, and said, "I'm sorry."

Over the years that Sylvia had worked with Peter, when he was the state's Indian Child Welfare Act liaison and she was a foster care supervisor, J. B. had heard many stories from her about Peter's uncanny ability to sense someone's emotions before they themselves felt them. This was the first time he had experienced it himself. "I should have told them she's like a mother to me," he muttered under his breath.

Peter sighed and mumbled, "Probably wouldn't have worked anyway," to which J. B. responded that then he wished he had told them that Sylvia *was* his mother.

"Her heart stopped." J. B. placed his hand on his own heart. "It just stopped."

Peter pushed his oversized glasses up on his nose. "I didn't know she had heart problems."

"She never said she did," J. B. said.

"Well." Peter paused and raised his eyebrows as if to say *Of course not.* Sylvia never mentioned *any* physical ailments to anyone.

"Yeah." J. B. sighed, his mind flashing back to those times Sylvia had put herself in harm's way and, without any complaint or even acknowledgment of pain, had been injured, once even hospitalized.

The ER door opened and a doctor in a white coat, with a stethoscope around his neck and a mask covering all but his eyes, walked in. J. B. jumped up from the plastic chair.

"Mr. Harrell?"

J. B., from force of habit even in the anxious state he was in, did a quick assessment of the doctor as he walked toward him. His posture was that of an accountant, precise and purposeful. He seemed too young to be a doctor, but his studious eyes made him look trustworthy.

"I'm Dr. James. Sorry you had to wait so long."

"How is she?"

"Ms. Jensen is still unconscious, but we were able to stabilize her, and she is resting comfortably."

"What happened? Was it a heart attack?"

"No. What Ms. Jensen experienced was a cardiac arrest. Her heart's electrical system malfunctioned, so her heart failed to pump effectively, and as a result she experienced a sudden loss of blood flow, which caused her to lose consciousness, stop breathing, and not have a palpable pulse. Sometimes heart attacks *cause* cardiac arrest, but that was not the case here. Ms. Jensen had no pre-existing heart problems that are the most common causes of cardiac arrest: no arrhythmia, no coronary heart disease, no enlargement of the heart. In fact, her heart looks good."

Fragments of the doctor's explanation spun around in J. B.'s head, gathering up new thoughts, creating more questions. As if anticipating one of them, Dr. James added, "If not treated within minutes, cardiac arrest is typically fatal. Quick use of CPR and a defibrillator saved Ms. Jensen's life. And without any fractured ribs. She was lucky."

J. B. closed his eyes and tried to process what he'd heard, which, in the end, came down to one thing. Sylvia could have died. She almost died. She still might.

"You're right," Dr. James said, as if reading his mind. "She's not completely out of the woods yet. Her recovery will depend on how much of a decrease in blood flow and oxygen there was to the brain. We'll transfer her to intensive care, where she'll be monitored closely, and run a few more tests."

When the doctor, with a quick nod, abruptly turned back toward the ER door, J. B. experienced a surge of anxiety that led him to spontaneously reach for the doctor's arm. "Wait! Please."

Dr. James turned around. "Yes?"

"You said her heart was good, and she didn't have any pre-existing heart conditions, so what could have caused her to have a cardiac arrest?" J. B. waited with breath held in, both expecting and fearing that the doctor's answer would confirm what he already suspected.

"All we know is that anything that causes severe stress on the body can lead to cardiac arrest," the doctor said. "Trauma, electrical shock, major blood loss, and the use of certain drugs, such as cocaine or amphetamines, all increase the risk."

"Sylvia doesn't do drugs. And she hasn't had anything to drink for over two decades."

"Right, that we know," Dr. James said. "Like I said, we'll run some more tests and keep you updated on her condition. The ICU is on the sixth floor. You'll find the waiting room there to be much more pleasant and comfortable."

With a sigh, J. B. walked back to the row of plastic chairs and sat down with his head in his hands. The doctor might not know what caused Sylvia to collapse, but he was afraid that he did.

"Something about Anthony Jordane triggered it." There, he'd said it out loud.

"She had a cardiac arrest because of Tony?" Peter's eyes were both apprehensive and filled with doubt.

"Look, she was just fine up until she recognized Jordane, and then she turned angry, made a snide remark, and then lost it completely, basically calling him a bastard and a liar in front of everyone before collapsing."

Peter flicked his fingers at J. B. "She must have mistaken Tony for someone else."

J. B. had already turned that possibility over in his head several times, hoping it was just a case of mistaken identity, but had finally conceded, based on how well he knew Sylvia, that it was not. "She knows Jordane," he said. "Either that or she knows something *about* him. Something so stressful, she wasn't able to handle it."

"What could be *that* upsetting about Tony? This doesn't make sense."

"I know," J. B. said. "Her negative reaction to Jordane is just the opposite of how you feel about him."

"Not just me," Peter added. "Our governor *must* have a very positive view of Tony, too, since she plans to endorse his candidacy. We'll need you there to cover the press conference when she announces that. Tony has assured me that he will work to protect our sovereign rights. But I don't need to tell you that; I mean, you practically endorsed him yourself."

J. B. nodded. It was true that he had written some positive things about Anthony Jordane in his recent article about uranium mining on Indian lands. Before Sylvia's outburst at the rally that morning, he'd planned to introduce himself to Jordane and shake his hand. But was there something about the man that he didn't know, but should?

Peter rubbed his chin and stared intently into space as if another answer to what caused Sylvia's cardiac arrest was floating in the air, and if he tried hard enough he would be able to grasp it. Finally, he turned to J. B. with an *aha* point of his finger.

"If something doesn't seem to make sense, that's usually because it doesn't." He paused, eyebrows raised. "But we both know Sylvia, right? And we both know that she's no fool, right? We know that whenever she's upset about something, there really is something to be upset about. Right? Am I right?"

"Truer words were never spoken," J. B. said, motioning with his hands for Peter to continue. If anyone could ease his mind by providing an alternative explanation about what had happened, it would be Peter. To Sylvia, Peter was the most levelheaded person she'd ever known, and over time, J. B. had learned to trust Peter's judgment and insights for himself.

"So, it seems clear, from Sylvia's behavior," Peter says, "that Tony's appearance at the rally stressed her out to the point that she had a cardiac arrest. About that, we must agree. But, the thing is, we don't know why, and there could be any number of explanations that we haven't even considered. What we do know is that, no matter what, we will still support Tony, because we need his help. It's all we've got."

Peter raised the palms of his hands, his gesture a declaration that if something about Anthony Jordane had caused Sylvia's heart to stop, he would not be the one to find out what it was. And, no matter what it was, he would be endorsing Tony as a candidate for the U.S. Senate. End of story.

So that left J. B. It was up to him. If anyone was to find the truth, it would have to be him. And didn't he owe that to Sylvia?

Chapter Three

1960

It's not even true. I'm in the back seat, mumbling under my breath.

What'd you say, sweetie?

Just talking to myself, Mom.

Oh, about what? Pinched voice. Drawn-out words. Gotta answer.

It's that sign, Mom. I jab my finger at the window. Welcome to Bigger, the Friendly City. Population 1,781.

What about it?

I don't know if she's curious or just glad I'm talking.

It's annoying, that's all, I say.

Bigger is a town, *not* a city. Not such a friendly place either. And that sign is ten years old so I know that number is wrong. But I swallow my opinion, and scrunch down in the seat. Don't care to be heard. Don't want to be seen either.

Mom sighs. She cranes her neck to get a better look back at the run-down houses that are in a little cluster on the outskirts of town.

You know, Harlan, I still say everybody has a God-given right to eat.

Come on, hon, you gotta admit my pa's got a point. That school cafeteria food belongs to the government. The principal and the cook don't own it. You can't have them secretly packing stuff up that isn't theirs and giving it away without even asking permission.

And you can't let perfectly good leftover food rot at the end of the week either, Harlan. Not when there's those in need of it. *That* would be the bigger sin.

Daddy laughs and pats her shoulder. What is Bigger's bigger sin? The bigger sin in Bigger is.

Mom pushes air through the gap in her two front teeth with a *fissst* sound. Daddy shuts up.

I study the houses, some more like shacks, unpainted, patched up with wood that doesn't match. Grandpa says the people who take the food every Friday night won't tell because what they're doing is illegal, and besides, that kind keep to themselves. I know what he means when he says *that kind* of people. He means dishonest. Greedy. Out of favor with God. In need of forgiveness. Lazy. He says the Bible tells us that laziness is a sin that can lead to poverty and distract people from their purpose. Whatever that is.

I bounce up and then land back down on the seat with a sharp jolt. We just crossed the railroad tracks. The train only passes twice a day, six days a week, coming in at five in the morning with all its cars empty and leaving fourteen hours later with all its cars filled with ore to be loaded onto ships fifty miles away. People living next to the tracks say they set their clocks by that train.

Daddy slows our car to a crawl. County Road 50 is now Main Street.

Fifty on fifty, ten on Main, and Bigger could be bigger! Daddy laughs like he's just said that for the first time instead of the hundredth and like it's the funniest joke in the world. Mom doesn't laugh. I don't either. But he doesn't notice.

This is the groovy end of Main Street. Anyway, that's what I think. People are jostling each other, walking from the House of Ale, Brewskies, and Afterhours on the north side to the Moose Lodge and Jordane's Beer Stop and Pizza on the south side. Grandpa says there's no need for *five* bars in a town this size, it's the devil's hand plain and simple. Well, it sure does seem that the devil knows how to show folks a good time. I wonder what it would be like to have that much fun, to laugh as hard as those people are laughing. I don't get why laughing is a sin, no matter what Grandpa says. Except when you laugh *at* other people. I don't know if that's a sin or not, but I do know it's not right and too many people in this town like to do that.

Now we're in the downtown business section. All two blocks of it. I look out the window and see three little wrens with their heads tucked into the eaves of the post office.

Wren Street. I like the sound of that. Daddy's teasing.

Now, Harlan, you know the city council is *never* going to change the name of Main Street to Wren Street. I can tell Mom is rolling her eyes.

I cross my arms. Why can't people just let those baby birds sleep in peace? They're not hurting anyone, poor things. Besides, they make that drab gray building more interesting. Don't people have anything better to argue about in this town?

The glass door to the post office is locked, and the wrens will soon be sound asleep on the roof. The neon sign is off in the window of Jensen's Hardware—Grandpa's store until he got cancer last year and turned it over to Daddy. It's Saturday night, so the downtown business section is empty. It feels lonely. Like an abandoned ghost town. The only lights on are inside the Piggly Wiggly. Daddy sees them and snorts.

I heard Speedy hired that floozy to stock shelves on the weekend. Looks like she's got that bastard kid of hers working tonight, too. Good. Keep him out of trouble.

Mom sighs. I mutter behind Daddy's head.

The kid's name is William James. Will for short.

What did you say, sweetie?

I said Will is probably the smartest kid in school, that's all.

Daddy snorts again.

Oh? Mom turns and looks at me in the back seat.

Yeah, we're in the same Advanced Chemistry class. That's how I know.

Isn't that nice?

Mom looks interested, like maybe she wants to hear more. I could say that Mr. Minor always asks Will the questions that no one else can answer, but I don't because Daddy's here, and like a lot of people in this town, he's going to think what he wants to think no matter what I say just because of where Will lives and what he looks like. I for sure would never tell my parents that I heard Will was going to ask me to the prom this year. Even if he had, I would have had to say no because Grandpa says dancing is a sin and so is mixing the races, which is only one of the reasons why Daddy wouldn't have let me go. And besides, I don't know how to dance.

At Fifth Avenue, Daddy turns right at St. Mary's church. The stained glass rose petals that radiate from the middle of the round window over the carved wooden doors make me feel warm and tingly inside.

He's wrong, I mutter under my breath.

Who's wrong, sweetie?

No one, Mom.

She doesn't know I told our preacher to his face that he was wrong, that my Catholic friend Becca was not going to hell, and furthermore that my Jewish friends, if I had any, weren't going to hell either. Reverend Cramer doesn't talk to me now, which is just fine, as long as he doesn't tell my parents what I said. I wish I could go to the Community Congregational Church across the street from St. Mary's. It has the most colorful stained glass windows, and besides, most of my friends go there. Daddy speeds the car up, passes those two churches like they don't exist, or he wishes they didn't.

I close my eyes when Daddy slows the car to a crawl because I know he's driving past Praise the Lord Free Church now. Our church. Except for a wooden cross on the roof that is painted white, and it being tucked farther back from the street, it looks just like all the other prefab white houses in town, right down to the American flag attached to the front. A church should look like a church. Ours doesn't. It's just another house like all the other houses that were built in that factory outside of town.

We live behind it, just across the alley on the next street. Daddy pulls our blue 1950 Nash Rambler into our driveway. Grandpa's standing in the picture window of the house next door, with his shock of white hair and his rail-thin shoulders. He's staring out at us with those penetrating steel-blue eyes of his. His bony hand goes up, real slow, palm open, then drops back down. Like a judge. That's what Grandpa does. He judges. Grandma's just the opposite. She's standing on the porch with her pudgy arms open and a smile so wide it makes her cheeks look like pink tennis balls.

Daddy gets out of the car and heads next door, says he wants to talk to his parents for a few minutes. Mom and I walk across our freshly and perfectly mowed lawn to the back door of our house. I wait until we're in the kitchen before I ask.

Can I go to Becca's for a sleepover, Mom?

You know it's Saturday night, sweetie.

Just this once?

Ask your father.

She always says that. Always with that sad look on her face, too.

I'll get up early in the morning for Sunday school and church, Mom. I promise.

I cross my fingers. Please, please, please say yes. Becca has never invited me to a sleepover alone, never without a bunch of her other friends, and she has a lot of friends, more than anyone else in school.

I have to go, Mom. I just *have* to.

Well, I guess it will be all right.

I quick run to my bedroom. I already packed my round navy-blue overnight bag, the one with a white stripe on the side that I got for Christmas last year but have never used.

Thanks, Mom.

I rush out the front door so Daddy can't see me and practically fly the whole seven blocks to Becca's house. All the street and porch lights are on, but I could find my way blind. I land on Becca's back porch with a thump. The door swings open. There's her big brother, red hair and all, grinning like a Cheshire cat. I step back and stumble, almost falling down the stairs. He laughs and yanks on my ponytail. Ouch! Why'd he do that? I see stars. Becca grabs my arm and pulls me into the kitchen, pushes her brother out of the way.

It's about time you got here, girl. Why do you tease Sylvie like that, Ray? Maybe cuz you like her, huh? Huh?

Her brother's beefy hand flies up and Becca ducks, just in time, so all he swats is the air a foot over her head. She laughs but I don't. My head hurts.

Nice try, big brother.

Becca winks at me. She reaches up and drapes her arm around Ray's shoulder.

So, big brother dear, you gonna give Sylvie and me a ride or not? If you don't want to, that's okay. I'll take your car.

You? *My* car? When hell freezes over, little sister.

Come on, Ray. You wouldn't have missed *your* senior kegger for anything. And we're not going to miss *ours* either!

I open my mouth, but my throat is so dry I can't talk, only cough. Becca pats my hand and glares at her brother.

Don't worry, Sylvie, we'll get there. We *have* to.

Where's everyone else, Becca? Are they already at the kegger or what? What's the plan? I didn't know . . .

Now don't you dare be telling me, Sylvie, that you don't want to go now.

She flashes her eyes at me in a way that makes me turn away. I stare at the kitchen floor, linoleum just like ours, same confusing pattern of squares and rectangles in different sizes and shades of brownish-tannish-orangish colors. Ray brushes up against my arm. I ignore him.

Don't flip your wigs, girls. I'll drive you. I'm just rattling your cages.

Becca shrieks and throws her arms around her brother's neck.

Let's go then. We're already late!

She grabs my hand and drags me out the back door and then past the pots of geraniums along the sidewalk that leads to the driveway. I turn, see her brother sauntering behind us like what's the rush. We get to his car, and he twirls keys around his little finger. He winks at me, runs his hand along the pale blue driver's door.

She's a beaut, hey, Sylvia? Got this tank before I even passed my driver's license. Only two hundred bucks for a 1953 Ford coupe. Who could pass up a deal like that?

Come on, Ray, you gonna make love to your car or are we gonna go?

Becca climbs into the front seat and slams the door shut. I slide onto the shiny plastic-covered gray and pink back seat. The car takes off, tires squealing. At each stop, I lurch forward, fall back, lurch forward again. When the car turns I either fall onto my left side or hit the car door with my right shoulder.

Main Street turns into County Road 50, and Ray's car zooms ahead with a roar. Thick, pitch-black woods whiz by. I smell pine and cedar. I press the lock down on the door, grip the corner of the seat with my right hand, and press my left palm against the back of the front seat. My armpits are wet. I close my eyes and see Mom's face. I didn't lie to her. I thought

I *was* going to Becca's for a sleepover. I forgot all about the kegger. Well, plans change, that's all. No need for my parents to know anything different. What they don't know won't hurt them.

Without warning, the car screeches to a stop, and I brace myself with both hands against the front seat. Becca slaps her brother's arm.

You trying to get us killed or what?

Stay cool, sis! I just missed that balloon marking the spot, that's all.

He backs the car up and then turns off the highway and onto a dirt road, slowing to a crawl, the whole time complaining that he can't see a darn thing. I roll down the back window and hear music, drums, muffled voices, laughing. I smell smoke.

Far out!

Ray honks the horn and points to an open field ahead. I see a bonfire in the middle, flames shooting up to the sky, sparks crackling and flying around the heads of human silhouettes. My stomach is doing cartwheels. And to think that I forgot this was happening tonight.

There's a helter-skelter of cars, trucks, and motorcycles parked at random around the edge of the field. Ray squeezes his car into a tiny space. Becca turns to me, jumping up and down in the front seat.

What a gas! Our senior kegger! Can you believe we're here, Sylvie?

I nod and swallow a laugh. I jump out of the car, drawn to the music, the laughter, the *fun*. My insides vibrate from the noise, from everyone shouting over everyone else. My skin prickles from the crackling fire, burns sweaty hot.

Doris and Cindy materialize out of nowhere, screaming and hugging and spilling beer all over us.

Hey, Becca! Gimme some skin!

Finally! We almost gave up on you, Becca!

I feel invisible until Becca points her notorious finger of blame at me.

Girl here was late!

Becca bumps her shoulder against mine like she's just kidding.

Hey, Becca, you know that guy at the basketball playoffs that you thought was so cute? What town was he from again?

He's here? Really? He's here? Where?

Becca squeals, jumps up and down, pokes me in the arm like I'm supposed to go look for him or something.

Here you go.

Ray shoves a red plastic cup in my hand. Foam dribbles over the edge. He nudges me with his elbow, and I bring the cup up to my lips. Beer trickles down the corners of my mouth.

Hah! You never had a beer before, did you?

What do you mean? Course I have!

I jerk my shoulders back, but the truth is I've never even tasted beer before. This is only the second time I have ever had alcohol of any kind, the first time being at a wedding reception when I was in the sixth grade, and I had a little sip of gin and tonic that sure tasted a whole lot better than this stuff. Ray taps my arm, and I bring the cup to my lips again, force a big gulp down my throat. He raises his eyebrows. I take another gulp, then another and another. It starts to not taste so bad.

I'll be right back. Getcha another one.

He reaches for my empty cup, and I turn to talk to my friends, only they're gone. I search the clusters of kids around me, bounce from one foot to another. Where did they go? What should I do?

Hey, Sylvia, brought you another beer . . . and something else, too. My buddy Tony here says he's been looking for you.

Hey, how ya doin', babe?

My knees buckle from the hot musky smell of Tony Jordane. His fingers brush my cheek. It feels soft as a feather. Bulky handsome, gorgeous, *the* most popular boy in school and three-time state wrestling champion, Tony Jordane has been looking for *me*? And he just touched my face? I think my heart just stopped.

Chapter Four

In the two days since Sylvia was transferred from intensive care to a room in the step-down unit, J. B. had slowly become acclimated to the antiseptic smells and the omnipresent bleep-blip sounds of the heart monitor and other machines that measured her breathing, blood pressure, oxygen saturation levels, and intake of IV fluids. The sweet funereal aroma of well-wishers' flowers hovering over the room, however, plagued him like the doctor's words: She's semiconscious and could either regain full consciousness or slip into a coma, we'll just have to wait and see.

"Will . . . Becca . . ."

"Will?" J. B. asked. "Becca? Who are you talking to, Sylvia?"

She had been muttering sporadically all morning, and despite his attempts to decipher their meaning, her words remained inscrutable to him, leaving him increasingly troubled.

"Where are the others? What's the plan, Becca?"

The adolescent tone in Sylvia's voice agitated him; it reminded him of the girls he had assiduously avoided in high school. But when he rested his chin and arms on the bed railing and looked down at Sylvia's gray hair, framing the creases in her face, he remembered his beloved foster grandmother and found comfort in that.

"Oh no . . . Will . . ."

J. B. put his hand on her cheek. "Who is Will, Sylvia? Who are you talking about?"

For an ever-so-brief second, she opened her eyes and seemed to be aware of his presence. "William James," she said. Then her eyes closed, and once again she seemed unaware of J. B.'s presence.

"Tony is looking for *me*? Really?"

J. B. practically leaped over the railing. "Tony? Tony *Jordane?* He's looking for you? Why? What is happening, Sylvia?"

"Oh, Will, I am so sorry! It's all my fault!"

Sylvia jerked her head back and forth with such force that J. B. was worried his raised voice might have startled or frightened her. "It's okay, Sylvia. It's me, J. B. You're in the hospital. Can you hear me?"

She stopped moving, the muscles in her neck went slack, and soon after, her chest started rising and falling ever so slightly under the sheet. She was asleep.

J. B. relaxed and sat back in the chair. How peaceful she looked. Nothing like the Sylvia he knew, the Sylvia who was not, by nature or by any stretch of the imagination, a calm and tranquil person. She most certainly was nothing like the naive, innocent-sounding girl who had been mumbling incoherently all morning.

Text alerts on his iPhone were a welcome distraction, an opportunity for him to slip back, at least for a few minutes, into the comfort zone of his normal life. To his editor's note about an incident in the Bronx, he responded that he would have his intern check it out. He reviewed the readers' responses to his latest feature article, all complimentary and needing no comment from him. He responded to a text from a colleague with whom he'd been collaborating to tell him no, he didn't know when he would be back in his New York office, but that he was still available by text, email, and phone. After reading the rest of his texts, listening to his voicemail messages, and jotting down a few reminder notes on his little notepad, he slipped his iPhone back in his pocket.

Then he opened a document on his iPad. He'd been recording Sylvia's every word, no matter how nonsensical or fragmented, along with his own observations, no matter how insignificant. He wasn't doing it to keep anxiety at bay or as a wishful attempt to ward off death. At least not consciously. It was just what he did. It was his journalistic default mode. He typed, *Find out what I can about someone named William James aka Will*, then noted that there had been a frantic tone in Sylvia's voice when she spoke about or to someone named Will. He typed, *Tony must be Anthony Jordane*, and then added the question, *Why did Sylvia seem enthralled and excited about him one minute and then extremely agitated the next? Who is Becca?*

He embraced his iPad as if it contained a treasure trove of clues, and when Nurse Sandy came into the room, she misinterpreted the gesture. "No, you mustn't give up, Mr. Harrell!" She reached for his arm with one hand and with the forefinger of her other hand motioned for him to stand up.

J. B. liked Nurse Sandy. She was always helpful and pleasant even when working double shifts. And so, he did as she asked and stood next to her at the bed railing while she talked to Sylvia.

"Good morning, Ms. Jensen. How are we doing today?" She nudged J. B. with her elbow, her eyes sparkling. "Did you see that? She just mouthed the word *fine* to let us know she's doing okay. That is good. Don't you see? That is very good."

After Nurse Sandy left the room, J. B. leaned closer to Sylvia and whispered, "You didn't say *fine*, did you? You said *fuck*." He chuckled at his attempt to get a rise out of her, hoping for a slight curl of her lips, maybe a tiny little grin, something, anything at all. "Okay, so it was a bad joke," he said, "But please, Sylvia, could you just tell me why Anthony Jordane is looking for you?"

He waited a few seconds before giving up and was still feeling discouraged when Mentayer called. As soon as he told her that Sylvia had been talking all morning, his wife squealed into the phone, "Yes! Yes! Yes!"

"It's true that she's talking." He hesitated, imagined the tears of joy and relief running down his wife's cheeks that he was about to wipe away. "But she's not talking to *me*. I don't think she even knows I'm here. Or where she is, for that matter."

"Oh." That one word carried the full weight of Mentayer's disappointment. Sylvia was as important to her as she was to J. B. Their personal histories with Sylvia were separate, but each of them had been children when they met her: in 1968, Sylvia had been Mentayer's third-grade schoolteacher in the Bronx; in 1972, she'd been a social worker on the reservation where J. B.'s birth mother lived.

"I worry that she's hallucinating," J. B. said. "I read that survivors of cardiac arrest often have brain damage."

"What does the *doctor* say?"

"He says she's minimally conscious and should be able to hear me and respond during moments of awareness."

"Then you must simply talk to her as if she *is* talking to you. And . . ." He could hear her suck in her breath before continuing, "Don't forget, J. B. *Most* people who experience cardiac arrest don't survive. So, despite all the odds, our Sylvia is not only alive, she's talking."

"You're right." His voice cracked. For the umpteenth time since they'd been together, J. B. was impressed by his wife's unrelenting determination to remain hopeful.

Feeling more optimistic after talking to her, and with his faith in his intuitive skills boosted, he pulled out his iPad and created his usual kind of worksheet. On the left side of the page, he typed what he knew, and there was only one thing—*Sylvia knows Anthony Jordane personally.* On the right side of the page, he started to type what he didn't know and needed to find out. *What kind of relationship does, or did, Sylvia have with Jordane? What does she know about him? Who is William James, aka Will? What happened in the past and why is it important now? Who is Becca? Does she know what happened?*

The list of everything that he didn't know grew and grew until he finally quit, exasperated. "I sure could use your help," he mumbled to Sylvia with a shake of his head.

He closed his *What I know and don't know* worksheet and opened the Internet instead. Two and a half hours after googling Anthony "Tony" Jordane and finding nothing he didn't already know, he rubbed his eyes and closed his iPad. He thought about what he'd recently written about him—"a successful businessman, and a supporter of sovereign rights known for his belief that you can make money by doing good, . . . a man with a steady moral compass that always puts humanity before profit"—and how those words were based on what people who claimed to know Jordane had said about him. It was one sentence in a five-thousand-word feature article about uranium mining on Indigenous land, not something that had required any research other than interviewing a few people who knew

Jordane. He reached in his pocket for his iPhone and called his intern at the *New York Times.*

"Rory," he said. "Yeah, I'm still in Monrow City. No, I don't know how long I'll be here. Thanks for stepping up while I'm gone. Listen, I know you're busy, but I want you to do some more research about Anthony or 'Tony' Jordane. Yeah, that's right, the guy everybody said was great. No, you didn't mess up. We did as much research as we needed to for that piece, but now he's running for the U.S. Senate. Yeah, that *is* a big deal. The governor's expected to endorse him next week. Oh, and while you're at it, see if you can find anything about a boy named Will. William James. He may have been from Bigger, the town Jordane grew up in, I think, but I'm not sure."

"J. B.! J. B.!"

He quickly ended the call, leaned over the railing, and looked into Sylvia's wide-open eyes. She was staring at him as if she had heard everything he'd just said.

"Anthony Jordane." Her eyes flashed, and her voice was unbelievably clear and strong. "He is not who everyone thinks he is. Ask Becca. She was there. She knows what happened."

• • •

Two days later, J. B. found himself double-checking the dusty odometer. Two hundred miles down, fifty to go. He calculated that, if all went according to plan, he should arrive in Bigger just as the sun was setting, but just then the car started vibrating. When he released the gas pedal and slowed down, the driver of the truck behind him did a quick swerve left and gave him the finger as he thundered by in the passing lane.

"Hey! You think *you're* frustrated?" J. B. yelled out the window. "You're not the one who has to drive this old beater!"

Well, he didn't have to drive Sylvia's car either. He could have rented a car. Or he could have gone for a test drive to make sure her ancient 1985 Toyota was up for such a long trip. At the very least, once he realized her car refused to go over fifty miles an hour without threatening to fall apart, he could have pulled off the highway and exchanged it for a rental. So why hadn't he done any of those things? He didn't think of himself as either sentimental nor superstitious, so it was hard for him to admit, even to himself, that he hadn't taken Sylvia's car just because she told him to. He took it because when he was in her car, he felt like she was there with him. He even found himself talking to her.

He hadn't wanted to drive to Bigger at all—not when Sylvia, in a moment of consciousness, told him to talk to Becca, not when Mentayer encouraged him to go, not even when she said she would come and stay with Sylvia at the hospital while he was gone. He didn't want to leave Sylvia's side, and he also didn't think he'd learn anything by going there. But yesterday, when his intern, Rory, called, that all changed.

"I haven't found anything new about Jordane yet," Rory had said. "But I did find an interesting newspaper article about a boy named William James, also known as Will, who must have gone to school with Jordane. I'm sending it to you now."

J. B. knew he was about to strike gold and so nearly forgot to thank Rory. He ended the call and quickly downloaded and opened the attachment. The headline of the Bigger newspaper article, dated June 7, 1960, said "Local Boy Found Dead." He read the first sentence —"Yesterday morning, the body of eighteen-year-old William James was found in the woods outside of town."

He had to sit back and catch his breath before continuing. The article provided no details about how the boy died, and only scant information about who he was. He had just been released from jail. He was an honor student and a quiet boy. His death was tragic. J. B., sure his intern must have forgotten to send the rest of the article, called him back.

"The answer is, no," Rory said. "There is no other information. Not that I could find."

"Not even cause of death?"

"Nope. Nothing. Nada. Zip."

J. B. had leaned over the bedrail and bombarded Sylvia with all the questions that were flooding through him and demanding immediate answers. "I know now that Will died, but how did he die, Sylvia? Why was it your fault? Why was Will in the woods? Why was he in jail? Why wasn't there any more information about his death? What do you know?"

Sylvia's eyelids had fluttered, and she opened her eyes, but only long enough to say, "Tony did it." Then she slipped away again.

And that was when J. B. knew he had to go to Bigger.

He looked at the passenger seat as if Sylvia were with him now. *Okay, we're almost there. Only ten miles to go. Before we get there, though, I already know one thing for certain. Whatever happened to Will was not your fault.*

As if answering for her, Sylvia's car started vibrating again. He slowed down and drove up the exit ramp to the last rest stop before the freeway's four lanes would merge into a two-lane road. He parked in a shady spot next to a picnic table and scrolled through the series of new messages on his iPhone. A text from Mentayer—*Plane just landed*—sent a wave of gratitude and love for his wife surging through him. He knew she'd had to rearrange her work schedule to fly to Monrow City and stay with Sylvia.

"Nurses' station."

"Oh, uh, Sandy," he said, expecting to hear Mentayer's voice and then realizing he had called the hospital number by mistake. "This is J. B."

"I'm sorry, Mr. Harrell . . . please hold a minute."

Why did she say she was sorry? Had she sounded worried or was that his imagination? His hands trembled, and his chest grew heavier with each minute he waited. Something must be wrong, he knew it, something was terribly wrong.

"Sorry about that, Mr. Harrell."

"What is it? What happened?"

"Oh no, no, no worries, Mr. Harrell. I was on another call, that's all. There's been no change in Ms. Jensen's condition. I'm sorry. I know how you worry."

"Is she still unconscious?"

"Minimally conscious," the nurse clarified. "Your wife just got here. Hold on, I'll connect you to the room."

Mentayer picked up the phone on the first ring, and J. B. showered her with questions like kisses—How was she? How was the flight from New York? Was it nonstop? How did she get to the hospital? How did Sylvia seem to her?

Mentayer chuckled and, with her hand covering the receiver, called out to Sylvia, "It's J. B. on the phone. Bombarding me with questions as usual."

Then, "Everything is fine," she told him. "Sylvia and I have been talking. Right, Sylvia?"

"She's talking?"

"Not really." After a brief pause, Mentayer said, "J. B. wants to know if you're glad to see me. You are, aren't you, Sylvia?"

"I get it," he said. "You're doing what you told me to do. You're talking to her as if she's talking to you."

"Exactly." The smile in her voice made him smile, too.

"Tell her I'm almost there, and her car is a piece of shit." He waited as Mentayer laughingly relayed the message to Sylvia, and then he added, "Seriously, hon, I couldn't have left her side if you weren't there."

"You know I had to be."

How true that was. Sylvia was like a mother to both of them.

"Keep talking to her," he said. "Let me know if she says anything at all that will give me something, anything, to go on while I'm in Bigger. I'll call you when I get there. Be sure to ask Nurse Sandy for a blanket. The chair in Sylvia's room is lousy, so you might want to sleep on the couch in the waiting room."

He hung up and got out of the car, then stretched his legs and walked to the restroom. On his way out, he bought a granola bar and a bottle of water from the vending machine. While he was sitting at the picnic table eating his snack, his iPhone pinged, this time with a text from Peter Minter. *The governor's press conference is in two days. Be there.*

He got back in the car. One day was plenty of time to find someone who could tell him what happened. After all, when a boy in a small town is found dead in the woods, well, that's not something people forget.

He kept driving until he spotted the town sign—"Welcome to Bigger, the Friendly City. Population 700."—and then pulled over to the side of the road. The wooden sign was shaped like a house, painted in red, white, and blue colors that were faded, the paint chipped away so it was mostly gray. Behind the sign, at a distance, a dark melancholic cloud hung over a cluster of what looked like abandoned shacks.

He got out of the car, thinking he'd take a selfie by the sign and send it to Sylvia and Mentayer. But when he was within an arm's length of it, he felt a tightening in his chest. He took a step closer and touched the faded wood—a tingling sensation, like an electric shock, made him pull his hand back. He dropped to his knees in front of the sign. There was no doubt about it. Something tragic had happened in this town.

Chapter Five

1960

Sylvie! Wake up!

Becca's yelling makes my head pound. I cover my ears. I roll onto my side. Two huge brown eyes stare at me. I shriek and slap them away.

Geeezus, girl!

It's just Becca's old stuffed bear. She grabs it away from me and presses its nose into the strawberry patch printed on the front of her pink baby doll nightie. She plops down on her bed, already made, God only knows how or when she did that. I sit up. My blouse is bunched up around my neck and my jean shorts dig into my crotch.

It's your mom, Sylvie.

Huh? My mom's here?

On the phone, silly.

I open my eyes and the sun shoots a sharp pain into them.

God, Becca, could you *please* close that curtain?

Hey, don't blame it on the sun, girl. You're the one who slugged it down last night.

Becca snorts and purses her lips. She's taking the pink rollers out of her hair. When did she have time to do her hair? And who is she to sound so high and mighty? Didn't she drink just as much as me last night? It isn't just the sun that's giving me a headache. Or my hangover. It's these nauseating Pepto Bismol pink walls and ceiling, the frilly pink lace and ruffled bedspread, Becca's pink pajamas. I cover my face with a pillow.

Your mom wants to know if they should wait for you at home or if you're going to meet them at church. It's almost ten. You better hurry.

Tell her I'm sick. I *am* sick. I'm not lying. Tell her.

I already told her you'd meet them at church.

I'm not going.

I know that if I miss Sunday school at ten, my parents will be mad. And if I don't show up for the service at eleven, Daddy will ground me. But if they knew what I did last night, oh God, I don't even want to think about what they'd do to me. I moan into the pillow.

Well?

I said I'm not going.

I'm not asking about church, silly. I'm asking about TJ.

Becca grabs the pillow from my face. I turn away so I don't have to look at her. But then, oh my God, then I see Tony's face instead. It feels like there's a pickax inside my head and it's loosening chunks of memory from last night bit by bit. The crackling fire. Music. Laughter. The smell of beer on Tony's breath. The touch of his fingers, his hands.

Well, did you go all the way, or did you just make out? What was it like?

Each question feels like a punch in the gut. A sharp pain shoots up my chest and into my throat. I whimper. I'm pathetic.

That good, huh?

Becca sits right next to me. She grips my shoulders. Her face is in mine. Her eyes flash. Her mouth is wide open, a starving bird begging for food.

I don't remember anything about last night, Becca. What time did we get home?

Oh, come on, girl, you're stalling. Tell me everything!

I gotta go, Becca!

I push her off me, swing my legs onto the floor, stumble down the hall to the bathroom. I can't tell her what happened. She's the biggest gossip in school. Everybody's probably talking already. Everybody saw me smiling and holding hands with TJ. I sit down on the toilet, my elbows on my knees, and my cheeks burn the palms of my hands. How could I have been so stupid? Stupid! Stupid! Stupid! I hate myself. I wish I was dead. I'm dripping with sweat. I'm gonna throw up.

Coming in, girl! I can't hold it anymore!

Becca barges into the bathroom, jiggling up and down, squeezing her legs together. Why didn't I lock the door? I splash cold water on my face and neck at the sink while she pees.

Well?

Becca's perfect eyebrows are way up in her hairline now. She barricades the door. I can't get past her.

I gotta get home. I can still make it to the service.

Not until you tell me about TJ.

Come on, Becca. You told my mom I'd go to church. If I don't show up, my dad is going to kill me.

She doesn't move, so I push her, hard, shove her away from the door. She's shocked. She'll never speak to me again. I don't care. I bolt out the door and run down the hall. A hand shoots out of nowhere. I scream. It's Ray, he grabs my arm, he's smirking.

Whoa! What's the rush . . . uh . . . babe?

Let go!

I dig my feet into the carpet. I glare at him. What's going on? Becca's brother never called me babe before. He's never leered at me like this either.

Hey, chill out . . . babe. I just wanted to let you know that I won the bet.

He lets go of me, raises his hands in the air like he's all innocent. I don't know what he's talking about. All I want to do is get out of here. I flick my shoulder, twist my body away, and stomp off to the kitchen, slam the screen door behind me. Hard. Then I run and run. Don't even stop to catch my breath.

I'm home, collapsing in a chair at the kitchen table, crossing my arms over my chest and rocking back and forth, back and forth. The telephone on the counter rings. I freeze. I know it's Mom. She wants to know where I am. I won't answer and she'll give up. Only she doesn't. The phone keeps ringing. I can't stand it anymore and grab the receiver.

I'm sorry, Mom, I—

Why'd you cut out on me like that, girl?

What bet, Becca?

Huh?

Your brother said he won the bet. What bet?

Oh God, Sylvie, don't tell me that's what got you all bent out of shape about . . . Guys make bets about us girls all the time.

What . . . bet . . . Becca?

It was just a joke, Sylvie.

Okay, fine, if you don't want to tell me. It's been nice knowing you.

Geeez, girl! Okay, okay. My brother bet that TJ would get you to . . . you know . . . do it . . . And all the other guys bet that you would never let him . . . So Ray won, what's the big deal?

I slam the receiver down. Slap at the tears pouring down my cheeks. Grab a sharp knife from the drawer and go to the bathroom. If they want to make me the laughingstock of the school, I'll show them. I stare at my face in the mirror. Hold the side of the blade against the jugular vein on my neck. First the left side. Then the right side. But then I think about Mom coming home from church and finding me dead on the floor. Lifting my head and holding me, rocking me in her lap and crying. Screaming for Daddy. Washing my blood from the sink, the floor, the side of the cabinet. Her heart breaking. No. I can't. I can't do that to her.

I'm like a zombie when I carry the knife to the kitchen and put it back in the drawer. When I go to my room, take off my clothes, and get in bed. Hide under the covers.

• • •

What's wrong, sweetie?

I open my eyes. Mom is sitting on the bed next to me. The palm of her hand is on my forehead. It's warm.

You don't have a fever.

I'm sorry I missed church, Mom. Becca and I stayed up late talking and eating junk food.

Well, then you'll be fine.

I hear the accusation in her voice. She kisses my forehead and leaves. Shuts the door. I stay in bed all day. Until I hear Grandma and Grandpa come in the back door. Then I quick change my clothes and go to dinner, act like nothing's wrong.

Under the weather today, young lady? Missed church this morning, did we?

She's fine now, Pa.

Grandpa's mouth always does the smiling while his eyes do the judging. Mom talks to him all nice-like. Her eyes are telling me *Don't let him bother you, sweetie, and whatever you do, don't argue with him.* I nod, force a smile. I don't say I still have a headache or a queasy stomach, because then Grandma will be all worried that I have the flu. Then everyone will start asking me questions and I'll have to tell even more lies.

We have dinner. I pretend to eat. Then we walk across the alley for the seven o'clock prayer service at church. It's like every Sunday night. Grandpa, Grandma, Daddy, Mom, and I, in that order, sit in the second pew from the front, same as always. When I was little, I used to wonder what would happen if someone didn't sit in their regular place, but no one ever does, so I don't think about it anymore.

Tonight, dear friends, we pray for forgiveness.

Reverend Cramer stands at the pulpit with his arms raised. He looks at me over his wire-rimmed glasses. They're always perched on the end of his wide nose except when he's reading from the Bible.

Tonight, my fellow believers, we will ask forgiveness for the stumbling blocks that keep us from dedicating our lives completely to God.

I quick bow my head before Pastor tells us to. Once he gets started, he looks like a toad to me, all the warts on his face scrunched together in the folds of his dry gray skin. I'm afraid I'll puke.

Dear friends, what is your sin? Is it drink? Lust? Greed? Lack of faith? Whatever it is, God is telling you tonight that if your right eye is making you stumble, it is better to tear it out and lose one part of your body than for your whole body to be thrown into hell. You are either in or out with God, there is no middle ground. Whatever your sin, it is time to pluck it out.

His voice rises to a fever, and then suddenly he goes silent. I roll my eyes. Why would God tell me to tear out my eye? Pluck it out? No kind of God would tell you to cut off part of your body. It's just Reverend Cramer talking.

So now, my dear friends. It is time to tell God what your sin is. Is it a desire to be liked or fit in? It doesn't matter if your sin is something you did or something you felt in your heart. It's all the same to God. Don't overthink it, dear friends. That, too, is a sin. If you are feeling shame, that is God talking to you. That is all you need to know.

His voice is soft, almost like he cares. I squirm. Is he looking at me or am I imagining it? I close my eyes and I'm back at the kegger. My jean shorts too tight and too short, my blouse too revealing. I'm smiling and flirting with TJ. The boys are laughing and leering at me like I'm a slut.

If you feel shame, then it is time to confess your sins to God. And the good news, my dear friends, is that our God is a forgiving God. All you need to do is turn your heart to Him and ask His forgiveness and it *shall* be granted.

I slump forward with my head on my knees. I'm shaking. Forgive me, God, for tempting TJ. Forgive me for wanting to be his babe. Forgive me for leading him on. Forgive me for my impure thoughts and behavior. If you will make me pure of heart, my lips will never touch alcohol again. I will cover my body. I will never ever go to another kegger. Dear God, I give myself to you.

Every time I make a promise, the pain in my head gets a little less. My neck and shoulder muscles relax. My heartbeat slows.

Amen.

Reverend Cramer's amen sounds like a tinkling bell, soft and clear and pure. I sit back in the pew and rest my head on Mom's shoulder.

And now, dear friends, may you go in peace, knowing that God has shown you how to put your sins behind you.

I close my eyes and whisper one last prayer. Dear God, thank you for sending Will last night to show me the error of my ways.

Chapter Six

J. B. drove at a snail's pace down Bigger's Main Street, at times talking to Sylvia, at other times recording his observations on his iPhone. He passed three bars that were boarded up, then three more with their doors propped open to let in the warm summer breeze. Even though it was that time of day when people usually gathered for drinks after work, there didn't seem to be many customers.

"Do you think you would have become an alcoholic, Sylvia, if you hadn't grown up in a town with so many bars?"

She had always been open with him about her recovery, but they had never talked about when her problems with alcohol started. Did she drink to forget and relieve her guilt about whatever happened to Will, he wondered? She was, after all, the most guilt-ridden person J. B. had ever known. Had she sentenced herself to a lifetime of atonement? But for what? Something she did? Something she didn't do? Something she had been unable to do?

When he reached the end of Main Street, J. B. stopped speculating about Sylvia and started to worry that he wouldn't have a place to stay if the motel he'd found on Google Maps had met the same fate as the abandoned gas station he'd just passed. But when he rounded a curve in the road less than a mile later he saw, with a sigh of relief, the flashing neon sign. "Ski Bum Motel. Vacancy. A Color TV in Every Room." He turned right off the highway and drove up to the small single-story motel, a string of only six or seven rooms with an office and restaurant and bar at the end.

He parked in front of the office. The door was open, but no one was there. The place had an abandoned feel to it, as if someone had brought in old stuff to be stored there and then walked away without turning off the lights or closing the door. But as he scanned the dozens of photographs of ski scenes covering the knotty pine walls, he imagined what the room would be like in the winter when the ancient black freestanding fireplace in the corner radiated warmth and cast a homey glow on its frayed braided rug, tattered plaid couch, and worn stuffed chairs.

He rang the bell on the counter. No one came, so he followed the sounds of voices, raucous laughter, the clicking of glasses, and jukebox music coming through the door to the attached bar. As soon as he stepped into the dimly lit room, the sounds of voices stopped and seven pairs of eyes stared at him from a round wooden table in the middle of the room.

"Good evening." He nodded and looked into the aging eyes of seven men, all wearing flannel shirts to ward off the chill of the rattling air conditioner in the corner.

Their silent eyes followed him. As he made his way across the warped and beer-stained wood floor. As he walked past the dozens of haphazardly splattered posters, photos, and artworks that obscured the color and texture of the walls. As he sat down on one of the four nondescript stools at the bar.

"I'm looking for a place to stay," J. B. said to the man standing behind what looked like a decently stocked bar. "I see the motel next door has a vacancy."

The man chuckled and his ample belly shook and his cheeks puffed up. "That's about *all* we have around here this time of year. I'm Mac. Mac Novak."

"I'm J. B. Harrell."

The man wiped his hands on a dishcloth and reached across the counter to shake his hand. A woman appeared and Mac put his arm around her. "This here's my wife Jill, Mr. Harrell. We own the motel. This bar and restaurant too."

J. B. smiled and said hello, amused to see how alike the couple looked: both in their early sixties with stocky builds, a few pounds and muscles shy of chubby, wearing identical bright red T-shirts that said *Retired Ski Bums* in bold white letters.

Jill Novak examined J. B. with eyebrows furrowed and eyes unblinking. Then, through slightly puckered lips, she said, "You must be looking for directions. It's another hundred miles from here to the rez."

Mac grimaced and dropped his arm from his wife's shoulder, but J. B. just smiled. He was used to these kinds of comments from people—considered them "slip-ups"—and hers was more creative than most.

"I thought I would be able to drive here from Monrow City and back in a day," he said with a shrug, "but the old clunker I'm driving took longer than I expected."

"I see," she said, with a set jaw frozen with stereotypes.

Mac Novak rolled his eyes, stepped away from his wife, and pointed to the door at the end of the bar that led into the motel office. "Well, Mr. Harrell, it is your lucky day. The best room we have just happens to be available. Come with me and I'll check you in." He started walking toward the door but then stopped as if having second thoughts and turned around.

"Hey, everyone," he called out to the men at the table. "Listen up! It's Jill's meatloaf special tonight, and drinks are on the house."

J. B. followed Mac to the office, impressed by what he had just witnessed. In one fell swoop, the man had revoked his wife's attitude, compensated for it by becoming more friendly, and then used her cooking to appease her and free booze to entice the wary men into relaxing.

"You're not from Bigger, are you, Mac?"

He chuckled. "Is it that obvious?"

While Mac checked him in, J. B. learned, without asking a single question, that he and his wife had been ski bums when they were young, they bought the motel at a steal after the previous owner died, the place had been closed for years so they had to fix it up a bit, and now it was a popular low-end place for skiers who couldn't afford the nearby ski resort that opened twenty years ago, which is what put the previous motel owner out of business. During the summer, there wasn't much—in fact almost no—motel business, but the old-timers claimed the bar as their hangout during the off-season, which was how Mac and his wife managed to stay afloat.

"I'm living the dream," he said. "It's an easy, laid-back retirement that suits me just fine." Then, with some hesitation, as if not wanting to be intrusive or impolite, he asked, "And what about you, Mr. Harrell? What brings you here?"

"I'm a journalist."

"Mmmm. Let me guess. You're writing a story about the demise of small-town America."

J. B. smiled. "In a way."

"Well, Mr. Harrell, those old guys next door can tell you all about what happens to a mining town when the ore runs out and they end up living in a small retirement enclave with their kids and grandkids only coming back for holidays and, more and more often, funerals."

"I'd love to hear their stories, but . . ."

Mac winked and raised his forefinger. "Now, don't you worry none, Mr. Harrell. Trust me, they will talk your arm off once they know you're willing to listen. Course, some of their stories are whoppers, so you gotta take 'em with a grain of salt. Now you just get yourself settled in and then come back for some meatloaf with mashed potatoes and the most delicious down-home gravy you ever tasted."

As soon as J. B. opened the door to room number 1, a mixture of smells washed over him like a foul sea wave. Once inside, several sources of the aromas became immediately apparent. A disposable air freshener in all its simulated evergreen pine glory hanging from a ceiling light fixture. Water dripping from a rusty showerhead. Dried flowers and crushed leaves that looked suspiciously like cannabis lying in a plastic bowl on the bedstand. A sticky fly strip hanging from a lamp, weighed down by corpses of flies and mosquitoes. Even though the room appeared clean, J. B. deemed it wise, while walking on the threadbare carpet, to keep his shoes on.

There was no air conditioning or ceiling fan, just a lone screenless window stuck open six inches above the sill. The bedspread on the worn-out double bed was stained and the pillows flat as biscuits.

Being both hungry and unaccustomed to staying in this kind of place, J. B. was eager to leave the room and get back to the bar. He looked at himself in the cracked mirror on the inside of the door and did a quick appraisal of his appearance—business executive hairstyle, pressed jeans with a crease down the front, bold NYU logo in purple letters on his white

T-shirt—and saw himself through the eyes of the old men next door. Presumptuous. Uppity. Or worse, a liar. No Indian went to NYU. Those old-timers had tons of information just waiting to be mined, but he knew he would have to work hard to gain their trust before they would give him any of it.

He stood outside the entrance to the Novaks' Ghost Skiers Haven bar for a few minutes, bracing himself for the challenge ahead, preparing himself for the worst. But, much to his surprise, when he opened the door, it was immediately apparent that the ambiance inside had changed. Yes, the old men still stared at him as he walked over to the bar, only this time with eyes that conveyed a *Who are you* curiosity instead of a *We don't trust you, go away* hostility.

"They always sit in the same places and bring their own cushions." Mac winked at J. B. and spoke in a low, confidential voice. "I told 'em you were a journalist doing a story about small towns. See that? They already squeezed in an empty chair for you. Go on. Jill will bring you a plate. Hey, guys," he then called out, "don't you be keeping Mr. Harrell here all night now."

"J. B. You can call me J. B.," he said with a smile as he joined the men at the table.

"A journalist, hey?"

"Doing a story about small towns?"

"In general?"

"So, why pick Bigger?"

"Why would anyone?"

"Yeah, why us? We're dying here."

"Or is that the point?"

The men continued to toss out questions, passing them around and across the table like a balloon volleyball game for seniors. Finally, a man who appeared to be a decade or so older than the others, probably well into his nineties, raised his hand and said, "Name's Jeremy Kuzik here. So, okay, Mr. J. B., who are you and why are you here? We are all ears."

J. B. took in a deep breath. This was it. He would have to tell them more than who he was. He would have to level with them about the real reason he had come.

• • •

"I'm a journalist." J. B. pointed to the front of his T-shirt. "Graduate degree from NYU's Journalism Institute." Judging from their smiles, it seemed like the old guys wanted to believe him or at least wanted to hear more. "I live in Manhattan and work as an investigative reporter for the *New York Times*." Noting the pursed lips and rolled eyes, he quickly added, "*But* I grew up in this state . . . in a *small* town east of here. Basko." There was a collective sigh, and then the men softened and leaned toward him. "When I was a kid, I also lived on the reservation for a while. Before I moved to New York, I lived for several years in Monrow City. That's where I got my start, as a reporter for the city newspaper."

"Okay, Mr. J. B., you've established your credentials," Jeremy Kuzik said. "Now tell us what is it exactly that you're investigating here in Bigger."

He took in a breath and let it out. That had been easy. Too easy. But now the moment of truth had arrived. This would be harder. He would have to take it one step at a time. *Kudos to you,* he said to Sylvia in his head.

"Let's start with Anthony Jordane," he said. "I understand this is where he grew up, and I need to learn more about him since I'll be covering his campaign for the U.S. Senate."

That did the trick, set off another string of comments around the table.

"Yeah, wow, Tony, a senator."

"Imagine that, huh?"

"Holy . . . you think he'll win, for real?"

"I hear the governor's gonna endorse him."

"Really? Where'd ya hear that?"

"I heard that guy Rodriguez was sick or something and that's why he isn't running for a second term."

"I don't get how that firebrand ever got elected in the first place."

"Ya think there's something suspicious about his sickness?"

"What race is he anyway, Puerto Rican?"

"Maybe Mexican? Same thing I guess."

"He's probably mulatto."

"Like a mongrel or mutt. A little bit of everything."

"As long as it speaks Spanish."

Mac brought J. B. a glass of water and a *Didn't I tell you* wink. The old-timers didn't even notice, just kept going on, laughing, patting each other's shoulders, one-upping each other.

"No surprise to me why the governor would support Tony."

"Me either. She is, after all, a woman."

"Which goes to show you what the world is coming to, don't it."

"No woman on this earth can resist Tony's charm, not even one sittin' in the governor's mansion."

"Ya got that right."

When there was a brief lull, J. B. moved in quick to take advantage of it. "So, was there a special girl in Tony's life? Did he have a girlfriend?"

At that, the men burst into laughter again, slapping the top of the table with their arthritic hands. Then one of the men, the one with a long white beard and no hair on the top of his head, picked up his fork and tapped it on his glass. "*All* the girls chased after Tony. He was always a ladies' man. Still is, I'm sure."

"It sounds like you all knew him very well," J. B. said.

"*Everybody* knew him. He was our three-time state wrestling champion, you know."

"That's right, he put Bigger on the map."

After that the men tripped over each other in their eagerness to tell their favorite Tony stories. He could get any girl he wanted. He tooled around town in his muscle car, honking and waving and smiling like he was king, which he kind of was. He was always the center of attention, at school, at parties. He came from one of the town's most prominent families, with his father being the chief of police and all. He was voted most likely to succeed in the high school yearbook. There had been talk a while back about changing the name of the main drag to Anthony Jordane Street, but nothing ever came of it. The men all agreed that if he became a U.S. senator, they'd go ahead and do it then.

Jill placed a plate of food in front of J. B., which he was happy to eat since the old-timers weren't about to be interrupted as they reminisced about the old days. How Bigger used to have both elementary and high schools until there weren't enough kids coming up, so they closed them down ten years ago, and now they had to bus the kids to Altos City, where everything's consolidated these days. How ever since the Piggly Wiggly store and the gas station closed they'd had to drive there to the big Walmart for food and gas, too. But at least they still had the park, a nice little place for the grandkids to play when they came to visit.

With a collective sigh, the men finally seemed to run out of steam. "Delicious," J. B. said as he pushed his now-empty plate back. "And you all have given me a pretty good picture of what Tony was like, and what Bigger was like back then, too." He noted their satisfied smiles. Time to take the next step.

"You know," he said, "interestingly enough, many years ago I met someone from Bigger. Name of Jensen."

"Oh sure. I remember the Jensens."

"None of them left now, either died or moved away long time ago."

"They were kinda odd. Different, as I recall."

"Me, too. Old man Jensen started that church, more like a cult."

"Right, I remember it died when he died. It's a house now, just sitting empty. I mean, who wants to live in a church, hey?"

"They had a daughter . . ."

"Yeah, she was in my class. Quiet, shy thing."

"Sylvia."

"Yeah, didn't Tony have a little fling with her?"

"That sure was a surprise to me."

"To everyone."

J. B. was jarred by each revelation, the questions piling up in his head. Had Sylvia had a relationship with Jordane that ended badly? Is that why she was so angry at him?

"Shortest fling in history," one of the men said.

"Lasted only about a minute," another one snickered, and that set off a round of sniggering.

J. B. told himself to act interested and yet aloof enough so they wouldn't know they were in personal territory now. "What happened to her," he asked in an intentionally nonchalant tone. "The Jensen girl?"

"Don't know."

"She left town and never came back."

When they shrugged like Sylvia was no big deal, J. B. had to restrain himself by curling his hands into fists under the table and counting to ten.

"Tony never came back either. Didn't even make it to our sixtieth class reunion a few years back. Too good for us now, I guess. Only a few of us from that class left now anyway."

"Not that many of us to start with. Only forty-two of us graduated in 1960."

"At least we had a high school then."

Some of the men sighed audibly, others quietly sipped their drinks.

"What about the Bigger newspaper?" J. B. asked. "That still published?"

"More like a monthly newsletter these days. The former editor's grandson goes into the building, mostly to dust is my guess."

"Yeah, he hangs out across the street at the post office—at least we've been able to keep that so far. That's where he picks up the monthly gossip."

"Mostly about which one of us died and who was at the funeral."

"Did you know that visiting priest that comes for confession and mass on Saturdays? He writes a column sometimes, too."

"Yeah, and don't forget the minister at the community church. He always adds a little reminder about church on Sundays for the ten or so folks who go to services there."

"We like it here though, Mr. J. B."

That set off another round of laughing and jostling.

"We have houses to live in, after all."

"Course, they're not worth anything."

"Hey, Mr. J. B., you want a vacation place away from the Big Apple? You could pick one up cheap here."

He laughed along with them. "You guys have seen it all, haven't you."

"Got that right," they said in unison.

The men, clearly pleased with themselves and having a good time, looked at J. B. as if anticipating his next question so they could go another round.

"Not long ago, I came across an old article that was in the Bigger newspaper in 1960. It was about the death of a boy named William James. Do you know what happened to him?"

Furtive glances practically flew around the table, passed from man to man. For just a second or so, it seemed as if everyone stopped breathing. J. B. leaned back in his chair and waited. Only then, one by one, the men started checking their watches, reaching for their wallets, and placing money on the table to pay for their meals.

"Time to call it a day," one of them said as he stood up and shook J. B.'s hand.

The others followed suit. Everyone thanked J. B., and when one of them said, "It's a good little town we got here, Mr. J. B. Every town has its quirks, you know," all the others nodded their agreement.

After the door had closed behind the last man, J. B. sat back down at the table with his notepad and pen. *What kind of relationship did Jordane and Sylvia have? Why won't anyone talk about Will? Is it about shame? Is it related to the guilt Sylvia carried all her life?* Whew! This town was full of secrets and lies. And in order to get to the truth, he would have to untangle a hairball of human bias, fear, anger, and pain.

He glanced at his watch. It was late. He put the notepad and pen back in his pocket and stood up to go to his room. That was when he spotted a note someone had left for him in the middle of the table. *I remember Sylvia Jensen. Meet me at the pavilion in the park at nine o'clock tomorrow morning.* The note wasn't signed, but he was pretty sure he knew who wrote it.

Chapter Seven

1960

The door is always propped open Monday mornings like none of us can wait to get back to school after the weekend or something. Well, not me. I *don't* want to be at school. I usually don't want to. But especially not today. I acted sick at breakfast, but Mom gave me her *Do you really think I'm going to fall for that two days in a row* look, so here I am. What else can I do?

Hey, guys! Wait up!

Doris and Cindy are standing by the door, their heads together, laughing. I smile and wave to them, trip over my feet racing up the steps. They turn around and go inside like they don't see me. I know they do.

How ya doin', hot one? My best buddy Tony says you loved it. So, got any for the rest of us, or are ya gonna save it all for the champ?

Jake smirks at me. He flicks his shoulder and it brushes my arm. I push him away and run inside. My eyes sting. Please, dear God, don't let me cry.

I walk fast and look straight ahead. But I don't have blinders on. I can still see them. The girls with their wide eyes and their open mouths. The boys with their tongues touching the backs of their upper teeth and their lips mouthing *Slut*. It's my fault. They saw me looking all lovestruck at the kegger. Smiling and holding hands with Tony. Walking off with him to his car. Being stupid.

My locker is right next to Becca's. She acts like I don't exist, which is hard to do with our shoulders so close they touch.

I'm sorry I hung up on you, Becca.

She ignores me. I put my hand on her shoulder.

I'm not mad at you, Becca. I was just upset about all the guys making a bet about me.

She turns around with her legs wide apart and her hands on her hips. She looks straight at me. I look straight back at her.

You know what your problem is, Sylvie?

I have lots of problems. I don't know which one she's talking about.

Why are you dressed like that anyway, girl?

She looks me up and down and rolls her eyes as if my biggest problem is what I'm wearing.

For your information, Becca, I'm dressed like this because it's the loosest-fitting blouse and longest skirt I could find in my closet.

Your problem, Sylvie, is that you're too thin-skinned.

So, what would you do, Becca, if all the boys made *you* the butt of a joke? Would you laugh it off?

I cross my arms over my chest. She sighs. I know she thinks I'm overreacting.

Oh, girl. Don't you know the difference between a joke and a compliment?

A . . . a *compliment*, Becca? You think I should be flattered when all the guys in school bet that I would let Tony have his way with me?

Is that what you think? That all the guys bet you would *want* to have sex with him?

Yeah. That's what I think, Becca, because that's what they did. Your brother was the only one who bet that I wouldn't let him.

No, silly. Just the opposite. All the guys bet that you would *never* let him, or anyone, have his way with you. Ever! Ray was the only one who bet that you *would*. That's why he won. I don't know, Sylvie, sometimes I think you're from another planet or something.

So . . . So . . . your brother thinks I'm *easy*?

Don't be stupid. He knows better than anyone what a Goody Two-shoes you are. He figured *someone* had to bet that Tony would score with you. No one was more surprised than him when he won.

He didn't win. He shouldn't have won.

Oh, Sylvie, Sylvie, Sylvie. Don't you know all the girls in this school would die to be you right now?

The first period bell rings and I jump. Becca gives me that little finger wave of hers like everything's okay with us and disappears down the hall. I grab my books and hurry to Advanced Chemistry. Keep my head down.

Hey, babe.

Oh my God. Tony is right in front of me. Big smile that shows all his teeth. I look down and try to get past him. He blocks my way. Starts talking really loud. He wants everyone to hear. He sounds all friendly, but his hands are cold and he's squeezing my shoulders so hard that it hurts. I almost scream when he pulls me close and acts like he's kissing me. But he isn't. He's jamming his tongue into my mouth so I choke. He holds me tighter and turns his head so his lips are next to my ear. Then he whispers. Hisses.

You will not tell anyone what happened. No one, right? Nothing, right?

He leans back and smiles, slides his fingers on one hand down the side of my face. His other hand jerks my ponytail back. Hard.

You hear me?

I nod. I shiver. I can't stop shaking.

He squeezes the back of my neck and presses his ear up against my lips.

Say it. Right here. Say you won't tell anyone.

I won't . . . tell . . . anyone.

He lets me go. Pats me on the back.

That's a good little bitch.

He didn't have to threaten me. I wasn't going to tell anyone. My eyes fill with tears. My hands curl into tight fists. He smiles and swaggers off. Big man in school. Hero who turned a virgin into a slut. Or made her the luckiest girl in school. Pick your lie.

There you are!

Mr. Minor, our Advanced Chemistry teacher, motions to me from outside the door to class. I take a deep breath, drag myself over to him. He holds the door open with a flair and a little bow.

I'm glad to see you decided to come to class today, Miss Jensen.

Sorry I'm late.

I turn my head away, don't want him to see I'm upset. I hurry past him and he closes the door.

Good morning, my dear students. And how are the crème de la crème of Bigger High School this morning?

Mr. Minor claps his hands and prances toward the blackboard in front. I slide into my desk next to Will's. He doesn't look at me. His head is down and his chin tucked into his chest like he's studying the cover of his notebook or something.

Hey!

I poke him in the arm. He doesn't look up. I tear a piece of paper from my notebook, scribble *are you okay* on it, and put it on his desk. He slides it into his notebook without looking at it. I write another note, *I want to talk to you*, and put it on top of his notebook. He shoves it off to the side and it falls on the floor. I pick it up and hold it out to him. He flinches. I mouth *Thank you for standing up for me.* He glances at me, funny-like, and turns away quick. But not quick enough. I see his black eye. I grab his arm. Oh my God, I whisper. What did he do to you? He sinks down in his seat like he wants to disappear, like he's not Will anymore, like he's not my friend anymore.

I crumple the note into a little ball. My cheeks are wet. I wipe them with my sleeve. Something happened on Saturday night after I ran away from Tony. I never should have left Will alone with him. I never should have gone off with Tony. If only I could turn back the clock. If only I had never gone to that kegger.

Chapter Eight

"Morning, Mr. J. B." Jeremy Kuzik used his cane to pull himself up from where he was sitting on the bottom step of the eight-sided gazebo-style pavilion.

J. B. greeted him with a smile and a hearty handshake. "I figured it was you who left that note on the table last night."

"Why? Because I'm the oldest?"

"Because it seemed like you were in charge."

"Guess I am, Mr. J. B. Yup. Guess I am." He laughed and pointed at the benches inside the gazebo. "Let's sit up there. I forgot my cushion, and let me tell you, these crumbly old steps are not friendly to decrepit old bones like mine. The roof will protect us from the sun, too."

Mr. Kuzik climbed the pavilion's six steps as if he were attempting the ten-hour hike from the bottom of the Grand Canyon up to its rim without having had any training. When he reached the top, he collapsed onto a bench with his hand on his chest.

"Used to have concerts here in the park," he said after his breathing returned to normal. "Dances in the pavilion. Only thing we do now is put lights on this here gazebo in December." He ran his fingers along the inside wall. "See this. Paint peeling off like wallpaper. No one notices."

"So, Mr. Kuzik, in your note you said . . ."

"They keep mowing the grass regular, though, gotta give 'em that." His rheumy eyes fluttered as he gazed out at the park grounds. "I was born in 1930, so if during my lifetime this lawn was mowed regular for ninety-four summers, how many total mowings would that be, do ya think?"

Despite himself, J. B. attempted a quick calculation in his head and then said, "That's a more complicated question than it seems, Mr. Kuzik."

"Yup. It depends on how often it was mowed. What about when it rained? And then there was that drought the summer of, yup, can't remember what year that was. This is how I pass the time these days. Trying to figure out stuff like that." He stared off into space as if searching for more puzzles to unravel.

"So, Mr. Kuzik, in the note, you wrote that you remember Sylvia Jensen."

"I graduated from high school in 1948."

"Twelve years before Sylvia graduated?"

"I worked in the mine after high school. Lived with my parents until I saved enough money to go to college."

"And Sylvia?"

"Oh. Right. Sylvia. I knew who she was. I'd see her around before I left for college."

"So . . . Sylvia was just a little kid when you finished high school?"

Mr. Kuzik shook his head, and his eyes wandered off into the distance again. "I studied sociology. Living in the big city was quite the eye-opener."

"Just so I understand," J. B. said. "In your note, you said you remembered Sylvia, but you were twelve years older than her and you were away at college when she was in high school, so how well *did* you know her?"

"Oh, right. Well, you see, Mr. J. B., I moved back here *after* college. Got me a job in the police department. I was thirty years old. That was back in 1960."

"The year Sylvia graduated from high school." J. B. made a circular motion with his hands in an attempt to help him focus.

"I was the deputy police officer. That was my job title. Chief Jordane's assistant."

"Anthony Jordane's father."

"Yup. That's right. First day of work, Tony's pa throws me the keys to the police car and shoves a gun to me across the desk. Then he takes the day off and leaves me in charge. What do you think of that? Only training I ever got. I guess he figured I knew everything I needed to know because of all those courses I took in criminology and deviance. Tell the truth, I did have more learning about police work than he probably ever did." He smiled, but J. B. saw a melancholy look in his eyes. "Yup, first day on the job was January 1, 1960. New Year's Day." He sighed, a very long sigh. "Last day on the job was less than a year later." He lowered his head, and a tear dropped onto his blue-veined hand. "Don't remember the exact date. Guess I didn't want to."

"What happened, Mr. Kuzik? When you quit the job, did it have anything to do with that boy who died? As soon as I asked about William James last night, everyone stopped talking. Is there something you want to tell me about him?"

"There is . . . there was, but . . ." The old man shook his head and stared down at his tightly clasped hands. Just then J. B.'s iPhone rang, the special ring tone he and Mentayer had agreed to use when the call was important. He had told her that he would be busy that morning. She wouldn't be calling if it wasn't urgent.

"Sorry. I have to take this call, Mr. Kuzik. It's my wife."

"I hate to interrupt, hon, but I knew you'd want to know right away." He held his breath. Was this it? Was it over? "Sylvia is sitting up in bed and, you won't believe this, but right now she's eating breakfast."

J. B. let out his breath and looked up at the cloudless morning sky, his eyes glistening.

"She even made me get her something from the coffee shop downstairs."

"'A plain croissant, or almond if they have one,'" he said, laughing louder and longer than he had laughed in a long time, maybe ever.

"J. B., are you in Bigger?" At the sound of Sylvia's clear voice in the background, he broke out in a smile that stretched from ear to ear.

"I'm sitting in the park pavilion."

"Why?"

Her terseness, so often irritating in the past, was music to his ears now. "Why? Because I am here talking to Jeremy Kuzik. He remembers you."

Sylvia cleared her throat. "Put him on," she said.

"It's Sylvia Jensen, Mr. Kuzik. She would like to talk to you." J. B. held out the phone, and the old man recoiled as if it were a grenade about to explode. His mouth twisted in pain. Tears ran down his cheeks. Then he clutched at his chest and J. B., now seriously alarmed, quickly told Sylvia he would have to call her back.

"She doesn't know," the old man whimpered. "Nobody knows."

"You can tell me, Mr. Kuzik. I'm listening," J. B. said as he pressed the record button on his iPhone.

"Will was in his cell. The boy didn't want any visitors, but Sylvia wouldn't take no for an answer. I only let her have five minutes. Didn't even let her go inside his cell, only talk to him through the bars. I heard her tell him she was going to get him out."

A few seconds of silence followed until J. B., worried the old man might have drifted off again, asked, "Why was Will in jail, Mr. Kuzik? Did Sylvia get him out?"

The old man didn't hear him, in fact didn't seem to be there, almost as if he were back in 1960 again. "I went to the bathroom," he finally said. "Only for a few minutes. That's all it was." He struck his knees with the palms of his hands, then winced and fell silent again.

"Mr. Kuzik? Was Sylvia still there when you went to the bathroom? Mr. Kuzik, can you hear me?"

The old man looked at him, his eyes open in surprise. "Oh no, Sylvia was there in the afternoon. It was later that night when I went to the bathroom. I left the keys on my desk. I never should have done that. And I never should have gone to the bathroom without first making sure the door to the station was locked." He gritted his teeth. "When I came back from the bathroom, my keys were still there, right where I left them. The chief was sitting at his desk. He said he came in to catch up on some paperwork, so I figured everything was okay. After about an hour he told me to go check on Will. That's when I found the cell door open. The boy was gone. The chief told me to stay there, and he'd go look for him, said he couldn't have gotten very far. When he came back, he said he'd looked for him everywhere. The alley behind City Hall. Up and down Main Street. All over town. I don't know how that boy escaped or how he could have disappeared so fast." He paused to wipe away a tear. "I told the chief the truth. I told him I left my keys on the desk. I knew it was my fault."

He wiped the tears from his face and, with a final very long sigh, said, "The next morning, Will was found dead in the woods, and at the end of the year, I was back to working in the mines."

The old man leaned back on the bench with a long sigh. Stretched his legs out straight, like he was finished, but J. B. was just getting started. He had even more questions than before.

"Mr. Kuzik," he said, "did you ever find out how Will got out? And why didn't the paper say anything about *how* he died?"

"The chief investigated, but we never did find out, Mr. J. B., and he thought it was best not to cause alarm in the town."

"But surely people would have wanted to know how he died. Didn't anyone ask?"

The old man looked at him, bewildered. "You don't understand, Mr. J. B. No one ever talked about what happened that night."

• • •

Two hours later, sunlight dappled the narrow path as Jeremy Kuzik walked away with a sprightly gait after shedding his decades-old shame. J. B. stayed in the pavilion to record their conversation on his iPad, typing what he knew in the left column and what he didn't know in the right column. He'd learned a lot but, as usual, that had triggered even more questions. Why was Will in jail in the first place? And how could he just disappear from his cell? Did he escape? Did someone let him out? Was he taken? Then his body, found the next morning—by whom? exactly where? how did he die? did someone kill him? how could no one know? And the one unanswered question that still weighed most heavily on him: *Why* was any of it Sylvia's fault?

He had asked Mr. Kuzik if Sylvia might have taken the keys from his desk, unlocked Will's cell, and helped him escape.

"No, not saying that at all, Mr. J. B.," the old man had said. "I must admit, though, that I did wonder at first if that was the case, because I heard her promise that boy, clear as anything that same afternoon, that she was going to get him out. But then, after he died, she went running around town, you wouldn't believe it, Mr. J. B., what she was saying . . . all kinds of crazy things . . . things that made no sense at all . . . So no, then I knew it wasn't her."

"What kinds of things did she say," J. B. had asked.

"Oh, hardly worth a mention, Mr. J. B. Too crazy to repeat. Uh-uh, don't need to fill your head with old rumors."

J. B. had prodded, asked for just one example of something Sylvia had said, but to no avail. "Okay then, one more question, Mr. Kuzik, if you will. Didn't you ask the chief how he thought Will got out of that cell that night?"

At that, the old man had given him a blank look. "No, why would I? I knew it was my fault. I told him it was."

"Do you know if *anyone* ever asked or talked about how Will got out of his cell?"

"Well . . . there was one person. Gerald Pelto. He's the only person I know of who ever said *anything* about that night. His older brother Stan was my best friend. We worked the mines together, and after Stan was gone, I visited Gerry a few times in the nursing home until he died, too. He claimed he knew things about what happened back in 1960 that he never told anyone."

"What kinds of things?"

"Didn't ask. Didn't want to know. Wouldn't be true nohow. He didn't lie exactly. It's more like he made up stories. They say it was his Alzheimer's. Poor guy."

"I've heard that typically a person with Alzheimer's is more apt to recall things from many years ago than more recent memories. Do you think he might have told his stories to anyone else?"

"Only one I can think of. Spencer Jackson. We called him Spence. He was a few years younger than Gerry, heard they played together as kids. Not sure if he's still alive, though. Last I heard he was in the Altos City hospice."

"Thank you, Mr. Kuzik. I'll check that out."

"Up to you, Mr. J. B., but if you want my opinion, I think you're wasting your time. Gerry and Spence, why, they were only little kids back when Will died, I don't know, eight, maybe ten years old at most. They don't know anything."

None of that mattered to J. B. A lead was a lead, and he always followed each and every one of them. He called up directions to the Altos City Hospice and Palliative Center on his iPhone, saw it was a twenty-minute drive from Bigger, and then returned to Sylvia's car to call her back. After ringing only once, someone picked up the phone in her hospital room and then dropped the receiver. After a minute of nothing but fumbling sounds, Sylvia's voice came on the line.

"J. B.? Is that you?"

"Sylvia! Why are you answering the phone? What'd you do with my wife?"

"She went to get more coffee. Are you still with Jeremy? Let me talk to him."

"He left, but he did tell me what he knew."

"Well, then you already know what happened. Anthony Jordane murdered Will."

"What? No! Jeremy told me that cause of death couldn't be determined. Could have been a suicide."

"Tony killed him!"

"What makes you think that, Sylvia?"

"I don't think it, I *know* it . . . and I know why he did it, too. Didn't Jeremy remember . . . oh, he probably didn't want to say. I mean, Tony's father was the police chief, after all. He covered it up to protect his son."

"What do *you* remember, Sylvia?"

"You won't believe me. No one ever did."

"Go ahead, try me."

After several seconds of labored breathing, Sylvia started talking again, only this time in a voice that was not her own but instead that of a distressed teenage girl.

"Everyone thinks you did it, but I know you didn't. Look at me, Will. Please." She choked on a sob, or was there a catch in her breath, J. B. couldn't tell. "I will get you out, Will. I'll tell them the truth about everything." Her breathing was coming in short, rapid spurts now. "Daddy! Mom! Listen to me. Will helped me and now he needs our help. You have to help him! You . . . have . . . to . . ." Her words faded into a long, drawn-out moan. "Stop yelling, Daddy. Please. I told you I was sorry I snuck off to the kegger. I'm sorry I got drunk. I'm sorry I lied to you. But I'm telling the truth now. Please believe me. Please." She stopped to blow her nose, and when she spoke again, her voice sounded bold and defiant. "So I'm a liar. So what? Maybe Grandpa's right. Maybe the devil *is* in me."

J. B. became increasingly worried as he listened. Re-living the past, which was what Sylvia seemed to be doing, was too stressful for her. Still, something told him not to interrupt. If the cardiac arrest had been triggered by an old trauma, then maybe this was what she needed to do. He curled his fingers around the phone and held his tongue. Sylvia was the strongest woman he'd ever known. She would be all right.

"Let it go, girl, it's none of your business." Sylvia's voice was sing-songy and sarcastic now, sounded even less like her than before. "Besides, how do you know Will didn't do it? Were you there, Sylvia? Did you see what happened? I mean, really, you were kinda busy with Tony that night, weren't you? Maybe you're just mad cuz he broke up with you. Seriously, girl? Have you lost your mind? You keep telling lies and you're gonna get yourself run right out of this town."

When J. B. heard a *whoosh* sound, as if Sylvia had just pushed all the air out of her lungs, he couldn't stand it anymore. "Stop!" His voice was like a slap that left her whimpering on the other end of the phone. "You're not in Bigger anymore, Sylvia. You're in Monrow City. You're in the hospital."

She sucked in her breath. "Becca?"

"You're not Becca. I'm not Becca. It's me, J. B. I'm talking to you on the phone. You're in the hospital. Mentayer is staying there with you. Everything is okay now."

That seemed to bring her back, because after a long sorrowful sigh, she spoke, and this time it sounded like her. "I told them Tony killed Will. That he had to get rid of him because he knew that Tony tried to rape me. I told them Tony was mad at Will because Will helped me run away from him. No one believed me."

"Tell me, Sylvia, how did Tony do it? How did Jordane kill Will?"

"He . . . he . . . I *know* he killed him, and I know *why*. But, but . . ." She groaned. “Oh no, I can’t remember *how*. How could I forget the most important thing? Why can’t I remember? What’s wrong with me?”

“It’s all right, Sylvia. You’re okay. The doctor said you might experience some temporary memory loss. Don’t worry. Jeremy Kuzik told me about someone who might know what happened.”

“Becca knows what happened, J. B.—Becca Milley. That was her name. Unless she got married. Then I don’t know what it is. I don’t know if she still lives in Bigger.”

“Okay, Sylvia. You rest now. I’ll go see what I can find out.”

“I am tired,” she said with a sniffle. “I am very tired.”

J. B. pressed his forehead against the steering wheel and closed his eyes. He had just met seventeen-year-old Sylvia, and it had been almost unbearable to listen to the fear, distress, and desperation in her voice.

He sat up, took in a deep breath, and let it out. He felt like his heart had just broken into a million pieces for Sylvia. But he had come to Bigger to find the truth for her, and in order to do that, he would have to set aside his emotions. He didn’t know if she’d been hallucinating on the phone, if she had brain damage, or if she was remembering or re-living something that actually happened. But he did know that if Anthony Jordane really was a rapist and a murderer, he would have to be held accountable.

Furthermore, he knew that Sylvia could not have been responsible for Will’s death.

He told himself that he had come this far and there was no turning back. Whatever the consequences, he would explore all leads, starting with the one Sylvia just gave him. He checked the white pages on his iPhone and found Becca Milley. She was still living in Bigger. He called her phone number, but no one answered, so he left a long message, explained what he wanted to talk to her about, and said he was on his way to her house now. But first, he texted Mentayer. *I’m worried about Sylvia. Call and let me know how she is.*

Chapter Nine

1960

Where is Will? He always eats lunch the same time as me on Mondays. Why isn't he here? I have to talk to him. I have to know he's okay.

I hear she's only fourteen. Her brother never should have brought her to the kegger in the first place. Don't you agree, Sylvie?

What?

Aren't you even listening? I'm trying to tell you about the girl who was raped on Saturday night. Her brother told my brother. They know each other from basketball. Ray says not to tell anyone. I'm only telling you, Sylvie, so you have something else to think about for a minute. I mean, girl, ever since we sat down all you've been doing is looking for Tony.

Raped? Who?

A girl from Altos City. She was raped on Saturday night. She's only fourteen. Poor girl.

I feel sick. I'm gonna throw up. If not for Will, that girl would have been me. Did Tony call her babe, too? Did he hold her down like he held me down? Did his hands grope her like they groped me? Did he hurt her like he hurt me? Force her into his car? Rip her clothes off? Push . . .

What's wrong, Sylvie? You're shaking like a leaf. Why, I believe you're even more lovesick than I thought.

Becca winks and puts her hand on my arm. I flinch, slap her hand away.

How?

How *what*?

How is she? The girl who was raped. Is she okay?

Don't know. Her brother says she won't talk about it. She doesn't want anyone to know. Just wants to forget it ever happened. I don't blame her, do you?

Becca shrugs. I shake my head. No, I don't blame her. I want to forget, too. I don't want anyone to know either. Only it's different for that poor girl, whoever she is. She didn't get away. I did. I was lucky. She wasn't.

Becca laughs and waves to someone on the other side of the room. She doesn't care about that girl. Not one bit. I grab my tray, throw my lunch in the trash can, then push the tray through the dishwasher window. Where is Will? I have to find him. I have to know he's okay.

I hurry to Advanced English. He's always early to class, never late, but he doesn't show up at all this afternoon. I can't pay attention. I have no idea what our teacher is saying about homework or anything. I run to senior study hall next, but Will's not here either. Tony is, though. He's parading around the room high-fiving his buddies. I scrunch down in my seat. My cheeks burn. I know they're beet red. I stare at my homework until the bell rings. Then I walk, don't run, out of the room, but I can't even try to act like I'm in my right mind any longer.

Becca is waiting for me. Leaning on my locker. Not smiling like she usually is at the end of the day. Her forehead is all scrunched up. Something's wrong but I don't ask her what. I don't want to hear anything else from her today, maybe never.

Excuse me, Becca, you're in my way. I'd like to get into my locker, please.

She doesn't move.

I need to tell you something, Sylvie. It's about Will.

Where is he? What happened to him?

She bites her upper lip and stares down at the floor. I grab her by the arm. Her books crash onto the floor.

Just tell me Will is okay, Becca! Tell me!

I know you like him, Sylvie, but . . . well . . . it seems that . . . Well, you know that girl I told you about at lunch? Well, they're saying it was Will who raped her.

I slam my fist into the locker door. She bends down and picks up her books, then squeezes them against her chest like she's protecting herself from me. She better.

Who is *they*? Huh? Your stupid brother? Who? Never mind. I don't care. They're liars. *All of them!*

I'm screaming. I don't care. Becca looks scared. I don't care.

I'm sorry, Sylvie. I wanted to tell you before you heard it from someone else.

You believe what they're saying, don't you? Tell me you don't, Becca! Tell me!

Look, Sylvie. Someone saw Will coming out of the woods with blood on his shirt. He got in his car and drove away. Fast. I really am sorry. I know he's your friend. I'm only telling you what someone saw.

Becca puts her arm around my shoulder, but I grab her hand and twist it off me. She yelps. Good!

No, Becca, you are not telling me what someone saw. You are telling me what someone *said* he saw. And I know who he was!

I just thought you'd want to know, girl. That's all. I don't know what's true and what's not true. And neither do you.

I know more than you think I do, Becca. I know that Will did not hurt that girl. He would never hurt anyone.

Then he has nothing to worry about. But then, if he didn't do anything wrong, where is he now? Why did he leave school? Is he hiding?

Stop! Just st-st-st-stop!

Becca gasps and wipes my spit off her neck, then rubs her cheek. Did I just slap her? I run away, down the hall, stumble out the door, almost fall down the steps. I'm crying and running, crying and running. *Be home, Will, please, please be home. I know what happened. I know Tony beat you up at the kegger. I shouldn't have left you alone with him. He was furious at me, and he took it out on you. You didn't do anything wrong, Will. You just stopped to say hi. You were just being friendly. Did you even know that you helped me get away from him? Tony's telling everyone that you raped that girl but I know it was Tony who raped her. I know you would never, ever do anything like that. I'm going to tell everyone the truth about what really happened.*

I'm crossing the railroad track, running to his house, tripping on the broken porch step, pounding on the door, looking through the window, bending over the porch railing and throwing up. *I am so sorry, Will. I will fix it. I promise. I will fix it.*

Chapter Ten

J. B. looked out the car window at the untrimmed branches of the overgrown trees in Bigger Park encroaching on the sidewalk, and the pavilion's sagging roof that was in dire need of repair. He gripped his iPhone. Why was it taking so long for Mentayer to call? It seemed like forever since he texted her, but then he glanced at his watch and saw that it had only been a few minutes. Just then, his iPhone rang.

"What is it, hon? What's wrong? Why are you worried about Sylvia? Where are you? Are you still with that old guy in the park?

"See, that's exactly why I'm worried. I talked to Sylvia on the phone after Jeremy Kuzik left, but she obviously forgot to tell you. It wasn't that long ago. I'm really worried about her memory. How does she seem to you? Do you think she has brain damage? Has the doctor been in to see her yet today?"

"Slow down, hon. You must have talked to her while I was out, and she was asleep when I came back. She just hasn't had a chance to tell me yet. That's all."

"I should have stopped her, Mentayer. You'd be worried, too, if you heard her. When I asked her about Will, she didn't just tell me what happened, it was like she was *re-living* it. Like she was seventeen years old again. She sounded so little, so helpless. Do you think she may have been hallucinating? I should have known it was too much for her. I should have stopped her."

"Sylvia is all right, J. B. The nurse just checked her vitals. She's stable. It's good for her to sleep. It was probably a huge relief for her to talk about everything."

"That's the thing, Mentayer. She didn't talk about *every*thing. She insists that Jordane killed Will, but she can't remember how he did it. Do you think she might be making things up in her head?"

"It's the trauma," Mentayer said. "I see it with the kids at my school all the time. Their brains protect them from remembering some things because it's too painful or unthinkable to remember them."

"Do you think Sylvia didn't remember *anything* that happened in 1960 before, and now she's just beginning to remember some but not all of it?"

"Sure. It could have been hidden in her brain for decades, and then the shock of seeing Anthony Jordane brought it out from the shadows. Maybe everything isn't all the way out yet."

"I think it might be best if she doesn't remember anything else. She's old, Mentayer, and she's fragile. It could be too much for her. It could kill her."

"Or it could be a chance for her to heal."

J. B. sighed. Maybe they were getting ahead of themselves. Maybe it wasn't even true that Jordane killed Will. Maybe that's why Sylvia couldn't remember how he did it.

"So, hon," Mentayer said, "did that old guy shed any new light on it?"

Without getting bogged down in the details, J. B. filled his wife in on what he'd learned from Jeremy Kuzik. "In a nutshell," he concluded, "Sylvia is sure that Anthony Jordane murdered Will but can't remember how, and the Bigger police couldn't determine the cause of his death."

"Mighty suspicious," Mentayer said. "Sounds like Sylvia may be right that the police covered it up. So, now what?"

"I'm on my way to see Sylvia's old high school friend Becca," he said. "Maybe she knows something."

When J. B. said good-bye, he felt better. Talking to his wife had helped, and he was ready now to take the next step. He opened Google Maps on his iPhone and entered Becca's address, then put the key in the ignition and listened to the engine roar to life.

> *In 400 feet, turn left at the stop sign. Go six blocks. Then turn right on Seventh Street North. Your destination is on the right.*

He pulled into the driveway next to Becca's pale yellow house, and parked behind a Ford Mustang that looked like it was in worse shape than Sylvia's Toyota, if that was even possible. There was a narrow sidewalk under the front window of the house, with weeds sprouting through the cracks, and the grass on the lawn looked like it hadn't been mowed all summer. It occurred to J. B. that maybe Becca no longer lived here, or maybe she was traveling, which would explain why she didn't answer the phone.

He knocked on the front door, heard rustling sounds inside, and knocked again. Out of the corner of his eye, he saw the closed curtain in the front window open an inch or two and then close. He knocked again. Louder this time. The door opened a crack. It was dark inside, too dark to see anything.

"Hello? I'm looking for Becca Milley? My name is J. B. Harrell. I called and left a message a few minutes ago. Sylvia Jensen asked me to talk to you. About William James. She thinks you might remember what happened to him. I explained it all in my phone message. Maybe you haven't had a chance to listen to it yet?"

Silence.

"Are you Becca? Can we talk? Just for a few minutes? Outside if you'd like."

"I don't know anything. Sorry."

The small opening in the door closed then with a finality that J. B. recognized. He knew from experience that if someone doesn't want or is afraid to talk, you can't make them. He also knew from experience that Becca was lying. He could tell she knew something.

He returned to the car, backed it out of the driveway. And, because he also knew from experience that Becca would watch until he was gone, he drove to the outskirts of town before stopping to search for directions to the Altos City Hospice and Palliative Center. Jeremy Kuzik could be right that he was wasting his time by going there, but after coming this far and learning a lot already, he wasn't about to stop now. And Spencer Jackson was the only other lead he had.

• • •

J. B. passed through several small towns, some similar in size to Bigger, a few smaller, one a mere hamlet of no more than a dozen houses along the two-lane road, before he reached the suburban density of Altos City with its neat rows of houses, apartment buildings, and parks. He drove past a shopping mall that was crowded with stores like Sears and JCPenney, chain restaurants like Papa Murphy's and McDonald's, a Super One Foods, and an ExxonMobil gas station—shops upon which folks from all the neighboring towns like Bigger depended. One mile later, he was at the Altos City Hospital and following the signage to the Hospice and Palliative Care Center, which led him around the corner to a square sandstone brick building that was tucked in the back.

What a peaceful place to spend your last days, J. B. thought, when he heard the quiet flow of water in the bamboo fountain outside the hospice center and then experienced the quiet serenity inside the vestibule. Stone fireplace, clerestory windows, vaulted wood beam ceiling. French doors that opened to different spaces—a community room, chapel, meditation room, sunroom, children's play area, administrative offices.

"May I help you?"

He turned toward the friendly voice, so entranced by the place that he hadn't noticed the desk to the left of the entrance or the gray-haired receptionist sitting behind it.

"Good afternoon," he said. "I'm here to visit Spencer Jackson."

"Are you a relative or friend?"

"My name is J. B. Harrell and I'm a reporter with the *New York Times*."

"I see." The receptionist tipped her head down and raised her eyes up. "And is Mr. Jackson expecting you?"

J. B. shook his head. "I'm writing a story about his hometown, and I was hoping he might help me with some background information. That is, if he's well enough to see me."

"Hold on," the receptionist said with a friendly midwestern smile as she reached for the phone on the desk. "Let me check with him."

She talked softly into the receiver for a few minutes and then said, "Mr. Jackson will see you. He says he's having a good day."

She gave him directions to an inner courtyard on the other side of the building, that was surrounded by eight apartments. He sucked in his breath when, waiting for him outside the door to apartment number 4, he saw a thin, pale man with skin so blotchy it looked like his blood could no longer reach all the parts of his body.

"Mr. Harrell." Spencer Jackson's voice was weak and shaky, and he had to pause between words to catch his breath. "A reporter, you say? With the *New York Times*, no less?"

"That's me. Only everyone calls me J. B."

"Okay, then. J. B. And everyone calls me Spence. Now tell me, why have you come to see *me*?"

"I just had a long talk with Jeremy Kuzik in Bigger, and he mentioned you and Gerald Pelto."

"Kuzik? He's still alive? Gotta be in his late nineties! What did he have to say about Gerry and me?"

"He remembers that the two of you played together as kids. I think he said that your fathers knew each other, too."

"And?" Spence Jackson raised his eyebrows. He held out his palms and splayed his fingers in a way that indicated to J. B. that his curiosity outweighed his sense of caution or suspicion.

"Mostly, Mr. Kuzik and I talked about a boy named William James. Everyone called him Will."

Spence pursed his lips and scrunched his eyebrows into a knot. "Does Mr. Kuzik know how Will died?"

J. B. shook his head.

"And he says that I do?"

"No, no. He only said that Gerry Pelto may have had some ideas about what happened. Maybe Gerry talked to you about that?"

"Well, Gerry did try to figure out for himself what happened to Will, after he overheard his father and some men talking about it. But he was only ten years old at the time."

"Did he tell you what he figured out? Or what he heard the men saying? Anything?"

Several seconds passed. Spence Jackson sighed a couple of times, stared at the floor and shuffled his feet.

"I'm sorry, Spence, about bombarding you with all these questions. I haven't even told you why I want to know."

Spence Jackson looked up with a shake of his head and then, sounding resigned and standing to the side as if he'd made a decision, said, "I guess you better come in then."

With painstaking slowness like it hurt his feet to walk, Spence led the way across the soft beige carpet toward a picture window at the end of his small efficiency apartment. Past a single bed with a bedspread in muted shades of browns and oranges and a small table with a lamp and tabletop humidifier on it. Through a sitting area with a reclining chair and a television along one wall and a small rectangular table with a wood bowl of fresh fruit along the other. He stopped when they reached double doors that opened to a garden flush with sun-drenched orange, pink, and purple wildflowers and decorative bushes that made the apartment seem like an extension of nature.

"It's a beautiful day." Spence walked through the doors and stepped out onto a small patio. He motioned for J. B. to sit in one of two comfortable-looking stuffed chairs and then slowly lowered himself into the other. He leaned back and crossed his arms, his eyes locked on J. B.

"Why is the *New York Times* interested in something that happened to a boy over sixty years ago in a small, insignificant midwestern town?"

"It isn't. I mean, I'm not on assignment. The *New York Times* didn't send me. A friend of mine did. Sylvia Jensen."

Spence Jackson uncrossed his arms, his mouth open in a silent O.

"Sylvia's in the hospital now. We think, I mean, I hope she's going to be okay, but . . ." J. B. rubbed his eyes and took in a deep breath. "But I worry about her. You see, she believes that what happened to Will was all her fault. I know, of course, that it couldn't have been, but I have to prove . . . I mean, I need her to know, before . . ." He bit his lip. "I don't want her to die feeling guilty about something she didn't do. So . . ." J. B. couldn't believe he had just blurted all that out. "So, I'm doing what I know how to do. Investigating, you know, following a trail of leads so I can find out what really happened."

"And I'm one of the leads you got from Jeremy Kuzik."

"Exactly. He said Gerald Pelto had ideas about how Will died, so I thought you might know what those were. Did Gerry ever talk to you about that?"

"Yes, he did. J. B., we were just kids." Spence paused to catch his breath. "When Gerry overheard some men who were meeting at his house with his father. He heard one of them say 'We're gonna have to take care of that injun ourselves.' And after Will's body was found, he asked me if I thought those men he heard had anything to do with it, and I said I didn't know. We were kids, you know, and I thought we'd both forgotten about it. But then I visited Gerry in memory care, just before he died, and he said he had finally figured out what happened to Will."

"And what was it? Did he tell you?"

Spence shook his head. "He figured the men were angry because Will raped a fourteen-year-old girl, and they didn't want him to get away with it. After that, everything got mixed up for him. At least that's what it seemed like to me. Anyway, nothing he said made sense to me after that."

Spence Jackson leaned forward in the chair, shifted his position. He bent over and held his head in his hands. He groaned and sat up. Finally, he looked J. B. straight in the eye and took a deep breath.

"I know what happened to Will," he said. "And Sylvia Jensen had nothing to do with it."

• • •

For a very long time, Spence Jackson was quiet. He looked up as if searching the sky for heaven, for mercy. "It's time," he finally said. "What I am going to tell you, J. B., is something I have never told anyone before."

This was it. J. B. felt it in every bone in his body. The truth was about to be revealed. The truth that would set Sylvia free. The truth that would either hold Anthony Jordane accountable or set him free as well. A lump formed in his throat, there was a burning sensation behind his eyes, and he tightened his jaw and clenched his fists to hold the tears at bay.

"Whew. Let me see," Spence said. "I don't how . . . ummm . . . where to start."

"How about with how you came to know what happened, Spence? Was it Gerry or someone else who told you?"

"My father. When he was dying." Spence's lip trembled, and he covered his heart with the palms of both hands. "He said he wouldn't be able to die until he got it off his chest. He told me he'd made a terrible mistake a long time ago. He was so ashamed of what he had done that he never told a soul about it."

Spence closed his eyes, breathed in and out several times, and then said, "My father wasn't a religious man, but he was confessing. When he told me what he'd done, he was really asking God, not me, to forgive him. A few minutes later, he died."

J. B. placed his hand gently on Spence's arm.

"He was my dad, you know, and I loved him. I still love him. But now that *I'm* dying, well, if you want to know the truth, I don't want to carry his shame with me to my grave either." After a heavy, drawn-out sigh, he added, "It's not just my father's shame, you know. It's mine. I'm his son. It's Bigger's shame, too. Everyone in that town who kept the secret. Including me. Until now." He slapped the arms of his chair, then cried out in pain.

"Whenever you're ready," J. B. said. "Take your time."

• • •

For more than an hour, Spence Jackson, his voice feeble and at times almost inaudible, had disclosed his father's, and Bigger's, shameful secret about the death of William James. When he was finished, he asked J. B. to help him into bed and, with the physical frailty of a man facing imminent death, asked to be left alone.

J. B. stepped out into the hall, careful not to make a sound when closing the door. He pressed his back against the wall with his eyes closed, his head in a fog, his heart shattered. *Lynched. William James was lynched.* He started walking. He had no plan for where to go, no sense of direction. Later he would wonder how he had ended up alone in the hospice meditation room with tears streaming down his cheeks, his feet cold, his nose stuffed up, and a tremor traveling up and down his back as it released all the emotions he'd intentionally suppressed while listening to Spence Jackson. A long-ago-closed channel to his heart opened and his chest expanded to make room for the pain. His head fell into his hands. *That boy, Will, that could have been me. Could have easily been me. He was me.* He lost all sense of time, forgetting where he was, who he was, what was happening.

A sound coming from his pocket frightened him at first until he realized it was a text notification on his iPhone. A text from Mentayer. After waiting for his head to clear, he read it. *Sylvia is awake now. She's waiting for you to call.* He took a deep breath in and let it out, then texted back: *I need to talk to you alone first.* Less than five minutes later, just as he was stepping outside the hospice center and breathing in the warm summer air, Mentayer called.

"I'm outside Sylvia's room. What is it? J. B., are you there? Are you all right?"

"No. I think so. I hope so." He lowered himself onto a bench next to the bamboo fountain in the middle of the patio in front of the hospice entrance.

"What happened?"

He blew air through his lips, and then the words came blurting out. "Will was lynched." He heard her gasp.

"Wait, J. B. Sylvia needs to hear this."

"No! It's too risky. She couldn't remember what happened because she couldn't handle it. You said so yourself."

"That was before, J. B. She can handle it now."

"Not in her condition, she can't. We can't take the chance."

With an almost imperceptible sigh and an ever-so-slight tone of irritation, Mentayer said, "Well, go on then. Tell me."

"Here's everything I know." He breathed in the sound of the water splashing in the fountain, then breathed it out until he was able to sink into a short version of the story.

"A fourteen-year-old girl was raped at the senior kegger. Tony Jordane told his father, the police chief, that he saw Will coming out of the woods that night with blood on his shirt. Based on that evidence, Will was arrested. But then the girl wouldn't talk, wouldn't even admit to being raped. So a group of men, enraged that Will was going to get away with it, took the law into their own hands. The police chief unlocked Will's cell, told him to go home until he got a call from the court, and then released him, knowing the men were outside, lying in wait to lynch him. The next morning, his body was found. There was no noose, no ladder, no way to prove he was lynched. No way, apparently, to determine cause of death." J. B. paused to catch his breath. His voice shook and he bit his bottom lip.

Mentayer didn't say anything for what seemed like an eternity, so he went on to tell the last part of what Spencer Jackson had revealed to him.

"Everyone in town thought that Will must have felt so guilty about raping that girl that he killed himself. Everyone except Sylvia, that is. But no one would listen to her, not her friend Becca, not her parents, no one. People said she was a nut job and spread terrible rumors about her. Tony Jordane bragged that she was a tight-ass bitch, but he got some pussy from her anyway, and all the stories she was telling were just her way of covering that up because she was so ashamed of her prissy self. She left town, didn't even go to her high school graduation, and never came back."

Mentayer sniffled, then blew her nose. "All these years," she said. "Sylvia felt guilty because she couldn't save Will. And she probably felt guilty about running away after he was killed instead of staying and trying to clear his name." She paused and then said, "I'll call you back in a little while. Remember, I love you." Then she hung up before he had a chance to say anything.

He stared at his iPhone. Whatever his wife was going to do, he wasn't going to like it or agree with it, but there was nothing he could do about it. Less than fifteen minutes later, while he was still sitting by the fountain, she called back.

"Sylvia knows," she said. "I told her everything. Here. She wants to talk to you. I'm putting you on speaker."

"Thank you, J. B. Now I know how Tony killed Will," she said.

"But Sylvia, Spencer Jackson didn't say Jordane killed Will. He didn't even say he was there the night they lynched Will."

Right away, J. B. kicked himself for saying that. Sylvia had had enough of people not believing her.

"I'm very tired," she said. "I need to rest now."

Then the phone went silent, and J. B. hung his head. He had gone and made things worse.

Chapter Eleven

J. B. leaned back on the bench and stretched his legs out in front of him. He was angry, at himself. And he was confused. Why did Sylvia still think that Anthony Jordane killed Will? Maybe what she meant was that Jordane had *caused* Will's death by providing false evidence that led to his lynching. Or did she really think that Jordane was part of the lynch mob, maybe that he led it? Had he in fact uncovered the truth about what happened to Will or was there still more to it, something else that Sylvia couldn't remember? Why did she end their phone call so abruptly? Something wasn't right. He couldn't shake the feeling that there was still more to the story.

His iPhone pinged. An alert from Peter Minter. *They moved it up. We need you back here tomorrow when the governor announces her endorsement.*

J. B. groaned. Peter was not going to want to hear anything bad about Anthony Jordane. He was not going to want J. B. to write anything that would interfere with the governor's endorsement or say anything that would jeopardize Peter's own support of Jordane's campaign. But what could he do? He was a journalist. He had always been committed to telling the truth.

With a sigh, he texted back: *Need to talk. Have uncovered some disturbing information here.* Almost immediately, the phone rang, and he took in a deep breath, prepared to tell Peter he was on his way to Monrow City and that he would tell him everything once he got there. Only the caller wasn't Peter. It was Mentayer calling again.

"Don't panic, hon," she said. "Sylvia is okay. But she's talking in her sleep, about things you should know about. Hold on, let me go see if the lounge is empty."

J. B. listened to the familiar hospital sounds in the background while he waited. If Sylvia hadn't revealed something very important, Mentayer wouldn't have called back so soon.

"Here I am, J. B. I wrote everything down, like you asked me to. Okay, here's what Sylvia said. 'Tony beat Will up . . . that's why he had blood on his shirt . . . Tony was mad because I got away from him . . . he blamed Will for that. . . Tony raped Patricia Grogan . . . he killed her so she wouldn't tell anyone . . . Will knew the truth . . . so Tony had to kill him.' That's all I wrote down, it's everything I could decipher."

"Wait a minute. Jordane raped a fourteen-year-old girl? And *killed* her? She died?" J. B. had to stop there for a minute before he could focus on details. "And the blood on Will's shirt was his own, not the girl's blood? And the girl's name was . . . Patricia? Grogan?" J. B. hurried to the car. Bent over and out of breath, he opened the car door, and the warm air inside hit him in the face. "I didn't know the girl's name before," he told Mentayer. "Maybe I can find some of her relatives. They'll know how she died. Call Peter Minter for me, okay? Tell him I plan to be at the governor's press conference tomorrow. I'm not ready to talk to him myself yet."

As soon as they ended the call, he leaned against the car, found the Altos City white pages on his iPhone, and scrolled down through the names of all the people whose last names started with *G*. There was only one Grogan. Julia.

He called the number right away. The phone rang several times, and he was about to give up when a woman answered, sounding out of breath.

"Is this Julia Grogan?"

"Yes. Who's calling, please?"

"My name is J. B. Harrell, and I'm wondering if you're related to Patricia Grogan?"

"She was my sister. Why?"

"I'm a friend of Sylvia Jensen."

"Who?"

"Sylvia Jensen. She grew up not far from here, in the town of Bigger? I'm sorry. Maybe you didn't know her. She . . ."

"You're right, I don't know her. Why?"

"I'm trying to help Sylvia. She lives in Monrow City now, and I drove up in her car to . . . it's hard to explain on the phone. I was hoping I might meet with you."

"I'm sorry. I don't know anyone named Sylvia Jensen, and I certainly don't know why she would have asked you to come and see me."

"She didn't. You see, Sylvia's in the hospital."

"Oh, so you're asking for a donation. Sorry, I can't help you. I don't take those kinds of calls."

"No, no, I'm not asking for money. It's difficult to talk about this on the phone, but it seems that Sylvia Jensen and your sister Patricia may have been raped by the same person, and—"

"Who the hell did you say you were?"

"J. B. Harrell. My friend Sylvia Jensen says the same man who tried to rape her back in 1960 raped Patricia, and then killed her to keep her from telling anyone."

"What? Are you for real? What?!"

"I'm for real. I am. I promise. Sylvia thinks what happened to your sister may have been her fault. She's very sick. I was hoping you could help me."

J. B. was disgusted with himself. What was wrong with him? Never before, even when he was a brand-new reporter, had he blundered like this—so badly in fact, that he didn't even know how to rescue himself. But then, much to his surprise, after an interminably long several seconds, Julia Grogan said, "You better come over, Mr. Harrell."

Ten minutes later, he parked Sylvia's car on a tree-lined street in front of a typically Midwest-style arts and crafts stucco and brick bungalow. And there, standing in the doorway with her hands on her hips, was Julia Grogan, an attractive woman in her seventies wearing a cobalt-blue ankle-length housedress, her silver hair tickling the top of stylish round blue-framed glasses.

They sat at an oval wooden table in a kitchen with dark woodwork and shelves that contained an organized collection of cookware, dishes, and utensils and smelled of freshly brewed coffee. J. B. was surprised at how self-possessed Julia seemed as she poured coffee and put a plate of chocolate chip cookies on the table, especially with an inarticulate stranger like him in her house. He was grateful to her for giving him a chance and careful, unlike on the phone, to clarify who he was. He knew that each of the wrinkles radiating from her eyes and down her cheeks contained a painful story, a story he was determined to learn. And so he eased into the conversation: shared a bit about himself and how he grew up in the general area, gave her ample background information about why he had made the trip to Bigger, and answered every question she threw at him. It was only when he told her, in person this time, that Sylvia said that Jordane had raped and then killed her sister that Julia's composure cracked. Her body tensed and a tear formed in the corner of her eye.

"My sister killed herself, Mr. Harrell. Momma's sleeping pills. She wasn't murdered, and I don't understand why your friend Sylvia would say something like that."

"I don't either," J. B. said. "She's been mostly semiconscious and mumbling, putting out bits and pieces of information. I'm trying to figure out what's true and what's not true."

"Look, you sounded sincere on the phone, but this story you've been told . . . I want to set the record straight. Pat, I mean Patricia, we called her Pat. She wasn't raped. You can tell your friend that, too. And if there's anything else I should clarify, let me know." She pursed her lips and pressed her hands on the table with an air of finality.

J. B., taken aback by her total denial, was careful to consider what to say next. "Maybe there's been some confusion," he said after sipping some coffee. "I hope you don't mind my asking, Julia, but what do you know about what happened to your sister? Do you know why she killed herself?"

"I was twelve. She was fourteen. She was my big sister. I looked up to her. I still miss her." The tear that had been sitting in the corner of Julia's eye escaped, and she removed it from her cheek with a napkin. "If something bad like that happened, why didn't she tell me?"

"The problem is," he said, "that Sylvia is sure that Jordane raped Patricia. And if he didn't, then she's been feeling guilty all her life about something that never even happened."

"I'm sorry I can't help your friend." Julia reached across the table and patted J. B.'s hand.

"What's even worse," he said, "is that a boy named Will, William James, was killed for raping your sister."

"What the hell? Who said that?"

Julia leaned forward and listened intently as J. B., in a calm and gentle voice, slowly recounted everything he'd learned. First from Jeremy Kuzik, who had been the town's deputy police chief at the time, then from Spencer Jackson, whose father had confessed that he and some other men took the law into their own hands and killed Will for raping Patricia.

"He was lynched, Julia." J. B.'s voice shook. He tried to stop the trembling of his hands. "That was horrible enough, but what if he was lynched for something that didn't even happen? Could that be true?"

Julia shook her head, a look of alarm in her eyes. "No! That is horrible! Horrible! But my sister never . . . I didn't . . ."

"There's no way you could have known that your sister was raped if she didn't tell anyone, and if Jordane didn't rape her, there would have been nothing for her to tell. And, the girl's name was never made public, so maybe it wasn't your sister who was raped? Maybe it was a different girl?"

Without any warning, Julia Grogan jumped up, pushed her chair back, and headed for the door, turning around only long enough to say, "I'll be right back," before walking out of the room. J. B. sat there, stunned, wondering if he'd blown it. Had he said too much too fast, maybe told her more than she could handle? He didn't have to wonder for long, though, because a few minutes later, Julia was back.

"I found this hidden in my sister's underwear drawer right after she died." She placed a pink imitation-leather diary in the middle of the table and sat down. "We always kept each other's secrets. When she killed herself, I hid this in my own stuff. I kept it all these years, but I've never read it, never even unlocked it."

J. B. stared at the lock on the vintage booklet and the embossed words *Five Year Diary* on the cover, imagining what secrets might be recorded inside. The rows of cracks in the cover seemed to match the wrinkles on Julia's flushed cheeks.

"I was too scared to find out why Pat killed herself." She shook her head, let out a long sigh. "I should have read this a long time ago. It's not right that I didn't, is it?"

"You were just a kid," he said. "You were trying to protect her."

Julia reached for the diary and with trembling fingers inserted a tiny key in its lock. She started to skim through the pages, pausing every now and then to dab her eyes with the napkin, and to mumble, "I can't help but feel like I'm violating her privacy." When she reached her sister's final entry, she pressed her finger on the page. "She wrote this two days before she killed herself."

"Would you rather . . ." J. B. hesitated, then said, "Do you want me to . . ."

She stopped him. "Please stay. I need to do this. It's way past time for me to do this." She took in a deep breath as if trying to force the moisture back into her eyes. Then she began to read, out loud but only in a shaky whisper.

"'Don't blame Donny.'"

She looked up at J. B. "Donny was our older brother. He was eighteen at the time."

"'He didn't want to take me with him to that kegger. But I begged and begged until he gave in. He said to stick close to him, but I didn't. It's not Donny's fault.'"

Julia set the diary, still open, down on the table and covered it with her hands. "If only I'd read this before . . . I could have saved my brother. Donny drank himself to death. He must have blamed himself for whatever happened. Oh God." She sat up, wiped away tears, and sucked in some air, then picked up the diary again.

"'Nothing that happened is because of Donny. I am the one to blame. The only one. I was stupid. I am stupid. Stupid. Stupid. Stupid. Stupid.'"

Julia repeated the word *stupid*, each time with a choking heaviness that dug deeper and deeper into her pain. Still, she kept reading in a voice now hoarse and hesitant, inhaling deep breaths of air after each sentence.

"'I was stupid to go into the woods by myself . . . so stupid I thought he was smiling at me when he was really snarling . . . too stupid to know that someone like him would never smile at someone like me. Senior boys don't notice freshmen girls and especially not someone as popular as him . . . he didn't even know who I was . . . I was too stupid to do anything when he touched me . . . too stupid to say anything. Too stupid to run away . . . too stupid to move, to even scream. It's my fault. I shouldn't have let him hurt me. I'm sorry for what I did and I'm sorry I didn't tell anyone. But I couldn't. Tony said he'd kill our dog if I said anything. But that's no excuse. I'm sorry. About everything. I don't deserve to live.'"

"If only . . ." Julia whimpered and pressed the open diary to her chest.

Tears welled up in J. B.'s eyes. "You didn't know. She never told anyone."

She took in a deep breath. "Tony. She said Tony."

"Anthony Jordane." J. B. nodded.

"The state wrestling champion?"

"And now would-be U.S. senator."

"And you said he tried to rape your friend Sylvia that same night?"

J. B. nodded again. "Only she got away, thanks to William James."

"You mean, the boy who was lynched?" Julia collapsed onto the table with her face hidden in her arms. "If only I'd read this. I could have saved that poor boy."

"No, Julia, you couldn't have. Will was already dead when your sister wrote this."

She shot up in her chair and hit the table with the palms of her hands. "If I'd read this right after my sister killed herself, I could have gone to the police and told them Will was innocent. I could have told them it was Tony. I could have done *something*."

J. B. sighed, thinking about the heavy burden of guilt and shame carried by so many. Julia, her brother Donny, Sylvia. Spence Jackson, Jeremy Kuzik. And how many others?

"Even if you'd known and could have told them that Tony raped your sister," he said, "they wouldn't have believed you, Julia. The police chief was in on it. Sylvia told them, and everyone said she was crazy and pretty much ran her out of town. Trust me, they wouldn't have listened to you."

"Your friend Sylvia was right in a way," Julia said with a sigh. "Anthony Jordane *did* kill Patricia. He killed my brother, too."

"And he got an innocent boy lynched for what *he* did," J. B. added.

Julia Grogan's face turned pale and clammy. Her breath started coming in short rapid spurts until she was bent over and gripping her stomach. J. B. rushed over to her, gently encouraged her to take deep breaths. Then he kept watch, silently waited for her to recover.

At last, after several long minutes, she did recover. Then she looked up and frowned, her lips pursed. "I guess I should thank you. Now I know why my sister took all those pills. She placed her hands palms up on the table, tilted her head up and pulled her shoulders back. "*But,* now that you have come into my life, Mr. Harrell, and opened my wounds, I will not let you leave me bleeding here alone. You will not walk away without doing something about that bastard Jordane!"

Then she pressed her forefinger on the cover of her sister's diary and shoved it across the table to J. B., with her lips drawn tight as she spit out the words "*Hell* no, you won't!"

• • •

J. B. opened the car door, then turned to wave good-bye to Julia Grogan. She was standing in the doorway with her hands on her hips just as they had been when he arrived. Only this time she raised her eyebrows and lifted her chin expectantly. And when he nodded back, she smiled in a way that made it clear that she understood his smile to be a promise.

He drove to the nearest gas station and filled the tank. Then he glanced at his watch and texted Peter Minter: *Need to talk. Be there by nine. Where should we meet?* Before starting the drive, he made a quick call to Mentayer.

"There's no change in her condition," she said when he asked how Sylvia was. "She's still asleep. Where are you?"

"I'm leaving Altos City now. With a pit stop, and depending on traffic, it may take me a while to get back."

"I called Peter right after the last time I talked to you," Mentayer said. "He said to tell you that everything's all set for tomorrow. They have a photographer lined up, and they're expecting key supporters from the community to be there. Oh, and he said the *Monrow City Tribune* wants you to cover the story for them, too. I told him you would call him later. I didn't say anything about Jordane's history and he didn't ask."

J. B. groaned. "I can't write anything positive about him, Mentayer. I just can't."

"You found something else?"

"I just came from Julia Grogan's house. It's in her sister's diary. Jordane raped her and threatened to kill her dog if she told anyone. For God's sake! How could I support a man like that? People need to know the truth about their political representatives, and it's my job as a journalist to tell them."

"You always do the right thing," Mentayer said. "That's who you are. It's one of the things I love about you. Of course, Peter will be disappointed, but you have to do what you have to do."

"I'll meet with him as soon as I get there. I need to tell him in person."

"Sylvia will be so relieved," she said. "No, she'll be delighted. I'll tell her as soon as she wakes up. And once she hears about the diary? She'll want to march right down to the prosecutor's office and make sure Jordane is charged with rape and convicted."

J. B. sighed. Even though there was no legal time limit in the state for prosecuting sex crimes committed against people under the age of eighteen, he knew it would be impossible to get a conviction, especially for a rape committed over sixty years ago where the victim was no longer alive. "Tell her not to get ahead of herself," he said. "Remind her to take it one step at a time. That's what she always tells me to do."

Thirty minutes later he had to tell himself to follow that same advice, when a car honked at him and he realized that he hadn't been paying any attention to his driving. He had been busy planning everything all at once—how to break the news to Peter and convince him not to trust Jordane, how to get his editor to approve an exposé about Jordane. He had even started to draft the article in his head.

Okay, so first things first. His meeting with Peter. He thought it would be best to start by recounting everything he had learned in the last twenty-four hours. That would make it clear to Peter that a man like Jordane was not the kind of person who would do anything he promised to do, that it was likely that he was lying to Peter right now. That a man like that wasn't fit for public office. To prepare himself, he made a list in his head of everything that Jordane had done in the past. Only he didn't stop there. He went on to imagine what kinds of things Jordane had likely done since then—sexual harassment and assault for sure, and lying and cheating were a given.

It's all my fault. My fault. My fault. He could hear Sylvia's voice so clearly, it was almost as if it were coming through the engine of her car.

"Listen to me, Sylvia," he said to her. "I am absolutely sure about one thing. Nothing that Jordane did was your fault. None of it."

J. B. was sure about one other thing, too: that whatever evil Jordane had done in his life, the man had never once been held to account for any of it. Until now. He grabbed his iPhone and dictated a text to Peter. *I can't support Jordane. Will explain. An hour away.* Then he pressed his foot down on the accelerator pedal and ignored the car's vibrations as it zoomed ahead.

Chapter Twelve

Driving through the heart of Monrow City's American Indian community on his way to meet Peter Minter, J. B. was struck by how much it had changed since his days as a novice reporter for the *Monrow City Tribune*. Where old houses occupied by multigenerational families once stood, there were now upscale apartment and condo buildings. The affordable Target store was replaced by a Whole Foods. The tribal-run public housing complex was still there, but instead of looking orderly and serene like it had back in the day, hundreds of people were crammed into tents pitched cheek by jowl on the strip of land between the street and the complex. The words *Forgotten Indians living on stolen land* were painted in red, white, and blue on the wall.

Four blocks later, when J. B. pulled into the community center parking lot, Peter was standing by the door waiting for him, wearing a black shirt and a turquoise and silver bolo tie with his white hair pulled back in a ponytail. J. B.'s stomach twisted into a nervous knot as they shook hands.

"Long day." Peter looked him up and down, his eyebrows knit together in a knot. J. B. quickly tucked his wrinkled shirt—nothing he could do about the perspiration under its arms—into his coffee-stained cargo pants. Too bad he hadn't worn his seersucker suit, that was at least meant to be wrinkled, or at minimum splashed some water on his eyes and run a comb through his hair.

"Let's get you some coffee and something to eat." Peter ushered him inside and led the way to the other side of the atrium.

"What happened to the Red Fox Den Café?" J. B. pointed to where the sign for the community's much-loved restaurant used to hang.

"Closed, ever since Sam died," Peter said. "We use it for meetings now." He opened the door, turned on the lights, and motioned for J. B. to sit at a table. The café looked pretty much the same, except the benches in the booths were cracked and worn, and it looked empty behind the counter without owner and chef Sam Chasa standing there with his trademark braids and grease-spotted vest.

"Everyone around here knows who you are. You know that, right?"

J. B. nodded and waited for Peter to drop the other shoe.

"Okay then."

Peter walked away, leaving J. B. to wonder if he had just been issued a warning. Was this a way to let him know that if he didn't support Jordane, there would be consequences? That people in Indian country would think of him, as Peter himself once had, as a white apple with the red skin peeled off and no core? Would they write him off as a big shot New York journalist who didn't give a damn about them? He lowered his chin and crossed his arms, preemptively peeved at the imagined injustice. What about the exposé he wrote a few years back about the Indian child welfare system? And the more recent article about the deadly health impacts of uranium mining? Hadn't he written the truth then? Wasn't he just as obligated to write the truth now?

Peter returned carrying a tray with two cups of coffee, a pitcher of cream, and a plate of golden fry bread sprinkled with powdered sugar, cinnamon honey butter on the side. "Leftovers," he said, "from the folks who were here making signs for tomorrow. So, eat."

J. B. held back at first, still smarting from the implications of what he'd perceived as a warning, accurately or not. But as soon as he bit into a piece of fry bread and gulped down some coffee, he realized he was starving and devoured the rest of it in a few bites.

"How long is it now that we have known each other," Peter asked after watching him eat for a few seconds.

"Over two decades," J. B. said with his mouth full. He reached for another piece of fry bread, topped it with honey.

"Right. I know you. You know me." Peter, with a sad smile, scrunched forward with his hands folded on the table. "All right then."

J. B.'s fists, as if they had a mind of their own, flew up in the air and landed on the table, splattering coffee in all directions. "Look, Peter. I just have to say it right out. Anthony Jordane should be in prison! Three people are dead because of him." He stopped, caught his breath. He'd intended to hold back his anger and was embarrassed. "Sorry." He shook his head, reached for a paper napkin, and dabbed at the spilled coffee.

Peter's eyes were devoid of any judgment or suspicion as he pushed the tray closer. "Eat. You are still hungry."

J. B. did as he was told, and when finished, licked a crumb from his upper lip and wiped his mouth with the back of his hand. Then he started to tell Peter about his trip to Bigger. He described the old-timers he'd met in the motel bar last night and was about to relate what he'd learned from them when Peter's raised left hand stopped him.

"No need. Tell me why you think Jordane should not be our senator."

"You're not going to like it." The corners of J. B.'s lips turned up slightly, an apology in advance. Peter didn't want to hear what he was going to say. He was sure about that.

"I already don't like it," Peter said with a shrug. He picked up his empty cup and walked toward the kitchen, leaving J. B. alone to wipe the sweat from his brow as he braced himself. "Nothing but grounds left in the bottom of the pot, I'm afraid," he said when he returned. "Brought you this instead." Peter handed him a bottle of water and then sat down with his hands folded on the table. "Okay then, let's get this over with."

"Right," J. B. said when a slight movement of Peter's hands gave him permission to continue. "Okay, bottom line . . . this is what Jordane did back in 1960." He paused, thought he heard a car drive into the parking lot behind the community center, then realized after a few seconds that he must have been mistaken. The last thing he needed right now was someone interrupting them. This was going to be hard enough. He loosened his arms and allowed his shoulders to sink down, tried to match Peter's neutral facial expression and tone of voice.

"Attempted rape . . . of Sylvia. Rape of a fourteen-year-old girl . . . who then killed herself. Lying, spreading rumors to get an innocent boy jailed for what he'd done." A plane roared overhead, flying low on its way to landing at the Monrow City airport, a twenty-minute car drive away. J. B. waited for the sound to recede and then, with a shaky voice, said, "Lynching an innocent boy. His name was Will."

Peter stared at him, eyes wide, jaw dropped. Minutes passed while J. B. waited for the inevitable questions, all demanding proof of his allegations. But instead, Peter stroked his chin with his fingertips. He curled his hand over his mouth. What expressions of doubt or anger or disappointment was he withholding, J. B. wondered? What was he *not* asking?

"Jordane's father was the police chief," J. B. continued. "He was part of the lynch mob. People in Bigger don't talk about Will or how he died." His hands covered his heavy heart. "Sylvia thinks that it was all her fault."

At that, Peter's lips puckered. *Why,* he mouthed.

"Because she wasn't raped, and the other girl was. Because her friend Will stood up for her, and he got lynched because of it. Because she couldn't save him. Because she couldn't get anyone to listen to her."

Peter grimaced. He sat still as a stone, gripped the table's edge with his eyes glued on the ropelike purple veins bulging on his hands. A streetlight outside the open café window had come on, the sky black and filled with clouds, no moon or stars. After several minutes, Peter slowly loosened his fingers from the table and rubbed his eyes, then stood up and with bent back dragged his feet over to the window. He stared out at the night with his arms tightly crossed over his chest while J. B. studied an old American Indian Movement photograph on the adjacent wall. There was a picture of Peter, his chiseled face strong and determined, holding an upside-down American flag while standing in line with other protesters along the freeway that ran through the center of the city.

Without warning, Peter hit the windowsill with the palms of his hands. "Okay then!" He strode back to the table, moving with surprising force for his age, the same look of determination that J. B. saw in the old yellowed picture on the wall.

"What Jordane did over six decades ago . . . whether it can be established as true or not . . ."

Every muscle in J. B.'s body tensed, bracing him for the doubts, the questions. He clenched his fists in an overwhelming urge to head off what he feared was coming. But he held his tongue. Peter had listened to him without interrupting. Now it was his turn to listen to Peter.

"What Jordane did is reprehensible." Peter scooted his seat an inch or two closer to the table, with a very long sigh that verged on loathing but didn't quite make it that far. "But here's the problem. No one else is even remotely interested in talking about uranium mining on our land and standing up for our sovereign rights. Jordane has promised to do both."

If J. B. had been sitting across the table from the *New York Times* editorial team, he wouldn't have hesitated to argue that Jordane was not the kind of man who kept promises. That to trust him would be foolhardy. That campaigning for him would be a setup for disappointment, and considerable damage. But this was Peter, not the editorial team. With him, the rules were different. Unspoken. Unwritten. Yet understood.

"Our survival is at stake." Peter paused for several seconds to let that sink in. "We have no other options." The headlights of a passing car outside lit up his face and then disappeared. "And since that is the case, it is best to let the past be the past."

J. B.'s mouth felt dry. His lips were stuck together. Which was a good thing. It kept him from saying what he was thinking. That the past isn't the past when the present is caught up in it. That Jordane had been getting away with doing whatever he wanted to do all his life, so why wouldn't he keep doing it. That you can never depend on someone like Anthony Jordane for anything, much less your survival.

"Peter." He said his name slowly, carefully, then tipped the water bottle to his lips and took a long drink. "Do you have any reason to believe that Jordane has changed?"

"Of course not. Do I distrust him? Absolutely. I have faith, unless proven otherwise, that the intentions of white men are always selfish, dishonest, and lacking in any concern about treating others fairly. We have always known not to trust them to change. That is why *we* are the ones who must change."

It started to rain outside, just a drizzle at first, but then it became a downpour, and when a heavy wind blew it into the room and started dumping puddles of water on the floor, J. B. rushed over to the window and slammed it shut.

"You see." Peter waited for him to sit back down. "Jordane's despicable past . . . and whatever his present might be . . . does not necessarily preclude him from doing something good." He paused, then raised his left forefinger. "Something we *need* him to do, J. B."

"So, you would trust someone like him to do something *good*?"

"Oh no. No, no, no, J. B. We know better than that." Peter leaned forward with raised eyes, a slight shake of his head. "But we have learned how to get the white man to do what we need him to do. That is why we have hope."

"And is hope enough?"

"Also no. However, in *this* case . . ." There was a knowing glimmer in Peter's eyes. "In this case, we have more than hope, because of Jordane's connection to the casino resort development industry." He raised his right eyebrow and left it up until he was sure this new information was sinking in.

"What?" J. B. was taken aback. "I asked Rory, my intern from Columbia University, to do some digging, and he didn't unearth any such connection."

"Ah, and that is because Jordane is a *silent* investor in casino resorts. The man's no dummy. He knows that people won't spend money at a resort if it's right next to a uranium mine. Even an abandoned one." He chuckled under his breath. "Radiation hot spots are *not* prime tourist attractions." He shrugged as if to say *So there you have it* and then added, "We know what he wants. Money, plain and simple. A lot of money. We know he's in it for himself and only himself."

J. B. wrinkled his nose in disgust.

"Ah, but his intentions are not what's important. What is important are the effects on our people." Peter raised his left forefinger again. "We can feed our families by working in casino jobs, or we can let our families sicken and die from radiation poisoning by working in and living next to uranium mines."

J. B. wasn't buying it. The chances were slim to none that Anthony Jordane could stop uranium mining. Even if he kept his word and tried.

"We are a realistic people," Peter said as if reading his mind. "By necessity, we always have been. But the reality is, no one's even thinking about uranium mining, and certainly not about our sovereignty. No one knows the dangers. No one listens to us. No one cares. We have no seat at the table. We know Jordane can't single-handedly pass a bill, but he *could* hold hearings about it. Get the press involved. Educate people. It's a strategy. A step at least: a chance for us to speak, maybe to be heard."

J. B. took a deep breath. How could he argue with that? He glanced at his watch and groaned. It was almost midnight. "It's too late to call Sylvia . . . I'm worried about her."

"Such a heavy burden of guilt our friend carries." Peter sighed, but then his face brightened. "But, as much as life takes, it also gives . . . if we can find the lesson in it. Maybe Sylvia has a chance to find that lesson now."

"Mentayer's with her. She knows a lot about trauma from her work with kids." He smiled, comforted by Peter's empathy, especially now; it was one of the reasons he'd felt connected to him right from the start.

"Astonishing, isn't it," Peter said, "how childhood experiences shape life trajectories. I always wondered why Sylvia was so driven. Do you think her life has been a search for redemption?"

"She does go to extremes sometimes," J. B. said with a nod. "Lost her job once. Even risked her own life. More than once. I never knew what she was going to drag me into next—first it was helping a foster kid, then a former student, then the son of an atomic veteran. Almost got *both* of us killed with that last one."

"We need more like her." Peter chuckled softly. Then his face turned dark. "Too many people are incapable of feeling guilt and are undeserving of redemption, not that they'd even think to seek it."

J. B. pursed his lips. "I can't hide what I know about Jordane, Peter. I won't lie."

"Then you must find the truth in the lie." Peter leaned back, looking exhausted, even more shriveled than usual.

"I have to . . . I don't know . . ." J. B. covered his face so his hands muffled the sound of anguish in his voice. He needed to be alone. He needed time to think.

"Open your heart and trust your own wisdom, J. B. Then what baffles you now will no longer trouble you." Peter walked him to the door. His parting words: "Just remember, J. B., in a storm, the tree that bends with the wind is the one that survives." Then he closed the door and locked it behind him.

It was still raining, a steady, unpleasant rain that had created so many pools of water in the parking lot, J. B. found it impossible to avoid them all. He opened the door to Sylvia's car, slid onto the seat, and put the key in the ignition. Sylvia had insisted that he stay at her apartment. It was only a fifteen-minute drive at this late hour, but he was in no rush to get there. Despite how exhausted as he was, he knew there would be no rest for him tonight.

Part Two

J. B. Makes a Decision

Chapter Thirteen

J. B. drove away from the community center just as the clouds broke open and released another torrent of rain. He turned the windshield wiper setting to fast and the wipers dragged themselves across the glass with a terrible chattering sound. He turned the setting back and the irritating noise stopped, but the slow wipers were no match for the rain, didn't even touch parts of the windshield. He could see nothing. It was as if he had gone blind or his eyes had been forced shut. He slowed the car to a snail's pace and steered straight, hoping the street was still in front of him, and with his foot off the accelerator neither stopped nor powered forward, just coasted along until he came to a streetlight at an intersection where he could see well enough to pull over. He smacked his forehead on the steering wheel, frustrated and exhausted, irritated with himself yet again for taking Sylvia's old clunker instead of renting a decent car.

He leaned back in the seat and listened to the pounding rain on the roof. A ray of light flashed in the window and then was gone, a car he hadn't seen coming. Peter's response was something else he hadn't seen coming. He hadn't expected him to be repulsed by Jordane and *still* support him. But he did understand what he'd said about how the survival of his people sometimes depended on getting the wrong person to do the right thing. Did that mean J. B. was the right person in the right place who was now being asked to do the wrong thing? Was that what Peter meant when he told him he must find the truth in the lie?

The rain finally let up so he could see the road ahead well enough to resume driving, only now he had a raging headache. Not a migraine, he'd never had one of those—but he didn't usually get headaches either, so how would he know what it was. He almost drove past the old brick building where Sylvia had lived for decades because now it was tucked in between and dwarfed by two new high-rise condo buildings where people with designer clothes and furniture lived behind floor-to-ceiling and wall-to-wall windows, their high-end cars tucked safely in reserved spaces underground while J. B. searched the narrow lot behind Sylvia's building for a parking space.

Inside, the lobby was brightly lit, but yet drab and eerily quiet; the building's mostly elderly residents already asleep for hours. The young people who'd once lived here were long gone, those irritating college students who, according to Sylvia, had wandered around at all hours of the day and night with perpetual sleep in their eyes and holes in the knees of their faded jeans. J. B. retrieved Sylvia's mail from the wall of mailboxes, then sorted through the mostly newspaper ads and grocery store coupons while riding the unnervingly slow elevator up to the fifth floor.

Her apartment was stuffy, with a not-lived-in feel to it that made it seem like it had been vacant for longer than a week. The gold and orange shag area rug in the living room was already dated when J. B. first saw it twenty years ago. Drab off-white walls that had never been painted. Old political posters from the '60s and '70s. The black imitation-leather couch from the Salvation Army, they didn't even make them in that style anymore. Dusty candles that had never been burned. An ancient scratched-up wood desk in the corner.

He walked over to the antique pulpit chair along the wall that had come from the Bronx, back when Sylvia's ex-husband was doing his seminary internship there and she could still tolerate going to church. J. B. tipped the chair sideways. And there it was. Just as she'd said it would be. A three-by-five card taped under the seat: *In the event of my death, ship to J. B. Harrell*, along with his New York address. He placed the chair upright and sat on its burgundy velvet seat cushion, felt the smoothness of its wooden arms, and rested his head against its hand-carved walnut-wood back. He closed his eyes, imagined Mentayer sitting in the cushioned chair next to Sylvia's hospital bed, and had an overwhelming urge to tell her about Peter, to ask her advice about what to do about Jordane. He reached for his iPhone but quickly put it away. What was he thinking? It was almost two o'clock, and she was probably asleep in the visitors' lounge. If he woke her now, she would never get back to sleep.

He sighed and went to stand by the sliding glass doors, watched the rain dripping off the edge of the patio roof, drops splattering onto the pots of geraniums and tomatoes. He slid the door open, breathed in some fresh air and listened to the now-soothing sound of rain for a few minutes, and then went into the kitchen to find something to eat. There was a cereal bowl with a few Cheerios and some milk gone sour in the sink, a glass with drops of orange juice pulp stuck to its side, a cup half-filled with coffee, Sylvia's old aluminum coffee pot with used grounds still in the basket. He thought back to a week ago when he picked her up in a cab. Had he been early? He must have been. He'd never known her to leave her apartment with dirty dishes in the sink. He opened the refrigerator—cubes of pineapple, cantaloupe, apple, raspberries, and strawberries—but couldn't decide if it was still edible, so he took out a chunk of cheese instead. He poured himself a glass of cold water and sat down at the table to eat it.

On the shelf above the stove there was an outmoded potato masher and the dented pot Sylvia used for boiling spaghetti. He shifted in his chair, rested his chin in his hand, wondering, for the first time, if maybe Sylvia had not lived like a pauper by choice. At least not consciously. Even with a decent income as a foster care supervisor, she would never buy anything new for herself, no clothes, not even a better coffee pot. He'd always accepted that she had made a principled decision to live simply. To question it would have been to question her values, and people's values should be respected. But now that he knew about Sylvia's past trauma, another explanation made as much, maybe even more, sense. Her guilt about not being able to save Will—perhaps it had not only evolved into a search for redemption that led her to believe she was never doing enough, perhaps it had also mushroomed into an unconscious conviction that she was unworthy and undeserving and thus destined to a life of deprivation. And wasn't that how saints were created?

How different he was from Sylvia. If she was a saint, then who was he? He liked shiny new things, expensive designer clothes, salon haircuts. He always bought the latest espresso maker. If Sylvia's moral compass always and unequivocally pointed toward justice, what did his ambivalence about whether to expose Jordane say about *his* moral compass?

He jumped up from the table as though he'd taken a wrong turn in a maze and couldn't right himself fast enough. He went into the living room and fell onto the couch as if the weight of responsibility had become too heavy for his legs to hold him up any longer. Sylvia's—and Julia Grogan's—determination to hold Jordane accountable for his crimes was deeply rooted in trauma and pain; Peter's determination to endorse Jordane for the greater good was deeply rooted in his Indigenous identity and community. So, what was his own indecisiveness rooted in?

J. B. looked at Sylvia's collection of Navajo pottery on the windowsill and thought about how his identity was more complicated than Peter's. He had no Indigenous friends or co-workers. The people he worked with were mostly white; there were only a few Asian and Black reporters. The people he and Mentayer socialized with were mostly Black, neighbors who, up until Harlem started to become gentrified, lived nearby. He had traveled the world. Covered a broad range of stories. His childhood had been different from Peter's, too. He lived most of his growing-up years in a small, all-white community. His white foster grandfather had drummed into his head the idea that he was special—in other words, not like other Indians—and had groomed him for success. And he had succeeded. Beyond all expectations. First Indigenous journalist at the *Monrow City Tribune* and later at the world-renowned *New York Times*. Pulitzer Prize winner. Would he be the author of his own demise now if he withheld critical information about a candidate for a major public office? Would he serve as an example in journalism classes of what happens to someone who violates the three cornerstones of journalism ethics—truth, accuracy, and objectivity?

There was a breeze coming through the open patio door now, but the air was still warm, the apartment too hot. J. B. took off his shirt and cargo pants, then walked over to the door and breathed in the air's fresh, clean smell. The rain had stopped, the sky now a hazy gray with bronze, orange, and yellow colors in between clouds. The beginning of dawn. He leaned against the door, clenched his fists in frustration. He was used to being sure, a trait he had scrupulously cultivated. In grade school he'd practiced being careful, sure-footed—staying out of trouble, lifting his chin and walking away whenever someone called him a dirty injun. In high school and college there had been ample opportunities to practice acting sure. He got so good at it that one day he realized he really *was* sure of himself. And now, because he hadn't been unsure of himself for such a very long time, he didn't quite know how to handle it. Just then his iPhone pinged, with a text from Mentayer. He shook his head in wonder. How did she always seem to know when he needed her?

It's early. You're probably not up yet but we are.

We? J. B. typed as he went to sit in the pulpit chair.

Sylvia and me. She's hungry. You should see her. She's ready to get out of here but I'm afraid it won't be as soon as she thinks. How are you?

Tired. Still don't know what to do. Don't tell Sylvia. She wants me to scuttle Jordane's campaign but Peter wants me to do just the opposite.

It's not a loyalty contest, Mentayer texted back. It's about doing the right thing.

That's the problem, he texted. They're both right. Exposing Jordane is a matter of justice. So is stopping uranium mining and trying to get a sovereign rights bill passed.

You'll know what to do. Just be yourself, hon.

He sighed. His wife wasn't used to him being unsure either, but unlike him, she was confident that he would soon be sure again. He texted her a confused emoji face and a good-bye wave.

Outside, the sky had brightened, and there were a few patches of blue peeking through the clouds. He had a decision to make. And he had to make it soon. But first things first. If he took a shower and got dressed now, he'd have time to get there early enough to find something to eat before he did whatever he decided to do. Whatever that was.

Sylvia's bathroom, like the rest of her apartment, was shabby and outdated. An old-fashioned claw-foot tub with a faded yellowish-pink shower curtain around it. Black-and-white tiled floor. A small crack in the lower right corner of the mirror above a coral-pink sink. A half-used bar of Dove soap. A bottle of shampoo with a dollar store sticker still on it. A freshly laundered beach towel, faded and thin from decades of use. An ancient but adequate hair dryer.

After showering and getting dressed, J. B. stood in front of the full-length mirror hanging on Sylvia's bedroom wall. His lightweight gray suit was a perfect fit on his squared shoulders. The streaks of gray in his stylish haircut made him look distinguished. His appearance pleased him, gave him confidence, a certainty that he would know what to do when the time came, and that he would do the right thing. And when he went to the hospital after the press conference, Mentayer would tell him he looked like a corporate model for *GQ* magazine and he would smile. And when Sylvia rolled her eyes and tried to muss up his hair, he would puff up his chest and take her teasing as a compliment.

But then his confidence was cut short by a text message from Peter Minter. *Don't try to be someone you're not. Open your heart to who you really are.* Those words literally knocked him off his feet, and he landed on the edge of the bed with his elbows on his knees.

There it was. The painful truth, inescapable, staring him in the face as he looked at himself in the mirror. *Don't try to be someone you're not.* But who was he, now, after he'd been groomed to be someone he wasn't? When he had been programmed to be white—not just to dress and act white, but to think white. Had living all but four years of his life in the white world erased him? Had his heart forgotten what he'd known briefly as a child? That he looked like his birth parents and siblings. That he was American Indian—100 percent Anishinaabe. Was it too late to open his heart to *all* his history, to *all* of who he was, who he *really* was?

Message received, he texted back to Peter. *Be there soon.*

He used a knuckle to dab a tear from his eye, then closed the patio door, left Sylvia's apartment, and went outside to hail a cab. When he spotted a taxi going in the direction of the state capitol, he stepped off the curb and lifted his arm like a man who knew where he was going, even though he still didn't know what he was going to do when he got there. What he did know was that the decision was his alone to carry. That he was the protagonist of his own life, that he would have to follow his own path no matter the result, no matter the consequences. He believed Peter; all the wisdom he needed was already inside him. All he had to do was open his heart and listen to who he was, to *all* of who he was it. Then he would know. When the time came, he would know.

Or would he?

Chapter Fourteen

The sky was blue, the early-morning sun already warm, a sign that, despite last night's cleansing rain, it was going to be a hot day. J. B. slid into the back seat of the cab. Thinking about what a physically and emotionally draining week it had been. Worrying about Sylvia. Driving to Bigger in her rattletrap car. Following one lead after another without taking time to rest or eat. Getting emotional about what he learned. Listening to Peter. Questioning himself, his identity. Losing his confidence. Finding it again. No wonder he was exhausted.

And yet, the more fatigued he felt, the more adamantly his mind went into overdrive. The governor would be late. She always was. She would announce her endorsement of Anthony Jordane's candidacy for the U.S. Senate. Everyone would clap. Jordane would speak. The press would ask questions. No other reporters from major papers would be there. *He* was covering the press conference for both the *Monrow City Tribune and the New York Times.* The two local TV stations would be there and would feed news clips to the national stations. And of course, corporate types like the PR person from the mining company would be there, ready to spin lies later. If he exposed Jordane, it would have to be during the question-and-answer period, a risky thing to do. Journalists could look like fools sometimes. He'd seen that happen. To others. Never to him. It wouldn't happen to him now either. Not if he focused on what he planned to do, but of course, he didn't know what that was. Yet. But he would. At least he hoped he would.

He repositioned himself so his head was resting against the back seat and slipped into his usual problem-solving mode—ask questions first, then weigh the pros and cons; always be objective. What would happen if he did nothing and Jordane won the election? Would he keep his word and introduce a sovereign rights bill? What if he did, but the bill didn't pass? That was a real possibility—actually, that was a certainty. What if Jordane *didn't* keep his word? That, too, was a real possibility.

Okay then, so what would happen if J. B. *did* expose the truth about Jordane's past, and he lost the election? Would more people, J. B.'s own people, sicken and die from uranium mining? Was there any other way to prevent that? And what about Jordane? If J. B. exposed him, would he be convicted of rape? The odds were against him even being charged, much less prosecuted. What would happen if J. B. wrote a feature article about William James, the innocent boy who was lynched for a rape that Jordane committed? Would anyone believe it? Would J. B.'s editor even allow him to publish an article based solely on a dying man's story about his father's deathbed confession? Would the people of Bigger deny it ever happened? Did any of them even know that it happened?

"More traffic than usual this morning. About ten minutes out yet." The driver honked his horn in frustration.

J. B. sighed and stared out the window. Even though doing what he usually did had always been reliable, and was as comfortable as wearing a pair of old shoes, it wasn't working for him this time. He had always been objective, had scrupulously avoided viewing situations through a personal lens, but he couldn't avoid it this time. Not when he was in the middle of the picture. He closed his eyes. *Just be yourself. Be true to who you are. Follow your heart. Trust your instincts. Don't try to be someone you're not.* The words triggered a memory from deep in his childhood of both his birth mother and his foster mother reading to him from *The Little Prince*—"It is only with the heart that one can see rightly; what is essential is invisible to the eye."

Would listening to his heart really be enough for him to see rightly, he wondered? Would it lead to the right decision?

He rested his head against the side window and dozed off. He didn't know if the loss of car motion woke him first or if it was the driver asking for his fare. With a mumbled thank you, he handed over a twenty-dollar bill and told him to keep the change. Then he stepped out of the cab and into the shadow of the twelve stone eagles guarding the gold leaf–covered dome on top of the marble and granite state capitol building. He walked up the wide granite steps heading for the marble statues that hovered over the main entrance, but when he reached the door, his instincts told him not to go inside. To turn around instead.

And that was when he spotted him. Anthony Jordane, standing at the bottom of the steps, looking utterly nonchalant in a pale blue short-sleeved shirt and a yellow tie hanging loose at the collar, upper arm muscles exposed, a power move even at his age, and a suit jacket draped over his arm, a nod to civility when he would put it on later. He leered at a young woman, shining his cocky high-beam smile right in her face.

Later, when it was all over and he'd had time to reflect on that day, J. B. still wouldn't be able to adequately explain what happened next, only that when his stomach muscles twisted into a hard knot and his heart started pounding against his chest, he knew what he was going to do. He just knew. And in the nick of time.

Jordane was headed his way. J. B. measured his progress by a cloud just starting to cross the sun, and determined he didn't have much time to consider. He could jump right in, lay out everything he knew about the man's sordid past right from the start. He could release the information little by little, let it build to a climax. He could schmooze a bit first, warm him up. He could ask a series of questions, always a good way to trap someone.

"Good morning!" Anthony Jordane, who had jogged up the last few steps, was suddenly standing a few feet in front of him with an overly familiar smile on his face.

J. B. ignored his outstretched hand and held up his press badge. "J. B. Harrell. With the *New York Times*."

"Yes, I know. Big day, hey? Sun even came out for us. You're early."

How satisfying it would be, J. B. thought, to puncture the man's remarkable arrogance by asking who he was, why he was here, and what made today such a big day. Instead, he simply smiled and said, "I was hoping we'd have a chance to talk before the press descends, Mr. Jordane."

"You're in luck, my good man." Jordane glanced at his watch, another show of self-importance. "A short interview over coffee, hey?"

They walked to the coffee shop in the visitors' center with Jordane making small talk—quite the thunderstorm last night, hey, but we needed the rain; they're predicting a sizzling-hot summer, probably worse on the East Coast where you live—and J. B. nodding agreeably, biding his time. They sat down with their coffee and croissants at a secluded spot in a courtyard surrounded by potted plants. J. B. reached into his pocket for the small brass thunderbird pin Peter had given him last night, saying it was *a symbol of our movement to protect our land* and that it would give him the courage and integrity he needed. J. B. placed the pin in front of him on the table. It was time. He was ready.

"How about we start, Mr. Jordane, with where you grew up? Are you originally from Monrow City?"

"Oh my, no. I'm a small-town boy, Mr. Harrell. Grew up in Bigger, some four hours north of here."

J. B. raised his eyebrows. "Isn't there a reservation somewhere around there?"

"Indeed. Not far from us. Not far at all. Unacceptably high unemployment, hey. *Huge* need for economic development. The governor knows I'm committed to that."

"That's what I understand. You must have gone to school with kids from the reservation then."

"Oh my, no. The rez kids got to go to boarding schools." He rolled his eyes and grinned. "Lucky bastards. They didn't have to take boring classes like we did."

J. B. curled his lips up in what he hoped would pass for a smile, despite the burning sensation in his chest and the sour taste in his mouth. "Tell me, Mr. Jordane, what was it like to grow up in a small town?"

"It was great, hey. Made me who I am today."

Jordane's pompousness was almost unbearable, but at the same time, it fit perfectly with J. B.'s plan. "You must have been the town hero. Being state wrestling champion three years in a row and all. Do you ever get back there?"

"Oh my, no," he said yet again, like a broken record. "Haven't been back in years. Not much there after the mines shut down. Not much there before that either. You see, Mr. Harrell, I was just a big fish in a very small pond." He lowered his chin and lifted his eyes, as if waiting for the compliment that usually followed such insincere nods to humility, but J. B. was too repulsed to oblige.

"So, tell me, when did you graduate?"

"Now, Mr. Harrell, are you implying something about my age?" With a chuckle, he made his left hand into a fist, bent his arm, and flexed his muscle. "See that? Born in 1942 and still fit as a fiddle, hey."

"Indeed. And here you are, small-town hero campaigning for a seat in the Senate of the United States of America."

Jordane puffed himself up. J. B. smiled as he imagined the man's pride growing so big that he exploded. He reached into his jacket pocket and pulled out his little notepad and a pen. "I want to make sure I have the details right. The name of your hometown? The year you graduated?"

"I grew up in Bigger, a small town of fewer than two thousand people. I graduated in 1960 with forty other kids."

"Well, I'll be." J. B. made his jaw drop and let his pen fall onto the table. "It really is a small world, isn't it?"

"Oh?"

"I believe I know someone who graduated with you."

"Really?"

"You said Bigger, right? 1960, right?"

Jordane's eyebrows scrunched together. He was curious. And, clearly, uncomfortable. "Isn't that something." J. B. waited several seconds more before dropping the other shoe. "I know Sylvia Jensen!"

The aging muscles on Jordane's face tensed into a grimace that he tried, without success, to disguise as a smile. "Hmmmm. I remember the name."

Such a flimsy effort! J. B. now knew exactly how this was going to go. It was almost finished. Just a matter of time now.

After an uneasy silence, Jordane flicked his wrist in an offhanded way and said, "I mean, I didn't know her personally." He paused, then shrugged. "But of course, I knew all about her."

J. B. heaved himself up in the chair and leaned forward, head tilted, eyebrows raised. He had the man on the line, all he had to do now was let him dangle from the hook, let him keep talking until he hung himself.

"Well, I don't know how well you know her, Mr. Harrell, and I don't mean to speak ill of anyone, but Sylvia Jensen was—well, let's just say different. A bit strange. Actually, everyone in town knew that she went plumb crazy." He chuckled, leaned his head back, and scratched his chin. "Hot little thing, though." He winked.

J. B.'s chest tightened. His stomach churned. He knew he could chew the man up and spit him out right then and there if he wanted to. And he did want to. He wanted to so badly he could taste it. He imagined shouting obscenities at this wannabe senator, calling him a rapist and murderer, grabbing him by the throat, slamming his head against the wall. But of course, he did none of that. Instead, he gritted his teeth. Warned himself to get a grip. This was not the time to blow it. Not when he was this close.

It took every ounce of energy he could muster, yet—squeezing the thunderbird pin tight in his fist—he did it. He pulled himself back from the brink.

"I admire Sylvia Jensen, myself." J. B. paused, forced himself to grin. "She's the most determined person I've ever met. Especially when she sets out to right a wrong that's been done to someone."

"Oh my, I do apologize, Mr. Harrell, if I spoke ill of your friend. I'm talking about a very long time ago, hey. We all change. Why, I'm sure I wouldn't even recognize her if I saw her."

"Oh, but she recognized *you*, Mr. Jordane. Just last week when you were here with Peter Minter. That's why she collapsed and had to be rushed to the hospital."

"*That* was Sylvia Jensen?"

"Yes, and I'm afraid I have some very bad news for you."

"Oh my, no. She didn't make it, hey." His fake concern was so transparent it didn't even come close to hiding the relief in his eyes.

"Oh, Sylvia Jensen is going to be just fine." J. B. paused to relish the satisfaction of telling him that. "I'm afraid I do have bad news, though, for *you*, Mr. Jordane. You see, I know about you and Sylvia."

"Now, Mr. Harrell, I just told you I didn't know her personally. I hope you aren't calling me a liar. There is no need for that. I already apologized."

J. B. sucked in his breath. An adrenaline rush of pure excitement surged through him. "I know what you did to her at the senior class kegger."

"Okay! Okay!" Anthony Jordane lurched forward and pounded his fists on the table. "I remember her, all right? She had the hots for me, okay? I didn't expect her to take it so hard when I rejected her. I'm sorry she went crazy, okay?" He flew back in his chair, shaking his head and muttering under his breath, something about bitches who couldn't take no for an answer.

The blow had landed just as J. B. hoped. He loosened his grip on the thunderbird pin and lowered his voice, kept it calm and steady. "You tried to rape her."

With a bang, Anthony Jordane jumped to his feet. His chair fell onto its side. "You tell that . . . that witch . . . she better be careful . . . she better stop lying." He leaned over, grabbed his suit jacket from the floor, started to walk away.

"Will. William James."

Jordane stopped. Turned around, his eyes wide.

"I know how he died."

Jordane narrowed his eyes into slits. He pursed his lips. Curled his hands into tight fists. The man, short on sense, looked ready for a fight. Maybe he'd snap. Maybe any minute.

"Come back here, Mr. Jordane," J. B. said. "You are going to want to hear this." He stood up, put the man's chair upright, and patted the seat as if giving instructions to a child. It took him a few seconds, but finally Jordane slumped down into the chair, his arms crossed over his chest.

"I know why William James was killed. It was because of what *you* did that night at the kegger."

Jordane turned away from him as if preparing to stand up and leave, so J. B. talked faster. "You tried to rape Sylvia. Will stopped you. You were pissed. You bloodied his nose. Then you raped another girl. Patricia Grogan. She was only fourteen. She killed herself. You may not have heard about that."

Jordane glared at J. B., his face twisted with rage. He leaned forward, stretched his arms across the table and shook his fists. "Outrageous! Blasphemous!"

J. B. kicked the table leg. "Your dad was the police chief. You told him Will raped that girl. As evidence, you said you saw him coming out of the woods with blood on his shirt."

"Lies! Lies!"

"Yes. *Your* lies."

Anthony Jordane shook his head and opened his mouth, but before he had a chance to say anything, J. B. jumped in. "I know how William James was killed." Emboldened by the flash of fear on Jordane's face, he leaned forward, ready for the home stretch. "I know your dad released him from jail. I know what happened in the woods." J. B.'s voice caught in his throat. His eyes stung. He paused and held up his hand, waited for a wave of anguish inside to pass. "I know what happened, Mr. Jordane. I know what you did."

"Too much, Mr. Harrell! Too, too much." Jordane's short, high-pitched hyena laugh made J. B.'s blood go cold. "Don't you see? Sylvia Jensen's lies just go to show that she is still crazy as a loon." He sounded both indignant and amused. There was a gleam in his eye and a smirk on his lips, as if this were a game, a con. "Now, didn't I tell you she was strange? Never did fit in. Same thing with that half-breed injun, or whatever the hell he was. I see what's happening here. You aren't taking any of this personally, by any chance, are you, Mr. Harrell?"

J. B. smiled and leaned back in his chair. The man had played the race card, a sure sign that he was nervous. "Perhaps you forgot, Mr. Jordane, that I am a Pulitzer Prize–winning investigative reporter. I do my own research. I search for the truth. And when I find it, I have an ethical responsibility as a journalist to expose it." He tapped his fingers on his press badge for emphasis. "So, you see, I went to Bigger myself. I did what I always do. Followed every lead. Talked to people. No, no, don't ask who. My sources are anonymous. Bottom line, Mr. Jordane, is that I unearthed the truth, and that is very bad news for you. I am only informing you out of professional courtesy. I've already written the article."

Anthony Jordane blinked. His jaw went slack. They stared at each other. For several seconds it seemed as if all the air had been sucked out of the room. The first one to look away, with an audible shudder, was Jordane. He shifted his legs under the table. Stared at the backs of his hands. Studied his fingers. Then he leaned so far back in his chair that it was balanced on its back legs and if it tipped over, he would land in a potted plant. And yet, to J. B.'s amazement, the man managed, even speechless, to still look cocky.

J. B. picked up his coffee cup and took a sip. While waiting for Jordane to find his voice again, he reached for his iPhone and typed what he would need to do next if his plan worked. Several minutes passed. Finally, Jordane brought his chair down with a thump. He sat up and crossed his arms over his chest.

"Okay, Mr. Harrell." He released a very deep, long sigh. "What do you want?"

Chapter Fifteen

The time had come. Just what J. B. had been hoping and waiting for. He leaned into it, sat very still.

"Mis-ter Jor-dane," he said in four very long, drawn-out syllables. "What you did to Sylvia Jensen, Patricia Grogan, and William James was criminal. Despicable. An outrageous injustice. And now, it must be put right." Their gazes locked as J. B. articulated each word with slow deliberation.

"Out of the question!"

"Ah, but I didn't ask a question."

Jordane pushed his chair back and leaned forward with his fists on the table. "I will not admit guilt for something I didn't do."

"Sit back, Mr. Jordane. Relax. This is your lucky day. But first, I'm going to read my article for both the *New York Times* and the *Monrow City Tribune*." J. B. brought his iPhone up to eye level so he appeared to be reading something instead of making it up as he went along.

> *Anthony Jordane, who is running for the U.S. Senate, stood by Governor Morcerber's side at the state capitol today as she announced her endorsement of his candidacy. Jordane, a newcomer to politics, grew up in Bigger, a charmingly typical midwestern mining town so small it has no stoplights. He was and continues to be the town's only hero, having won the state wrestling championship three years in a row when he was in high school.*

J. B. paused, noticed that Jordane had begun to relax, had even managed a slight smile. He smiled back at him and then continued reading.

Every spring, Bigger high school seniors would gather around a bonfire in the middle of an open field surrounded by a forest to celebrate the end of the year with a kegger of beer.

Jordane coughed into his hand. Tiny beads of sweat, indiscernible to the untrained eye, bubbled up on his forehead. Satisfied, J. B. cleared his throat and pretended to read on.

Jordane, affectionately known as Tony, went to the kegger when he was nineteen years old and about to graduate from high school. There, a classmate of his was sexually assaulted, and later that same night, a fourteen-year-old girl from another town was raped.

"Wait a minute!" Jordane was visibly sweating now, a look of horror on his face.

J. B. silenced him with a raised hand. "You can read all these details yourself. I'll just skip to the last part."

According to a prosecutor with twenty years of experience who was interviewed for this article, many rape cases such as this have been successfully brought to trial and the perpetrator convicted, even when the crimes were committed decades ago.

Jordane stared at him, slack-jawed and so red in the face that J. B. prepared to duck in case the man threw his coffee at him or, worse, threw a punch. But instead, like a deflated balloon, Jordane leaned forward with his hands holding up his head and a look of utter despair on his face. It almost seemed that he might cry.

"Almost done," J. B. said. "I'll jump ahead to the last paragraph."

The people in Bigger didn't know how William James, an innocent boy falsely accused of rape, died. If they were told he was dragged into the woods outside of their little peaceful town, where he was lynched, it is likely they wouldn't believe it. They believe things like that only happen in the south, not in the north, not in their town. "We're good people here," said a resident of Bigger after learning what Jordane, the town hero, had done.

J. B. lowered his iPhone. Jordane's eyes shifted from one look to another to another in such rapid succession that, J. B., while usually very good at reading people, realized all he could do in this case was wait and see where the man was going to land.

"What . . . ," Jordane finally said with lips pursed in a thin line and eyes squeezed almost shut. "What the hell do you mean this is my lucky day?"

"I mean it's your lucky day because my article will not be published as long as you . . ."

Before J. B. could finish the sentence, Jordane shouted, "As long as I what? Confess? Withdraw from the race?" Then he dropped his face into his hands as if to say *Why are you doing this to me?*

"No. I want you to do much more than that, Mr. Jordane."

"So, is it money? How much do you want?"

J. B. ignored the insult. "What I want is for you to make amends for what you did." He held up his iPhone. "Give me your number. I'll text you the list of amends you will make. There are six demands."

Jordane gave him a long, hard look, then reached into his briefcase and pulled out his phone. "How about you give me *your* number, Mr. Harrell."

J. B. indulged him. Even when cornered and feeling desperate, the man still managed to act tough.

Two seconds later, J. B.'s iPhone pinged, and he texted a list of six demands back to Jordane's number. Then he sat back and, a few minutes later, much to his surprise, saw a look of relief on Jordane's face.

"Okay, Mr. Harrell. I have already promised to do this.aH" He tapped his finger on the face of his phone and then, at J. B.'s request, read the first demand out loud. "'If I am elected, my immediate and number one legislative priority will be to ensure that Indigenous people have all decision-making authority over any new uranium mining operations on their lands and that all inactive mines will be cleaned to pre-mining conditions.'" He plunked his phone face down on the table as if that took care of everything.

J. B. motioned for him to pick up his phone again. "Okay. On to number two then. Read it, please."

"'I will work with Peter Minter and other Indigenous persons of his choosing,'" Jordane's voice oozed with irritation and impatience as he read, "'to write legislation . . . blah, blah . . . hold hearings . . . blah, blah . . . bring people to Washington to speak . . .'" He looked up from his phone. "I have already consulted with Peter about these things, Mr. Harrell."

"Not consult," J. B. says. "*He* decides. *His people* decide. *Them*, not you."

Jordane shrugged and rolled his eyes.

"That's all right. You make the promise today." J. B. shrugged back. "Peter will let me know what you do to keep it. Number three?"

With his chin tucked down like this was a huge waste of his time, Jordane muttered in a low, almost inaudible voice, "'Expand the Radiation Exposure Compensation Act . . . remedy harm from uranium mining . . . doubled cancer rates . . . contaminated water . . . blah, blah.'" He scratched the back of his head. "Haven't we already covered this, Mr. Harrell?"

"I take that as a yes?"

"Of *course*! But now," he paused to look at his watch, "I'm afraid I must leave. I told the governor I would come to her office early."

"Only we are not yet finished, Mr. Jordane. Number four?"

Jordane sighed, so overdramatically that J. B. almost laughed. Then he shrugged his shoulders, a quick irritated jerk, and looked down at his phone again. "Sign on to the UN Declaration on the Rights of Indigenous Peoples?" He covered his face with his free hand and groaned. "Are you fucking kidding me? Congress will *never* endorse that!"

"Nonetheless," J. B. said. "You *will* introduce the bill. And you *will* hold a hearing on it. You *will* get the issue out there in that and every other way you can."

"But they won't . . ."

"This is not a negotiation, Mr. Jordane. If elected, you will devote all your time and resources to making these amends." J. B. raised his eyebrows and waited for Jordane to nod before continuing. "Okay, on to number five. An easy one. If elected, you will serve only one term in office. You will not run for a second term."

"Wait a minute! Surely you don't expect me to accomplish all this in just one term, do you?"

"What I expect, Mr. Jordane, is that for the next six years, you will devote all your time, energy, and resources to making Congress and the public aware of these issues and the need to take action."

Jordane released a very long sigh.

"I take that as agreement then?"

After a quick nod, followed by an exaggerated look at his watch, Jordane stood, and at the same time silently read the last demand. "You can't be serious!" he shouted. He dropped his phone onto the table, plopped back down in the chair, and slapped his hands on his knees.

"*Dead* serious," J. B. said.

Their eyes locked. Neither of them moved. Was this going to be a standoff? The make-or-break moment? It might be a bridge too far to ask Jordane to give back to the reservations all the profits he made from casino development investments as long as he was in the Senate, but J. B. stood firm. Undeterred. He pushed his shoulders back. This was not the time for any second-guessing or regret or worry.

"*There* you are!"

Startled by the sudden appearance of someone standing next to him—a woman in her fifties, leaning way too close—Jordane clutched at his chest, his eyes wide as saucers.

"I'm sorry, Mr. Jordane." The woman blushed and took a nervous step back, straightened the jacket of her pale green linen suit. "I tracked you down." She held up her phone. "The governor is waiting."

"Certainly." Jordane had recovered enough to flash her a fake smile, but not enough, it seemed, to engage in his usual banter.

J. B. stood up with his hand out. "J. B. Harrell," he said. "I'm with the *New York Times*."

"Ruth Adamson. I'm the governor's executive secretary."

The two of them shook hands and J. B. said, "I've already written an article about Mr. Jordane. Here, I can send it to your office."

Jordane shot him a warning glare and then jumped up, shoving his chair back so hard it knocked a potted plant over onto its side. He wiped the moisture from his brow. Looked down at his watch.

"Or maybe, Mr. Jordane, you'd like me to send the governor your six-point platform instead?" J. B. then turned to the woman as if to explain.

"We were just talking about all the things Mr. Jordane is promising to do if he wins the election." He looked at Jordane, raised his eyebrows. "I have the list on my phone if you'd like me to send it to the governor."

"Thank you, Mr. Harrell, but there's no need," Jordane said through gritted teeth. "I'll talk to the governor about them myself."

J. B. looked at Ms. Adamson, whose eyes had been moving back and forth between him and Jordane, and said, "Tell the governor his commitments are truly impressive."

The governor's executive secretary nodded, then glanced down at her watch, said the governor was expecting them.

"There are *six* of them. Six promises. That's right, isn't it, Mr. Jordane?"

Jordane jerked his chin up, ever so slightly, in agreement and then, despite being caught over a barrel, swaggered out of the coffee shop as if he thought he was still in charge.

Chapter Sixteen

When the press conference was over, J. B. stepped out of the building into a bright hot sun and clear blue sky. The air was fresh and clean after last night's storm as he made his way briskly down the steps to where a cab had just dropped someone off. It was only a ten-minute drive to the hospital, a brief chance to rest—just enough, he hoped, to make it through the rest of the day. Writing the article about the governor's endorsement today would not be difficult. Facing Sylvia would be. With a long sigh, he rested his head on the back of the seat and had no sooner closed his eyes when he heard Mentayer's ringtone on his iPhone.

"Sylvia and I just watched the news."

That was it? No hello? Not even was Sylvia okay, or what did she think, or what was her first reaction, or? Mentayer didn't sound angry or surprised or pleased or confused. In fact, she didn't sound like anything. His head spun with the many things such a neutral tone could mean. Maybe she didn't want to get into it on the phone. Maybe she didn't want to ask, in front of Sylvia, why he hadn't confronted Jordane at the press conference. Maybe she was just keeping an open mind, waiting to hear his explanation.

"How is Sylvia?"

"The doctor says she's doing very well. She can go home soon."

"And?"

"She wants to know when you'll be here."

J. B. waited for his wife to say more, to at least give him a heads-up about Sylvia's reaction. Was she disappointed? Angry? Surprised? A clue about what he should expect when he got there would have been nice.

"Soon," he said. "Tell her I'll be there soon." He slipped the iPhone back in the pocket of his suit jacket with a groan. So much for trying to get a little rest. The taxi had already pulled into the driveway and was now stopping under the awning over the entrance to the Monrow City Hospital.

The sliding glass doors opened automatically, and he stepped into the spacious lobby with its soothing calm atmosphere, its ample spaces between comfortable seating areas offering privacy, the young man sitting behind the desk marked Patient Information offering a friendly smile.

The smell of coffee and the sign to Lobby Espresso sent him in search of a quiet place to finish his article about the governor's endorsement—he had already pretty much written it in his head—and submit it in time for tomorrow morning's edition of both the *Monrow City Tribune* and the *New York Times*. He paused outside the hospital gift shop, thinking maybe he would bring Sylvia a peace offering, if one proved to be necessary. But then he remembered, a long time ago, decades now, when he had flowers delivered for her birthday and she scolded him. "If you have to give me anything, J. B., don't go wasting money on things that are just going to die." So, for her birthday the next year, he gave her a book called *Daily Reflections for Women's Spirits* with a note that said, "So you'll remember me every day." It turned out that she not only had that book but every other meditation book he'd looked at as well, and she said she already thought about him every day and had ever since he was seven years old.

And so, no gift. He kept walking until he reached the coffee cart at the end of the hall. He bought a large coffee and found a private space to sit, a cushioned chair in a far corner next to the floor-to-ceiling window. Just as he'd expected, the article practically wrote itself. An introductory paragraph about Jordane's Senate campaign and the governor's endorsement, then a list of promises in Jordane's platform, which was basically a cut, paste, and edit of the six demands J. B. had extorted from him. He ended the article with two sentences—"If he wins this election, will Anthony Jordane keep his promises? That remains to be seen." With a satisfied flourish, he pressed the Submit button, then slipped his iPad back in his briefcase.

On his way to the bank of elevators that would take him up to Sylvia's room, his iPhone pinged. A text from Mentayer. *She wants to know when you'll be here.*

On my way, he texted back as he stepped into the elevator. "Stand clear of the door," a voice said as he pressed the button for the eighth floor. A woman near Sylvia's age stood in the back corner, one arthritic hand gripping the handrail and the other clutching some papers, a worn wedding band hanging loose on her shriveled ring finger and a look of worry and sadness on her face. J. B. turned around and stared at the numbers above the door, a lump in his throat as he imagined what she was facing. When the elevator stopped at the second floor, which was labeled Surgery, three people got on: a disheveled man who looked like he hadn't slept in days and his two teenage daughters hanging onto each of his arms, none of them with dry eyes. One of the girls pressed the button for the first floor, unaware that the elevator was going up. No one talked.

The sense of brokenness in the small space gave J. B. pause. A week ago, he thought Sylvia would die, and now she was going to go home. And while he worried that she might be disappointed in him for not exposing Jordane's past today, he didn't have to worry about their relationship ending, not after all these years, not after everything they'd been through. The elevator stopped at the fifth floor, and he held the door open with a silent blessing for the older woman as she exited with painstakingly slow effort. Before getting off on the eighth floor, he placed his palms together and nodded another blessing to the family of three clinging to each other in the back.

When he got to Sylvia's room, he stood in the doorway for a few seconds before going in. He took a deep breath. Squared his shoulders. The television in the room was on the news, its volume turned up. Sylvia was sitting in the same cushioned chair that J. B. had slept in for three nights after she was moved here from intensive care. It was encouraging to see that she was out of bed, but she looked quite frail. Mentayer, sitting in a straight-backed hard chair next to Sylvia, saw him come in and clicked off the TV with the remote control, then rushed over to the door.

"Brace yourself," she whispered in his ear while giving him a long, warm hug.

J. B. walked over to Sylvia and reached down to hug her, but when he saw the look on her face, he drew back and sat on the edge of the bed instead.

"I hear you're feeling better," he said with a smile. She nodded. "And you get to go home soon?"

"That's right," she said after an agonizing moment of silence.

J. B. recognized the expression on her face, the clucking sound she made with her tongue, the way she held her hands in her lap and squinted up at him. He gripped the edge of the bed. The Sylvia he knew and loved was back, as much a force to be reckoned with as ever.

"Maybe," he reached into his briefcase for his iPad, "I should read what I wrote about today. I just sent it to the papers."

The ever-so-slight upturn of her lips was encouraging; the glint of expectation in her eyes was worrying. Reading the article to her might not be the best way to start after all. Maybe he should first explain why he'd decided *not* to write an exposé about Jordane. Or, maybe he should first acknowledge her disappointment, tell her he was sorry, that he knew it wasn't what she'd wanted him to do. Better yet, maybe he should just ask her what she thought of the news coverage.

"Go ahead and read it," Mentayer said, sensing his doubts and unscrambling the options for him.

So, that was what he did. The article was short, and he read the whole thing without looking up. If the hope in Sylvia's eyes were to fade away while he was reading, he didn't want to see it, couldn't bear it if she felt that he'd let her down. Even when he was finished, he kept his eyes down, hoping that somehow she would understand why he did what he did.

"Fool!" Sylvia spit the word out with a sneer that startled J. B. into looking up.

He wanted to believe that she was calling Jordane a fool for letting himself be bamboozled, wanted to believe that it was Sylvia's way of saying that Jordane was no match for someone as savvy as him. But *wanting* to believe wasn't the same as believing.

"Lies! Lies! Lies!" Sylvia's hands slapped the arms of the chair. The scowl on her face made it perfectly clear that she was calling *J. B.* the fool, not Jordane, and just to make sure he got it, she pointed her crooked forefinger at him. "Didn't I tell you he was a liar!?"

J. B. sighed. Okay then. He sat up with his back straight. Things were going to get worse before they got better. It sometimes went that way when the two of them disagreed. Only this time was different. This time it felt personal. Raw. Gut-wrenching. He blew the air out through his mouth and planted his feet on the floor, his palms uplifted.

"Yes, Sylvia. You told me. And yes, I know that Jordane *is* a liar. He only made those promises because I blackmailed him." He paused, then said, "Well, actually, I threatened him . . . so, I guess that would be extortion, wouldn't it."

Sylvia shook her head, her eyes wide. It was the first time he'd ever seen her speechless.

"And, no, I do not trust him, Sylvia. Not for a minute. I know he's a liar."

"Then, why?" Wrinkles creased her cheeks and forehead as if finding her voice again had required her to put her whole face into the effort.

"It's complicated. So much has happened in the last few days. I don't know how . . . or where . . . to start." He knew he was asking Sylvia for help. And he knew that she couldn't help. She had no way of knowing that the trip to Bigger had turned him inside out. How much he had changed just in the last twenty-four hours. Maybe *resurrected* was too big a word, but that was what it felt like. Tears started to well up in his eyes. He pushed his tongue into the roof of his mouth, tried to hold them back. What was wrong with him? Why was he, all of a sudden, so shaky?

Mentayer came to sit next to him on the bed, put her arm around his shoulder. He pressed his cheek against hers, felt her soft feathery lips on his skin. He squeezed her hand and breathed in her belief in him, as if he could make it his own.

"Okay then." He got up from the bed, walked over to the straight-backed chair, ready to explain his decision to Sylvia. He would start with what Peter said, then tell her about the insights he'd had as a result, and, finally, tell her how all that came together so that, as soon as he saw Jordane gawking at a young woman that morning, he'd known what to do. He lifted the chair and turned it around, then sat down facing Sylvia so he could gauge her reactions as he talked.

"I am not excusing Anthony Jordane for *anything* he did. It was reprehensible." He spewed out the word *reprehensible* a second time, then paused to give her a chance to confirm that at least they were starting on the same page. But all he saw in her eyes was a despair so painful that he had to look away.

"So what, J. B.? So what?" Sylvia stopped to catch her breath, then leaned forward. She clenched her fists, her jaw. Her face was bright pink, the wrinkles an even deeper beet red. "So what if he gets elected? A senator who raped a *child*? A senator who murdered a boy? So what if he made promises? He won't keep them. And you know that. I know you do!"

She started coughing and fell back in the chair, the sweat running down her cheeks in a stream of disappointment and hopelessness. J. B. wanted to reach out to her, but his hands flopped helplessly on his lap and his chest was pounding so hard it felt like all the blood in his body had rushed into his heart. He pressed his index and middle fingers into the soft hollow of his neck, to the side of his Adam's apple. His pulse was regular. Was he having a panic attack? It was exhaustion. Too much stress. No sleep. But then, he'd done all-nighters many times in the past and had been fine. He managed to pull himself up from the chair. Mentayer, alarmed at how unsteady he was on his feet, started toward him, but he waved her away.

"Take care of Sylvia," he said. Then he dragged himself out the door.

• • •

All he needed was a few minutes to pull himself together. To regain control of himself. He had always known how to sort things. First, you ask questions. That was how you figured out what had happened. So, what had upset him so much about Sylvia's reaction? It wasn't like they had never faced off before. What was different this time? Why did he feel so diminished, so little? This was not like him. Not like him at all.

J. B. staggered down the hall, the white, vinyl-floored hallway swallowing him up. The bright fluorescent lighting and beige walls. Antiseptic smells, intermittent clouds of bodily stench. Alarming sounds—the beeping of machines, people crying out in pain. He hurled himself into the waiting room at the end of the hall, slammed the door shut. He flopped down on the couch—thank goodness no one was there—and slumped over, his hands gripping clumps of his hair. A chill came over him and he shivered, tapped his arms with trembling fingers. His eyes burned. He sniffled. Then the floodgates opened and an avalanche of tears coursed down his cheeks, releasing the pain of loss and trauma that had been hidden in a corner of his heart and merging the past with the present.

When it was over and there were no more tears to cry, J. B. pulled himself up to a sitting position, reached for the box of tissues on the table next to the couch, dried his cheeks, dabbed at his drenched shirt, and blew his nose. He felt strangely calm and relaxed. He breathed in the air, marveled at how fresh it smelled. The room was as quiet as if it were soundproofed. A green spider plant sucked in a bright ray of sunlight. His head felt as clear as the cloudless blue sky outside the window. He went into the bathroom, splashed cold water on his red, puffy eyes, and combed his hair.

Then he went back to Sylvia's room. The TV was off. The monitoring machines were unplugged and pushed into the corner. Sylvia was slumped over in the cushioned chair, chin resting on her chest, eyes closed, snoring softly. Mentayer was in the straight-backed chair studying her iPhone, but she sensed his presence and looked up.

"Are you okay? We . . . ," she tipped her head toward Sylvia, "we were both worried about you."

With a light step, J. B. walked across the room and hugged his wife, felt her body relax into his.

"I'm all right now," he whispered. "What about Sylvia?"

"Worn out."

"Shouldn't she be in bed?"

Mentayer shrugged, rolled her eyes. "I tried. She insisted on waiting for you first. She feels bad. She didn't mean to be so brutal."

Sylvia's body twitched and her eyelids fluttered. And when J. B. touched her bony hand lightly with his fingertips, her eyes popped open. She reached out for him and tried to stand up, but he shook his head and leaned down to hug her instead.

"I'm sorry, J. B." Her voice shook.

"No need," he said, "no need." He lowered himself onto the floor in front of her, sat back on his feet.

She leaned forward. "I shouldn't have . . ." She stopped, out of breath, then fell back, exhausted.

"It's okay, Sylvia." He hoisted himself up and moved a few inches closer to her. "I just needed time. I had a lot to sort out."

"You did what you had to do, J. B. I know that."

"You understand?"

She shook her head. No, she didn't understand.

"It doesn't matter," she said.

But it *did* matter to J. B. He wanted, no, he needed her to understand. He needed to tell her what had happened to him, needed to explain why he'd done what he did, and why it made sense to him. Only it would have to wait, because a heavy weariness had settled over Sylvia and it looked like she was going to pass out any minute.

Chapter Seventeen

The high ceilings, large windows, and table and seating arrangements in the hospital's light-filled cafeteria were designed to provide comfort and inspiration. J. B. and Mentayer found that and more on the outdoor terrace overlooking Monrow City as they sat at a table surrounded by raised garden beds of herbs grown for use in the cafeteria and plugged their iPhones into a nearby power unit.

"The nurse says Sylvia is okay," Mentayer said. "She'll probably sleep for the rest of the day and all night now."

J. B. nodded, distracted. His hand was unsteady as he reached for the handle of his cup and some coffee splashed on his designer shirt and the lapel of his expensive summer-weight suit jacket. He dabbed at the spots with a napkin, vaguely aware of how dreadful he must look after the meltdown he'd had in the visitors' lounge. But then, he realized with surprise, he didn't care all that much about his appearance, because he felt as if a swarm of bees were buzzing around inside his head, each one carrying a piece of his history and demanding his attention at the same time.

"After I left Sylvia's room . . ." He pinched the bridge of his nose. "Well, it's a good thing no one was in the visitors' lounge."

Mentayer took a bite of her cinnamon roll and sat back in her chair, asked him what happened.

That was all it took. A scramble of words flew unbidden from his mouth and he leaned forward as if he'd been propelled by a heavy wind. "I lost it. It was like I was a child again. Jamie. Little Jamie Buckley. One little, two little, three little, four little, now *five* little Buckleys." He laughed. A child's giggle. "We played that a lot. At first. My sister and three brothers.

Mostly my sister. She took care of me. They had a welcome party. Just for me. The whole reservation came. I learned how to fish. From my birth dad. I learned how to dance. From my birth mom. Me and my brothers slept in the same bed."

He blinked, both baffled and embarrassed by his outburst. It was so unlike him. But then he recognized the look on Mentayer's face. It was the look she had when one of her students had recovered a traumatic childhood memory.

"Well . . . ," he smiled, "you pretty much know everything already."

That was partly true. When they were first getting to know each other, almost twenty years ago, he had told Mentayer about how, when he was seven, Sylvia was the social worker who took him from the foster home where he'd been placed at birth and returned him to Josie and John Buckley, his rightful parents.

"I know everything you remembered *then*," Mentayer said. "And how you understood it *then*."

They sat in silence for a few seconds.

"Funny, isn't it." He rubbed his chin. "I remember what everyone else looked like that day *except* Sylvia. Even now I can't conjure up a young version of her."

But when he closed his eyes again, he had no trouble conjuring up multiple images of how his life had been turned upside down in just one day. From living in a comfortable middle-class home on a quiet tree-lined street in a small town to living in a two-room house that had once been a chicken coop on a weed-filled piece of land surrounded by a forest of trees. From having a spacious bedroom all to himself filled with more toys and books than he could possibly play with or read to sharing one bedroom with the whole family, his birth mother and father and sister in one bed, he and his three brothers and his dog Tick in the other, two pegs on the wall reserved for his clothes. From a reliable basement furnace that kept him toasty warm in the winter to an inadequate wood-burning stove in the room next to the bedroom and gaps in the walls stuffed with newspapers that still didn't keep the cold reservation wind at bay. From being doted on and adored as a special only child to being one of five. From cupboards filled with anything he wanted to eat at any time to not enough government surplus bags on the floor in the corner for all the mouths needing to be fed.

"They told me I was going there *just* for a visit. But I never saw my foster mother again." He stood up then, reached for their empty cups, and said, "I'll go get us refills."

The walk to the coffee bar inside was just the break he needed. Midafternoons were always quiet in the cafeteria, and the soft hush of the few voices there calmed him. Two young men in their twenties, one wearing a magenta T-shirt and the other a blue flowered Hawaiian shirt, sat at a table in the back corner whispering to each other. Along the opposite wall, a bald man was speaking softly to two women, presumably his daughter and granddaughter.

The comforting aroma of dinner preparations in the cafeteria reminded him of the warm, heady smells—roasted garlic, a simmering stew, hearty meatloaf, homemade bread—of dinners at the kitchen table with his foster grandparents. Grandma Rose trying to fatten him up, Grandpa Harold grilling him about his day at school. His bedroom with two walls blue and the other two white, the red and white striped curtains Grandma Rose sewed for him, crispy new Mickey Mouse sheets on his bunk bed. Long hot baths in his own bathroom, the luxurious and fresh-smelling towels.

J. B. placed the cups down on the coffee bar counter while his head kept spinning with memories. How he'd run away from the reservation and ended up living with his foster grandparents. How he forgot that he was Jamie Buckley, son of John and Josie Buckley, and came to identify with Grandpa Harold and his world, even adopting J. B. Harrell as his professional name in honor of him.

He reached for the coffee pot and refilled their cups, one sugar packet and a creamer for Mentayer, black and bitter for him, and carried them back outside to the patio.

"You know, hon," he said as he handed a cup to Mentayer, "when we get back to New York, I think I should see a therapist."

He placed his cup on the table without spilling a drop and sat down, staring out at the high-rise buildings beyond the patio instead of drinking his coffee. Who would he be today, he wondered, if it weren't for Grandpa

Harold? He owed him a lot, but at what price? He was caught between two conflicting worlds now because of him. But what did that matter? He'd had to make a decision, and he had. As a distinguished investigative journalist, he was compelled to tell the truth about Anthony Jordane; as an Anishinaabe, he was compelled to do what was in the best interests, even survival, of his people. An impossible choice. And so, he had found a third way.

"What are you thinking," Mentayer asked.

"When Sylvia wakes up, I want to tell her why I decided not to expose Jordane," he said. "I'm clearer about it now."

"As I knew you would be." Mentayer smiled and reached across the table for his hands.

"I did what I thought was right," he said. "Only, I'm not sure it really was the right thing to do."

Mentayer chuckled. "Sylvia knows it wasn't. You heard her: 'Mark my words. That man will never keep those promises.'"

He cringed, held his forehead in his hands. "What if she's right?"

"Well, J. B., all I can say is that you better keep your eye on him. Best to be prepared."

• • •

J. B.'s article about the governor's endorsement of Jordane's candidacy ran on the front pages of the morning newspapers. By the end of the day, plans had been made to discharge Sylvia from the hospital tomorrow; her next-door neighbor would drive her home and then be available to help with whatever she needed after that. Mentayer was already on a flight back to New York City, where she could prepare for her school's second summer session. In a few hours J. B. would follow her on a red-eye flight, and by eight o'clock tomorrow morning he would be back at his *New York Times* desk, responding to unanswered calls that had been stacking up and covering the immigrant crisis that was building up in the Bronx.

J. B. and Sylvia were alone in her hospital room. They had been sitting by the window ever since Mentayer left for the airport, talking and munching on the tuna salad sandwiches, potato chips, vegetables, and oatmeal chocolate chip cookies that the food service worker had placed on small tables next to each of their chairs. After sleeping last night more deeply and longer—fourteen hours!—than he ever had in his life, J. B. had woken refreshed and with a heightened need for Sylvia to understand his decisions about Anthony Jordane, even if she disagreed with them. After sleeping straight through from yesterday afternoon until this morning, Sylvia had been alert and loaded for bear.

"When I went to Bigger, I didn't expect any of this to happen." J. B. had waved his hands in a circle. He felt as if he had encompassed the world in less than a week.

That was how he started his conversation with Sylvia, before going on to describe everyone he'd talked to on the trip and everything he'd learned. From the old-timers in the motel bar—that Anthony "Tony" Jordane was the town hero, his father was the police chief, and no one would talk about Will's death. From Jeremy Kuzik, deputy police officer at the time—that Will had escaped from jail and his cause of death was never determined. From Spencer Jackson, a dying man—that his father and other men, including the police chief, had decided, since there was no evidence to charge Will with rape, that they would *take care of that injun* themselves.

He paused to sip some water. "They lynched him." He choked on the word, had to drink more water to calm himself.

Sylvia leaned forward with her hands on the chair's armrests. "Jordane killed Will. How many times do I have to say that!"

He raised his hand in a stop sign. "I'm just telling you what I was told."

Sylvia pursed her lips and crossed her arms over her chest. "And I'm just telling you what I know."

He took a deep breath. He didn't want to argue. He wanted Sylvia to understand what had happened to him, what led him to his decision.

"I know you don't believe me, J. B. You don't get it. You're just like everyone else."

"I am not like everyone else!"

She scrunched up her face and sat back in her chair with an impatient wave for him to continue.

"I'm not like everyone else, Sylvia. I'm like Will. Don't you see? I fell apart, almost as if *I* was lynched."

That was when Sylvia's eyes went soft. And when she reached for his hand, he was able, after taking a deep breath, to continue.

"The last person I talked to was Julia Grogan. Her younger sister, Patricia, wrote in her diary that Jordane had raped her and threatened to kill her dog if she told anyone."

Sylvia recoiled and hissed as if she were a snake ready to strike.

"Jordane didn't kill her, though," he said. "Patricia died by suicide."

"That's just semantics!" Sylvia's eyes flashed hot rage. "She still died *because* of him, and he should be in prison!"

"That's exactly how I felt." J. B. pursed his lips. "On the drive back, I drafted a scathing exposé in my head, a front-pager. The headline was 'Why Anthony Jordane Is Unfit for Public Service.'"

Sylvia had looked satisfied, but J. B. knew the hard part was yet to come, and he braced himself for it. "But then . . ." He blew the air out through his mouth. "I talked to Peter Minter." He breathed in, breathed out. "Hear me out, okay? He was repelled by what I told him about Jordane, *but* he urged me to support his candidacy anyway."

He could tell that Sylvia had to work hard to hold her tongue while he explained Peter's argument about thinking long-term about the health, the very survival, of his people.

"Okay, I get it! I get it," she said when he paused. "But you don't put your faith in a liar, J. B. Just don't. And, frankly, I don't get why Peter thinks Jordane can be trusted, even for a minute. It doesn't sound like Peter. Not like him at all."

J. B. went on to explain that Peter did *not* trust Jordane, nor did he have to, because Jordane had invested in the development of casino resorts, and uranium mining would interfere with his pocketbook.

"Snake in the grass," Sylvia said with a snort.

"Yes, he is," he said. "We all agree that Jordane cannot be trusted."

"It's still hard for me to understand why you went along with it, J. B. Why?" Sylvia shook her head, and tears of frustration filled her eyes.

He reached for her hands. "I know this is hard for you to stomach. I know how badly you want me to expose Jordane. But I want—no, I *need* you to understand what went into my decision." He pulled his hands back and ran his fingers through his hair as if massaging the explanation out of his head. "I was an Indian kid, a misfit in a white town. I was a target like Will was. And when Peter told me to remember who I was, and to not try to be someone I wasn't, all hell broke loose inside me. To be true to yourself, you have to know who you are, right? I realized that I had never come to terms with who I am, and that led me to some very dark places. To old and long-forgotten childhood memories from back when I was Jamie Buckley."

Encouraged by the pained expression on Sylvia's face, J. B. jumped to his feet and paced back and forth, back and forth, talking about all the things he'd completely forgotten or denied or had hidden in his unconscious until now. He tripped over his words, knowing Sylvia was with him, that she was listening to more than his words.

"Bottom line," he said, "my identity was erased when I stopped being Jamie Buckley."

"No!" Sylvia slapped the armrests of her chair with that determined look he'd seen so many times before. "You never stopped being Jamie Buckley. He never left you. He's always been inside you. Remember back when Anthony Little Eagle died in a foster home, and you charged into my office saying it wasn't an accident? It was Jamie who told you to do that. He told you to write that series in the *Monrow City Tribune* exposing the foster care system. And that feature article in the *New York Times Magazine* about the history of Indian kids and boarding schools . . . and when you cried about Will . . ."

J. B. smiled. "That was Jamie crying for Will and for me," he said, finishing her sentence.

"See? You never forgot who you were," she said.

He sat down, felt his body relaxing. Everything made sense. His childhood grief had played itself out in the present. The part of him that never forgot he was Jamie Buckley wanted to expose Jordane and get justice for Will, but at the same time, wanted him *not* to expose Jordane but to do what was best for his people. *His* people. And he simply couldn't do both of those things at the same time.

"No wonder it was so hard to make a decision," he said. "Just as I learned to respect my identity and skills as a journalist, I had to learn how to own and respect my Anishinaabe identity as well."

Sylvia raised her eyebrows. She understood. Now she understood. "And reclaim Jamie Buckley," she said with a smile.

"Right, and once I did that, well, then I knew what to do. I tell you, Sylvia, the minute I saw Jordane standing at the bottom of the capitol building steps, I just knew!" He pushed his chair a few inches closer to Sylvia and looked into her eyes. "I knew what I did when I extorted promises from Jordane instead of exposing him. I knew I let him off the hook. But I didn't support him. I don't. And I don't want him to win this election."

"You did what you had to do," Sylvia said in a whisper.

Just as Sylvia had done what she had to do when he was seven, he thought but didn't say out loud. She knew she was breaking his heart that day she drove him to the reservation, but she was doing what she had to do. And, it had been the right thing. He understood that now.

"Yes, I did," he said. "But I don't know yet if it was the right thing to do. That remains to be seen. If Jordane doesn't keep his promises, then . . ."

"When. *When* he doesn't keep his promises." Sylvia wagged her finger at him.

"We'll know if he doesn't," he said.

"No, you won't, J. B. That man is very good at keeping secrets."

"We'll watch him. I'm getting a new intern. She starts tomorrow. I'll assign her to do research, to dig in on what Jordane's up to. I'll brief her about him as soon as I get back to my office."

"Research?" Sylvia flicked her wrist at him. "He doesn't exactly leave a paper trail. The only way to know what he's doing is to see him doing it, and even then, he'll deny it."

"You're right," he said. "We need to have someone on the inside. Someone who has access to Jordane and his whole operation. My new intern is from NYU and her resume indicates she's very capable. If she's willing to take on the assignment, maybe I could send her to Monrow City to work as a volunteer in his main campaign headquarters. I would have to be open with Jordane about who she is, which means he might hide information from her, but it could still be a good learning experience."

Outside, the sky was dark, the lights of the city turned on in the windows of buildings, the street lampposts, the headlights of cars. He looked at the clock on the wall. It was time for him to leave for the airport.

Part Three

Sylvia Takes Action

Chapter Eighteen

I have to tell J. B. and Mentayer that I'm going to Bigger tomorrow. He'll try to talk me out of it. She'll support me but worry about my health. They'll both be upset, argue that I haven't been out of the hospital long enough, that I'm not fully recovered yet. That's why, before getting into our Zoom meeting, I did that photo booth thing to see how I look on the screen, and it's pretty damn good. My hair is pulled back in a bun, my cheeks are rosy, and I've gained some weight, too, although this old housedress has always been too big for me so they may not notice that.

"You look absolutely fantastic, Sylvia!" Mentayer breaks out in a huge smile. She's almost giddy. This is good. Just as I hoped.

"We're sharing a bowl of salted caramel ice cream from the Sugar Hill Creamery a few blocks away from here," J. B. says. "Come to visit and we'll take you there."

I hold myself back from breaking the news. I hate to upset them right away when they look so happy, so comfortable and relaxed sitting next to each other on the couch in that nice Harlem apartment of theirs with their after-dinner cups of chamomile tea.

"We'll take you up to the Bronx, too," Mentayer says. "See all your old haunts." She reaches for an eight-by-ten black-and-white family photo on the glass coffee table and holds it up to the screen for me to see. It's the one with her grandmother laughing and slapping her knees, Mentayer and her brother Markus on each side of her with silly grins on their faces. "Remember this picture, Sylvia?"

I smile and nod, but inside I'm about as antsy as I've ever been, thinking about how I am going to Bigger for Patricia Grogan. She was only fourteen. For myself. I was seventeen. For all the other girls back then who Becca knows about, because she always knew everything about everybody. For all the women who Jordane sexually assaulted over the years. And now for Emma, J. B.'s intern.

Yes, Emma, too! She called me last night in tears, told me Jordane had hurt her. In the background, I hear Mentayer's voice, and I can pick out the words even though her voice is like background noise to me right now.

"I still have Grandma's chair, too." She points the camera at the overstuffed chair in the corner, its arms frayed where her grandmother's hands once rested, its cushions still shaped to the form of her ample body. "I know it's an eyesore." Mentayer laughs and turns the camera back on her and J. B. "But I can't let go of it."

"I love your gran's chair." J. B. puts his arm around her. "And I love when you tell me her stories. I can just see you sitting on the floor with your gran fixing your hair in braids and telling stories about how your great-grandmother secretly taught children on the slave plantation how to read and write."

"Grandma *preached*," Mentayer says with a chuckle. "She said I come from a long line of educators, so teaching was in my blood, and if I ever forgot who I was she would come back from the grave and shake it out of me."

"The past is never really the past," J. B. says. "It lives inside you. Right, Sylvia?"

They don't wait for me to answer. I'll wait for them to ask me what I've been up to and then I'll say, *Well, since you asked, I'm going to Bigger tomorrow. Becca remembers something, and I'm going to get her to tell me what it is.*

"Grandma always said that about the past, too," Mentayer is saying now.

"And isn't it the truth." J. B. rests his head on the back of the couch like I've seen him do whenever he thinks he's encountered a big thought. "The more I unlock my own history, the more I realize that it never does go away. Like the other day, I was walking to the subway when I saw a woman with gray hair in a loose summer dress who looked just like a woman who taught me some Anishinaabemowin words and how to play the flute. And then I remembered, a long time ago, Sylvia, when you told me about a woman named May Goodheart who told the juvenile court judge that I belonged with my birth parents, with my own people. So, there you go, you see someone on the street who looks like someone you once knew, and another piece of the puzzle falls into place." He lifts his head. "I only stayed on the rez for five years, though. It was never home. More like a place in between places."

J. B. scoops out a spoonful of ice cream and hands the bowl back to Mentayer to finish off. Enough is enough. I can't wait any longer. If I don't break the news to them now, I am going to lose my mind.

"There's something I want to talk about," I say.

"If it's about Jordane," J. B. says, "you don't have to worry. Emma is on the case. She's reporting to me regularly from his campaign headquarters. She's so conscientious, Sylvia, the sharpest intern I've ever had. Probably the best volunteer any campaign has ever had, too. She's helping them with all kinds of things—getting access to Jordane's campaign finances, phone calls, meetings, reports."

I don't know what to say. I can't say that it was Emma's call that did it for me, made me decide to go to Bigger. She begged me not to tell J. B., said she doesn't want it to interfere with the undercover work she's doing for him.

"Sylvia? Are you okay?"

"I'm going to get that bastard, J. B. By the time we are finished with him, he will be convicted of rape and sentenced to prison for a good long time."

"Oh, Sylvia, Sylvia, Sylvia . . ."

"Don't 'Oh, Sylvia' me," I say. "Just don't."

J. B. leans forward and runs his fingers through his hair, his face so close to the computer that it's all I can see. I can't tell if he's angry or just determined or what, only that his lips are drawn into a thin line and his eyebrows are a black knot on his forehead.

"Listen to me, Sylvia. Jordane will *never* be convicted. He won't even be charged. No prosecutor will even look at the case, much less take it. It happened over sixty years ago. There's no rape victim. No witness to testify. Patricia Grogan's diary could have easily been forged, and there's no other evidence. It's not going to happen."

"You don't know everything, J. B. Just wait. You'll see. You'll all see." I shut my mouth, refrain from saying, *He tried to do it to me, then succeeded with a fourteen-year-old, and who else? He's still at it, you know. He even did it to Emma! Your intern. And I'm going to Bigger to find out who else he hurt!*

"I just don't want you to be disappointed," he says.

Whoa! Really? "J. B." I'm shouting now. "I know what I know, no matter what you or anyone else says. And I do not like or need to be protected. You of all people should know that!"

He sighs and backs away from the camera. Maybe I shouldn't have yelled at him, but at least his face isn't filling up the whole screen now so he looks like a monster. He throws up his hands and mumbles under his breath, but I can still hear him say "Nothing but a fool's errand." And he says it two times!

Mentayer places her hands on his arm like she's trying to hold him down. "Sylvia is going to do what she has to do, hon."

"I am," I say, "and I don't have to do it alone either. Julia Grogan is helping me. She was here."

"Julia Grogan was where? At *your* place?" J. B. sounds indignant now.

"Yes."

"How did *that* happen?"

"What do you mean how did that happen?" I wave my hand in front of the screen. "You told me her name and that she lived in Altos City. All I had to do was find her phone number and call her."

"When was she there?"

"Last week."

"Why didn't you call me? I would have liked to have talked to her."

"Yeah, well, after reading your newspaper article about the governor's endorsement, she doesn't want to talk to you. She thought you were going to expose him. She feels betrayed. Says you broke your promise."

J. B. squeezes his eyes shut, pinches the bridge of his nose with his thumb and forefinger, and mumbles under his breath, "I didn't promise anything."

"Anyway, whatever, we're going ahead."

He clenches his fists and grits his teeth. "Are you going to talk to Peter Minter before you do anything?"

I shrug. No point in responding. Nothing, no one, is going to change my mind.

"I know you and Peter don't agree," J. B. pushes. "But this is more than a disagreement. The two of you are working at odds with each other."

"I'm sorry, but Peter is naive, J. B. He doesn't know Jordane like I do. That man will *not* keep his word."

"Only, in this case, maybe he *will* keep his word," J. B. says, "because he makes money from his casino investments if he does."

I let out a long, exasperated sigh. "All I want is justice. All I want is for Jordane to pay for what he did."

"That's what Peter wants, too, Sylvia. Only he's found a way to make Jordane pay without him knowing that that's what he's doing."

I look at him blank-faced. "Make him pay without him even knowing it?"

"That's right, by giving him a chance to pay for the lives he took, by saving other lives now."

J. B. starts talking about the article he wrote—the numbers of abandoned and contaminated mines, uranium found in newborns, radioactive water, birth defects—but I stop listening. I know about the lives already lost due to uranium mining, but I can't allow them into my heart. And besides, it's a waste of time. Jordane does not save lives. He only takes lives. Why don't they get that?

"Could you just hold off for a while, Sylvia? Jordane promised to call for a hearing about a bill that some leaders in Congress are racing to pass right now that includes a major nuclear energy package. See if he does that. Jordane may be the wrong person, but he could be in the right place at the right time, and even more so if he wins the election. It will give him a chance to make up for, to pay for, all the bad things he's done."

"Please, J. B., exactly how does that make Jordane pay when he doesn't have to accept any responsibility or own up to what he did. Doesn't even have to know he's making up for it."

"Think about it as giving him a chance to make amends, Sylvia. Like that time you helped that frazzled young mother with a colicky baby in the grocery store, and you realized later that it had been your way to make amends for snapping at one of those arrogant young college students in your building."

I clench my jaw and hold up my fists, ready to fight. I do not appreciate him using my recovery like this. Next thing I know he'll be throwing my own words back at me, things I've said about the importance of forgiveness and not holding resentments. I force my breath out through my lips, and it leaves an angry *whoosh* sound hanging in the air.

"Don't talk shit to me, J. B. I am going to get Jordane. Whatever it takes. And *just so you know*, after he's charged with rape, I'm going after him for murdering Will."

"Oh God," he groans. "A group of men lynched Will."

"Yes, I know that's what a dying man told you, J. B., and I'm sure he believes it. But that doesn't make it true. Doesn't make it the whole story." I lean back in my chair with my chin jutted out and my arms crossed over my chest. Do I really have to keep doing this with him? With everyone?

"There is no evidence that Jordane was even there, Sylvia."

"I'm telling you that I *know* he killed Will. I just don't remember how." I swat at the tears suddenly filling my eyes.

"It's okay," Mentayer says. "When you're ready to remember, you will."

Her voice calms me for a second, but then J. B. slaps the palms of his hands on his legs.

"You can't remember something," he says, "that never happened!"

Mentayer purses her lips. "Think about what you just said, J. B.," she says. "If not remembering something means it never happened, then what about all the memories you've been recovering lately? Just because you didn't remember them before, does that mean they never happened?"

He groans and flicks the palm of his hand at her. "I can't just sit back and let Sylvia go around saying that a candidate running for the U.S. Senate killed someone."

"Pffft!" I slap at J. B. on the screen. He doesn't seem to notice.

"I can just see her walking into a Monrow City police precinct and saying, "'I'm here to report a murder.

"'And what is your name, ma'am?

"'Sylvia Jensen.

"'And the person who was killed?

"'William James. Will. He was my friend.

"'When and where did this happen, ma'am?

"'In Bigger. In the woods. June of 1960.

"'O-kay. And you witnessed this murder?

"'No.

"'Did anyone else witness it?

"'I don't know.

"'So, ma'am, how do you know your friend was killed?

"'I just know.

"'O-kay. So, ma'am, uh . . .

"'You probably want to know why I'm reporting it now.

"'Well, actually, ma'am . . . I was going to suggest that if there was a murder, there should be some record of an investigation.

"'What do you mean *if* there was a murder? Will *was* murdered. And I'm here to press charges against the man who did it. There never was an investigation because the murderer was the police chief's son.

"'O-kay, ma'am. And what is the name of the person who allegedly killed your friend?

"'Anthony Jordane. Yes, I know he's running for the U.S. Senate.

"'Excuse me for a minute, ma'am. I'll be right back.'"

"Stop it, J. B.! Sylvia is not going to do that. She would never do that!" Mentayer shakes her head, her voice sharp as the blade of a knife. "You need to apologize to her."

J. B. throws up his hands. "For what?"

"You practically called her a liar. Or delusional."

"I did not! All I said was that you can't remember things that didn't happen."

"*And* that she's on a fool's errand." Mentayer crosses her arms and shifts away from J. B. on the couch.

The rays of the midafternoon sun stream through the tall windows of their high-ceilinged living room and dance across seven multicolored pillows on their pearl beige sofa, then fall onto the boldly patterned and beautifully crafted area rug that was in Mentayer's South Bronx apartment.

I remember when I brought J. B. there the first time. That first meeting did not go well, to say the least. J. B. jokes that he fell in love with Mentayer's rug before he fell in love with her. And now here they are. Fighting. Over me. About me. As if I'm not even here. I shift around in my seat. I still haven't told them that I'm going to Bigger tomorrow. Well, there's nothing they can say or do to stop me anyway. I'll let them know once I get there, or maybe when I'm on my way. So be it. I press the Leave Meeting button without saying good-bye and turn off my computer.

Chapter Nineteen

May I have your attention please. The northbound bus is now boarding at gate number two. The coach operator will be at the entrance door to take your ticket.

Whew! Finally. I've been sitting on this hard bench for over an hour, that's how early I got here. I took an Uber, first time by myself, had to figure out how to download the app, put in my credit card information, go through that whole routine of finding a driver at the best price, and don't even get me started about what it took for me to figure out how to leave a tip. Then, when I got here, the only way to pay for my round-trip ticket was with a credit card. Doesn't anyone take cash anymore? There's something wrong with that.

"Altos City coach boarding at gate number two. All aboard please. And thank you for riding with Greyhound."

I hand the driver my ticket. He smiles at me. People usually do smile back when you smile at them first.

"Good morning, ma'am. Here, I'll help you with that."

I let him take my overnight bag even though it's not heavy. I don't make a fuss when he puts his hand under my elbow to help me up the steps, but it's awkward. He's on the portly side, so it would be easier to use the railing and pull myself up, but okay, if it makes him feel good. He looks to be close to retirement and I've heard that's tough on men.

He puts my bag down on the front seat and points to the seat next to it, by the window. People seem to like to do that, show older people what to do. They mean well. The bathroom is way in the back of the bus. Good thing I thought to go while I was in the station. Maybe the driver wants company, since I'm the only one on the bus, and that's why he put me in front. I wonder how Greyhound stays in business.

I only took the bus once before, from the Bronx to Chicago. It was back in 1968, the only way Frank and I could afford to join the peace action outside the Democratic National Convention. Whew! That was some trip, a twenty-hour bus ride, this one is only six hours, nothing compared to that. The driver is giving me a thumbs-up now. We're on our way.

I sit back and think about how Jordane got away with raping Patricia Grogan and trying to rape me. He did it by pointing the finger at Will. And then he killed Will to make sure the truth never came out. Everyone believed Jordane. No one believed Will. No one believed me. And now Emma is afraid that no one will believe her. That they'll say it was her fault. That it will affect her work, ruin her internship.

"Did you say something, ma'am?"

I shake my head. Was I thinking out loud? I hope he doesn't think I'm crazy. I remember only too well when everyone did. Well, I'm not losing it now any more than I was then. Pffft. Just last week my doctor said it was obvious to her that I'm sharp as a tack so there was no need for me to take one of those cognitive tests. I open the clasp on my purse, reach inside for my phone. Time to send a text to J. B. and Mentayer. They should have stopped arguing by now.

> *I'm going to Bigger. On my way now. I tried to tell you last night. Don't worry about me.*

That's enough to say. The more they know, the more they'll fret. Even if I told them the doctor says both my heart and blood pressure are good, they'd still worry. Nothing I can do about that. Nothing they can do to stop me either.

I tuck my phone back in the bottom of my purse and snap the clasp shut. I run my fingers along the embroidered rose flowers, not a single thread loose and the colors as bright as when I bought it, so long ago I don't remember when that was. I hold my purse next to the embroidered roses on my peasant blouse, an almost perfect match, like I bought them together, which I didn't.

I put the purse on the seat next to my travel bag and lean back against the headrest. Maybe I could have avoided making this trip if Becca had talked to me on the phone, but she never answered any of my messages. She was a shitty friend, truth be told, one of those popular narcissistic girls that everyone, including me, would have died to be friends with. But, who knows, she may have changed—we all do, don't we? She might not be home when I get there, so I'll just wait until she is. And if she refuses to see me, well, I'll keep going back until she does. I can't let this go. I won't. I know she's hiding something. And whatever it is, it might help Emma.

I close my eyes. Just for a few minutes. These seats are very comfortable. And the humming of the bus is soothing. I must have slept for a while because when I open my eyes again, everything looks different outside: rolling hills on both sides of the highway, political signs on the edges of cornfields, pro-gun, pro-Trump, pro-religion messages. I look out the front window of the bus and it feels almost like I'm driving, which of course I would never do for a trip this long, especially since my car won't go over fifty-five miles an hour without squealing at me. J. B. calls it a piece of junk, but it's my junk, and it works well enough for me, especially since I don't use it much.

"Ma'am, is that your phone ringing?"

"Oh! Thanks." He probably thinks I have a hearing problem, but I just had it tested and it's fine, must be the noise of the engine. I take my phone out of my purse, see on the caller ID that it's Julia Grogan.

"Hi, Julia! Yes, I'm on the bus right now and we're supposed to get there at . . ." I look at my watch. "At one o'clock. I look forward to seeing you, too. Okay, I'll look for you outside the front door of the bus station. A red Fiat, okay, got it. No, thanks, I have a sandwich with me. I want to go to Bigger right away. See you soon."

"Only a little over an hour to go, ma'am," the driver says while I'm putting my phone away.

I nod, then reach into my overnight bag for my apple and the peanut butter and jelly sandwich I made last night. The bread is stale, but no matter, it's enough to hold me over. Julia wants to take me out to dinner tonight but I'm too anxious to think about that right now. When I was in my late twenties and early thirties, I believed what some people said about anxiety, that it was inhibited excitement. Pffft. What I'm feeling right now is not excited, inhibited or otherwise, it's more like dread. Or fear. I bite into my sandwich. Then eat a slice of apple to get the peanut butter off my teeth. Drink some water to wash it down. Stay in the moment. As if that's ever worked for me.

The driver steers the bus off to the side of the highway and stops by a dirt road that I recognize is the one that goes to the reservation.

"I was a county social worker here in the early 1970s," I say. "In the spring, that road was impassable, nothing but a sea of mud after the snow melted. I can't believe the Bureau of Indian Affairs still hasn't blacktopped it."

"It's a county road," the driver says.

"Pffft. That's what the BIA told us when we asked them to blacktop it. So, we asked the county to do it, and they said it was a BIA road."

The driver shrugs. "It's still a dirt road." He opens the door and cranes his neck like he's looking for someone, glances at his watch, then closes the door and starts driving again.

"I drove this stretch of road so many times," I say, "I could almost do it with my eyes closed."

"Me, too," he says.

I sit back and look at the familiar landmarks outside that are mixed in my head with a flash of images from back in the day. The old guy in the county garage wiping the grease from his hands, then handing me the keys to a car and wishing me a good day. Men and women, girls and boys, riding in the county car with me from the reservation, making trips to the doctor for an appointment, the grocery store for shopping, the county courthouse for a hearing, the hospital for visiting someone. Too much remembering. Too much unmet need. Too much wrong in this world. Too long ago to remember so much and so vividly. It makes my eyes burn. I close them. So many memories, all so clear, so vivid. So why can't I remember how Jordane killed Will?

"And here we are, ma'am."

The driver stops the bus and opens the door. I reach for the gold chain on my purse and pull it over my head, drape it from one shoulder to the other. "I've got it," I tell the driver when he tries to grab my overnight bag. He nods and takes my free hand, helps me down the steps. Then I pull my shoulders back and at a brisk and steady pace walk through the door to the bus station, past the rows of benches inside, and out to the street. Julia is right outside the door, leaning against the fender of her red car parked by the curb. My shoulders relax and I breathe out through my mouth.

"Look at you." She grabs my overnight bag.

I look down, check for peanut butter on my white blouse and my long denim skirt, then run my tongue over my teeth.

"Your vintage look, I mean," she says with a flick of her hand. "It's the latest thing these days."

Oh my. Well, let people think what they think. Wear what they want to wear. I personally don't see the point of buying new clothes when your old ones are perfectly good and if you wait long enough will be back in style again. But if buying a pretty, light purple dress—expensive linen is my guess—makes Julia feel good, who am I to judge? It's just not for me, that's all.

"Want to stop for coffee?" she asks after I buckle my seat belt. "Or drop your things off at my place first?"

I shake my head. "No, no, no. I need to get there."

Julia tucks a strand of silver hair behind her ear and adjusts her oversized glasses before putting the car in gear. Both she and Peter seem to like big round glasses. What's with that, I wonder.

"Have you seen his campaign ads on TV?" Julia is driving on the highway now. "What if he wins? Everybody's been telling us that it's a waste of time, that we don't have a chance in hell to get him convicted of raping my sister."

Well, she is right about that. Everyone we talked to last week said the same thing—not just the lawyers we paid but also the advocacy folks from places like the sexual assault hotline, the Sexual Violence Law Center, the Center for Victims of Sexual Assault, and the local Legal Aid office—*In order to press rape charges against Jordane, you have to have a victim who isn't dead and some evidence that is credible.* There was one lawyer who told me that since Jordane had sexually assaulted me, I could file a civil suit for damages. Hah! Like I want his money!

"We can't give up," I say. "He's still getting away with it."

Julia looks at me like she's about to ask me how I know that, and I'm ready to say that I just know it. But just then my phone pings. I dig in my purse for it and see that it's a text from Emma.

Do you think it's too late for me to go to the police?

I look out the window and imagine Emma at the police station. Alone. They'll probably tell her it's too late, that she shouldn't have waited for two days to report Jordane. She needs someone to go with her. Someone who knows how the system works and how it's stacked against her. Someone who won't let the police dismiss her. And I think I might know just the person.

"Julia," I say, "do you remember the attorney who gave us a lot of advice about how to go about building a case against Jordane? I think she was with a law firm of, oh, something that had Confers and Roberts in the name or something like that."

"Karen Roberts," Julia says. "I sure do remember her. She met with us in her office for over an hour and didn't charge a penny. She wouldn't take the case, though."

"No," I say, "but she did say we could call her anytime."

I type a text to Emma. *It's not too late and I think you need to do this, but don't go to the police alone. Call Karen Roberts. She's an attorney with the law firm of Confers and Roberts. Say it's urgent and you need her help. Tell her that Sylvia Jensen and Julia Grogan sent you. I'll tell her to expect your call.*

• • •

I stare out the window. We're almost there. I feel it more than recognize it. Were there always this many trees alongside the road? Were they always this big?

"See that sign, Julia? It used to be red, white, and blue. Look how faded it is, so much of the paint is chipped off. Can you see what it says?"

Julia slows the car to a crawl and squints at the sign. "'Welcome to Bigger, the Friendly City. Population 700.'"

"Only seven hundred? There were almost two thousand people living here when I was growing up."

"The mines closed," Julia says with a shrug. "That's what happened to all the small towns around here."

I look across the field, a short distance behind the sign. Where's the green house with white trim and a broken swing on the porch? It was Will and his mother's house. I turn sideways in the seat and strain to see it.

"It's gone," I say. "Will's house is gone!"

Julia's knuckles turn white on the steering wheel. "Do you really think Jordane killed your friend Will?"

She asks the question like she doesn't want to ask it. I ignore it. "Nothing there but weeds," I say. "It's like they erased all traces of Will." A tear hits my hand. I wipe it off with the hem of my blouse.

Julia drives over the railroad tracks, and just like I remember, it feels like we're going over a speed bump. This is the part of Main Street with all the bars. The devil's work, Grandpa used to say. But where are they now? The House of Ale and Brewskies are gone. Afterhours and the Moose Lodge are there but they're closed, boarded up. There's only one bar still open.

"See that bar, Julia?" I point at the brick front of Jordane's Beer Stop and Pizza. "When we're done, and he's convicted of murder, no one's going to want to go to a bar named after him."

Julia raises her eyebrows, but this time she doesn't say anything, just keeps driving, past the boarded-up Piggly Wiggly grocery store where Will's mother used to work and where Will stocked shelves on the weekends.

"Stop here for a minute." I point at the American flag in front of the post office and she parks by the curb. I open the window all the way, stick my head out, and look up in the eaves. "There used to be cute little wrens nesting up there," I say. "Where are they? Why did they kill them? They never hurt anyone." I fall back in the seat, my whole body shaking.

"What is it, Sylvia? Did something happen here?"

I look at her, think about her question. It's only the post office. Is it just about the wrens? Why can't I make my hands stop trembling? Then it hits me. Like a two-by-four to the head. Bang, and it's all clear.

"I remember now," I say. "I was running out of that glass door right there. I had just heard that Will was dead and I was crying. I ran smack into Tony, and when he saw how upset I was, he laughed. He *laughed*!" I stop to catch my breath.

Julia shakes her head. "No wonder you stuffed *that* memory away."

"I was mad," I say. "I asked him what was so funny about Will dying, and he said, 'Well, they never should have let him go, should they.' I remember thinking what a strange thing for him to say. Now I know it was because he killed Will. *That's* why I've always been so sure."

Julia reaches across the front seat and takes my hand. I smile. "Now I know. This is good. Now I know." I blow air out my mouth. "So, let's go find Becca."

We turn right onto Seventh Street and drive past rows of the prefab houses that were produced and assembled at a manufacturing plant just outside of town, back when the mines were booming. So many are in disrepair now. Some look abandoned. Three For Sale signs in less than two blocks.

"I remember when all these houses were delivered," I tell Julia. "A whole new section of town sprang up overnight. They're all the same. Three bedrooms. One bathroom. Back yards big enough for a clothesline and a garden, a small patio, maybe. They were all white except for Becca's. Hers was yellow."

"Which one was yours?" Julia asks.

The trees and bushes in front of the houses are so big now I'm having trouble reading the numbers, even if I remembered what our house number was, which I don't. Really? I can't even remember what my own address was?

"I *think* it may have been that one." I point at a house that seems strangely familiar even though it's different. There used to be saplings on each side of the front sidewalk, but now there are two poplars there instead, and they're so tall they shade the whole house. The house is dark blue with a pinkish color trim instead of white, and there's a wreath of pink plastic roses hanging on the front door.

"My father's parents lived next door," I say. "It's that one. It still looks the same. See that big picture window in front? My grandfather was always standing there when Daddy drove into our driveway. He looked so stern. He never smiled."

I remember that the church was behind our house, across the alley. I look for the steeple but it's gone now. I search for more memories, try to pull them apart layer by layer like peeling an onion. Tears fill my eyes, but none of them are connected to any specific memory or feeling. It's almost as if I never lived here. Which may be true. It may not be the right house. Or maybe it is, only I'm no longer the girl who lived in it.

"How long since you've been back here, Sylvia?"

"More than sixty-five years."

"So how does it feel?"

I can't answer her because I don't know what I feel. I'm not angry. Not sad. Not nostalgic. Not happy. Nothing. Just empty. "You don't have to drive this slow," I say. "There's no one around. Becca's house is a few blocks down. It's next to the Catholic church."

I point to the house next to the empty church parking lot, and Julia pulls up to the curb in front of it. Becca's house is still pale yellow with brown trim around the windows and door, but there are two massive evergreen trees in the front yard that weren't there before.

I pat the tight bun at the back of my head to make sure no stray hairs have escaped. Maybe I should have gotten my hair done. Becca's hair is probably still blond—dyed now, of course, but still slathered in place with hairspray. Good God, here I am in my eighties and stubborn as sin—J. B.'s words, not mine—and I still feel that same sense of inferiority and inadequacy now that Becca brought out in me when I was a teenager.

"I'll wait here," Julia says. "You'll be fine. Text if you need me. You can do this."

I pump myself up with deep breaths, then get out and close the car door. I stand up straight, shoulder blades back, and tug my skirt down. I walk up the driveway, not the front sidewalk, and head for the back yard, an old habit. We always went in the back door. The yellow paint on the side of the house is peeling, the brown window trim flaking, the concrete sidewalk along the back of the house crumbling. The edge of my sandal catches on a jagged piece of cement and I almost lose my balance. A hand pulls the curtain in the kitchen window back then quickly closes it. I used to fly up the three stairs to the kitchen door without thinking, and here I am holding onto the railing before even lifting my foot onto the first step. My heart is pounding and I stop to catch my breath, but everything is okay, and I am ready. Becca is home and the truth is behind this door.

Chapter Twenty

I've knocked three times. I know Becca's in there. I'm not leaving until she talks to me.

I put my hand on the doorknob. No one locks their doors in Bigger. When we were kids, we would go in and out of each other's houses all the time without knocking.

"Becca! It's me! Sylvia Jensen. Let me in!"

I turn the knob and the door flies open. I stumble into the past. Same white Formica countertop and tan steel cabinets. Ancient brown refrigerator and matching stove. Linoleum flooring with brownish-tannish-orangish geometric shapes. Threadbare orange and white striped curtains. The only thing different is the strong smell of chlorine bleach.

Like a gloomy cloud, Becca appears from behind the door. Stooped over. Missing a tooth. Wearing a dingy white T-shirt, a yellow stain on the front. Short gray hair that looks like she chopped it off without using a mirror. She runs her fingers through it. When it was blond, long and fluffy, she would flick it back with a shake of her head and a flutter of her eyelids. What happened to beautiful, sexy, popular Becca? The girl I felt so inferior to?

"I wasn't expecting anyone," she says. There are blotches of pink on her neck.

"I took the bus," I say. "My friend J. B. asked to see you and you wouldn't talk to him. I left you several phone messages and you never called back. So here I am." I didn't mean to sound so harsh. Or did I? Well, it's too late to take it back.

"You've changed, Sylvia."

She half smiles, takes a small step toward me. I step back. This isn't a high school reunion. "I *am* different, Becca. Of course, I'm old. We both are. But that's not what I mean." I pull a chair out from the kitchen table and sit down. "I'm here to talk about Tony Jordane. But you already know that."

She reaches for a chair across the table, as far away from me as possible, and lowers herself into it real slow. She folds her hands on the table, like she's praying. I count to ten. To fifteen. To twenty. I'm waiting for her to ask me what it is that I want to know, but she won't even look at me. She tucks her chin down like she's afraid I'm going to hit her or something. I need her to tell me what she knows about Will's death. I need her to not be afraid of me. I need to change my attitude.

I lean forward, with my arms on the table and my hands open, and smile, sympathetically, I hope.

"Becca, I spent my whole life forgetting about Tony and what he did," I say. "I thought it was all in the past. But then, a couple of months ago, I saw him."

Her head jerks up. She unfolds her hands. They're trembling. "You talked to him?"

"Oh *no*," I say. "But *he* said something that made my heart stop. For real. I had a cardiac arrest. I almost died."

She cups her cheeks in her hands and wrinkles her eyebrows like she wants to know more but maybe is afraid, or doesn't want, to ask.

"I was at a rally, and he was smiling at all the people there," I say, "but I felt like he was looking straight at me. Then he said the same thing that he said to me at our senior kegger." I take in a deep breath. I'll be damned if I will let that man, or his words, have power over me ever again. "The exact same words he used when he tried to force me to have sex with him." I take another breath. I'll be damned if I won't say those words out loud. "He said, 'Now it's time to deliver the goods.'"

Becca gasps. Her hands fly up and cover her face. She lets out a wail, a long, high-pitched cry. I hurry over to her, alarmed, my arms open to her. She buries her face in my chest. She sobs and sobs and sobs. I feel terrible. What have I done? Does she need reassurance that she wasn't the only person who didn't believe me back then?

She chokes, like she's trying to say something, but I can't make out the words. I hold her tighter. Finally, after what feels like an eternity, she pulls away and wipes the wetness from her cheeks with the backs of her hands. My legs are tired. I sit down in a chair next to her. My blouse is soaked with her tears and clinging to my skin.

"I'm so sorry, Becca. I didn't mean . . ."

She raises her hand and puts her fingers on my lips, shakes her head. "He said the same thing to me, Sylvia." Her voice trembles. "And I *did* 'deliver the goods.' Many times."

My jaw drops. Becca and Tony? How? When?

She lets out a strangled cry, her eyes pleading. What does she want from me? Forgiveness? Understanding? I squeeze her hands, and her story pours out like a faucet turned on full blast.

Tony seduced her at our high school graduation party, the one I didn't go to. It was what she'd always wanted. What every girl in Bigger wanted. They had sex in his car that night and every night after that. Sometimes she didn't want to, but she did it anyway. She got pregnant and thought he would do the right thing and marry her. But he was furious and ordered her to *get rid of it*. When she told him she was Catholic, and abortion was a sin, he threatened her. He'd say it wasn't his, he'd say everyone knew she was a slut who slept around. Then he dropped her. Just like that. Never talked to her again. Filled with shame, she left the state to have an abortion, then came back with a serious infection that almost killed her. She made it through with the help of her brother, Ray, who kept her secret until he died earlier this year.

She never did tell Jordane what happened to the baby. He left town and she never saw him again.

"And now look at me, Sylvia," she says when she's done. A tear escapes from the corner of her eye. She swats it away like it's a nasty mosquito.

"We were young," I say. As if that explains anything. As if my head isn't spinning. As if I'm not burning up inside, torn apart by a deep sadness for Becca on the one hand and a murderous rage against Anthony Jordane on the other. I grip the edge of the table and say, "I need to use the bathroom."

The only door open in the hallway on the way to the bathroom is the one to Becca's bedroom. Same pink walls and ruffled bedspread. Everything the same nauseating Pepto Bismol color. What's different now is that it smells clean and it's in meticulous order, like no one sleeps there, like it's never used for anything but looking at. Like it's a museum. I go into the bathroom and press my back against the closed door. Remember how special I felt when Becca invited me to spend the night at her house, just me, without all the other girls. How shy and innocent I was back then. How naive. I was a perfect target for Jordane. Something Becca most certainly was not. At least that's what I've always believed. Until now.

I splash cold water on my face. I look in the mirror at how much I've changed, and I smile. Each wrinkle on my face tells a story, and they all come together to create a lifetime of experience. Each gray hair on my head is a strand of hard-earned wisdom. And my eyes, well, my eyes reflect a strong determination than is undeterred, unstoppable, and something Becca needs right now.

I go back to the kitchen. She's still sitting at the table. Staring into space. I sit next to her.

"Listen to me," I say. "You and I almost died because of Tony. And that fourteen-year-old girl he raped, well, she *did* die." Becca looks surprised. "Patricia Grogan was so ashamed, she committed suicide. All three of us were ashamed. We believed that what Tony did was our fault. And you know what? We're not the only ones. Tony Jordane has ruined the lives of other women, too. Other women are still living in shame because of him. And as long as predators like Tony get away with it, as long as women like you and me continue to take responsibility for *his* actions, his *crimes*, he will continue to be a predator."

Becca stares at the table. "We're old now." She sighs. "And so is he."

"Huh! You should see his bulging muscles," I say. "Believe me, Anthony Jordane is still getting away with it. And he will continue to get away with it even more if he becomes a powerful U.S. senator." I put my hand on her arm. "It's not too late. We need to stop him. For your sake and mine. For the sake of other women just like us."

She yanks her arm away from me. "No, Sylvia! You can't tell anyone.

No one else knows." Her eyes close and her body shrinks like she's collapsing into herself. She says, "I'm tired. Please. You need to leave now."

• • •

Back in the car, I fasten my seat belt and scrunch down in the seat. "I blew it," I say.

"I think that's your phone." Julia points to my purse.

I recognize J. B.'s ringtone. Bad timing. I don't feel like talking right now, but he's probably worried about me. I dig into the bottom of my purse for my phone.

"Are you there yet, Sylvia?"

"I'm sorry I didn't let you know. I'm in Bigger. With Julia Grogan." I scrunch up my eyes. Might as well tell him. "I just saw Becca."

"And?"

I groan. "I screwed up."

"So, she wouldn't talk to you either?"

"Oh, she talked."

"Did she tell you how Will died? Does she know?"

"She kicked me out before I had a chance to ask." I close my eyes and blow my breath out through my teeth. "It's a long story."

"Oh?"

I moan. Julia's eyes question me. I shake my head. "I can't talk about it right now," I say. Even if I wanted to, Becca begged me not to tell anyone about what Jordane did to her. I didn't promise anything, but I need some time to think about it.

Julia grabs the phone from me. "Hi, J. B. We're heading back to Altos City now. I'm taking Sylvia out to dinner." He says something to her, and she nods. "Just a minute, I'm going to put you on speaker." She turns up the volume and lays my phone on the dashboard, then says, "Okay, we can both hear you now. Tell Sylvia what you just told me."

"Jordane has already been breaking his promises." J. B. blurts it out, his voice angry, disappointed, shocked. "Emma found all kinds of evidence. It's damning. Downright damning!"

Emma? Has she told him what Jordane did to her? But before I can ask, J. B. goes on to rattle off all the other things that Jordane has been doing. None of it surprises me. Taking contributions from advocates of nuclear power and uranium mining, whose interests are antithetical to what he promised. Seeking the support of Christian nationalist groups and, the gall of him, even the anti-abortion Evangelicals, getting their money by assuring them that he agrees with and supports their positions.

"Peter Minter's not surprised," he says, "because Jordane's been stonewalling him for weeks. He says this is just another broken promise by a white man in a long string of broken promises by white men. He's totally on board with it."

"On board with what?" Julia and I both ask at the same time.

"With me writing the exposé now," he says. "We've already identified some sources to interview. Don't worry, my interns are fact-checking every bit of it so Jordane won't be able to dispute it, no matter how hard he may try."

"All right!" Julia raises her fist in the air. "All right! All right!"

"Wait a minute," I say. "Back up. Have you talked to Emma?"

"Of course! She's the one who dug up all the evidence while she was volunteering at Jordane's campaign headquarters. She sent me a whole slew of evidence—his financial records, meeting dates and times with influential people, all kinds of things I'll be able to use in the exposé."

I ask, "When did you talk to her?" but before he can answer, Julia lets out a whoop and interrupts. "I'll send you the excerpts from my sister's diary, too," she says. The enthusiasm on her face is so bright I can see it reflected in the dashboard. "You'll probably need my permission, so I'll get that to you in writing, too. Just let me know when you want to interview me. Is there anything else I can do to help?"

A second of silence, and then J. B. says, "Thank you, Julia, but I'm focusing *this* exposé"—he pauses—"on how Jordane is deceiving voters *right now*. The kinds of allegations that we can prove, you know, with solid, concrete evidence, in writing."

Julia shakes her head and throws herself back in the seat. "And I don't have *solid* evidence?" she spit-mutters under her breath, more to me than to him. "What about Pat's diary? It's all there, *in writing*. We could even include a picture of it in the article." She stares out the window, her arms crossed over her chest.

Several seconds of silence go by. I'm overwhelmed. Confused. When Emma asked me not to tell J. B., I assumed she hadn't talked to him at all, but clearly she did talk to him. She must not have told him what Jordane did to her, though, because if she had, surely J. B. would have started with that. And then there was Becca and her shocking revelation. What am I going to do about her now?

I reach for my phone on the dash, turn off the speaker. "Can we talk again later, J. B.?" I'm pretty sure I hear him let out a long sigh of relief before he says that will be fine.

I drop the phone back into my purse. Julia turns the key in the ignition, presses her foot down on the gas pedal, and revs the engine. She's pissed. Really pissed. So, first things first.

"J. B. really *does* believe that Jordane raped your sister," I say. "You know that, don't you?"

She nods. "I do. It's just that, for a minute there, I thought this was going to be my chance to get justice for her. *Our* chance."

With chin jutted out and lips pursed, Julia slowly drives away from the curb and heads up the block at a snail's pace. She needs time to calm down, so I stay quiet, do my own thinking. About Julia's sister, who couldn't live with the shame of being raped. About Becca, whose shameful secret kept her from living. About Emma, and how, just two days ago, she was too upset to tell me what Jordane did to her. About Will, whose life was ended just as he was about to graduate from high school as valedictorian. The more I think, the deeper I dig my fingers into my palms, the more rage I feel traveling up my arms, my neck, freezing my jaw.

I look out the car window. We're on Main Street again. No one here. So many people are gone now. A shell of a town, haunted by the secrets left behind. Finally, after what seems like forever, Julia drives onto Highway 50. My shoulders go down.

"The Ski Bum Motel." I point at the flashing Vacancy light. "New name. That's where J. B. stayed. He talked to a bunch of old-timers in the bar there."

Julia slows down and turns on the blinker. "Maybe there's some folks in there now that you know."

"No, keep going." I push against the dashboard with both hands as if that will make the car go faster. "I can't think of anything in this world, in this whole universe," I say, "that I would hate more right now than seeing *any* of those 'men'"—I made big air quotes—"who worshipped Jordane in high school and admire him still to this day."

Just imagining their eyes on me if I walked into that bar makes me shiver. My muscles tighten into a coil ready to strike. A body memory, is what my therapist calls it. I look out the car window, try to focus on the passing scenery. The huge pine trees looming over the highway. The open fields, their crops soon to be harvested. The political signs. American flags.

"Look at that, Julia!" I point to the billboard by the highway, the largest one I've ever seen. A baby, asleep on its side, thumb in mouth, a white gift bow on it. Above, in extra-large red letters, the words *Stop Killing Babies.* Underneath the picture of the baby, "*Jordane for U.S. Senate. Vote for our hometown boy.*"

What if the people who paid for that billboard knew that Jordane had ordered Becca to get rid of a baby, I wonder. Would he insist it was just a lie and call Becca all kinds of names? Of course he would. And they would believe him, too. They would attack *her*, not him. I shouldn't have pushed Becca to take action. I shouldn't have suggested that she go public with her story. I should have known better. In fact, I did know better. I wasn't thinking.

"Sylvia," Julia says after we drive a couple of miles in silence, "I know you still believe that Jordane killed your friend Will."

I suck in my breath. Does she not know that one of the reasons I made this trip was to find out *how* Jordane murdered Will. Not *if* he did.

"I already told you that I *know* he did," I say through gritted teeth. "Why do you keep bringing it up?"

"Well, because when J. B. told me that Will was lynched," she glances at me sideways, "he was really upset about it. So, when you say you're sure that Jordane killed Will, I keep wondering . . . well, how can both of those things be true?"

I stare out the window at the darkening sky. We speed past a bright yellow deer crossing sign, and suddenly, with no warning, I feel desperate. Like an animal. Like a deer caught in a car's headlights at dusk. I freeze. Make myself take a few deep breaths. Then, unlike a deer whose life depends on turning and running away from the light at the last minute, I know, in the deepest part of me, that my life depends on going *into* the light. Toward the truth. The truth about everything. About how Will died. About all the women Jordane has sexually assaulted over the years. About what he did to Emma.

I reach into my purse for my phone. "I have to talk to Becca again. I'm calling to tell her we're coming back tomorrow. *Both* of us this time, okay?"

"Okay," Julia says. "Maybe that will help us find another way of getting Jordane."

"We will get him," I say. "Trust me. We will."

Chapter Twenty-One

The three of us sit in silence, sipping coffee from mugs that Julia collected over the years in her travels to Venice, Prague, and Rome with her husband Ron, after he retired and in what she calls their magical life before his heart attack. Becca is staring out the kitchen window with resignation in her sad eyes. There was no such magical time in her life.

Yesterday I called to tell her I was coming back to Bigger to see her again, but she said she had to pick up groceries today at the Altos City mall anyway, so she'd come to Julia's house instead. I almost didn't recognize her when she got here. Today she's wearing an attractive aqua cotton knit dress, midi length, her hair wrapped in a matching headscarf, with dark brown mascara and eyeliner, subtle blue eyeshadow, and a touch of dusty rose blush that emphasizes her high cheekbones. In the kitchen now, she stares past me at Julia's organized shelves of dishes and cookware, and I can tell that her face, even with makeup, is filled with wrinkles. So is mine, only without makeup. I can tell that her body is lumpy under her loose dress. But then, so is mine, under my wrinkled and faded yellow blouse. I tuck a loose strand of hair behind my ear, look down at the old flip-flops on my feet, and shake my head, annoyed at myself for forgetting, even if it was only for a few seconds, that Becca is no longer the girl I once envied, and I am no longer the shy, innocent girl she once overshadowed.

We've been talking at Becca nonstop for almost an hour now, first Julia about how her sister killed herself at fourteen after Jordane raped her, and then me about how my own shame triggered my alcoholism and screwed up my life. All the while, Becca nibbled on a croissant, maybe listening, but if so, in a detached kind of way.

"He's still doing it," I say, "still grabbing and sexually assaulting and raping women at whim. I talked to Emma, J. B.'s intern, again last night, and she gave me permission to tell you what he did to her. I can't believe how arrogant he is. It's mind-boggling. He knew Emma was an intern at the *New York Times*. She told him that when she first started volunteering at his campaign headquarters. He even knew she was working for J. B., the very same man who extorted him and had the power to expose him. And none of that stopped him."

Becca fidgets in her seat, runs her finger around the rim of her coffee mug. "Did he hurt Emma?"

"It's still hard for her to talk in detail about what he did. She said she got away from him, but she ended up with six stitches on her arm and three on the left side of her face. Despite all that, she is a very courageous young woman."

Julia and I exchange meaningful glances across her oval wooden table. We have to be careful not to reveal J. B.'s plan to publish an exposé about Jordane. That's why we can't tell Becca about how Emma went to Jordane's campaign headquarters early the morning after he assaulted her and sent all the damning evidence she had gathered to J. B.

"Emma was so brave," Julia says. "The next morning she marched right back to his campaign headquarters, left a note and the keys on his desk, and walked out. Just quit her job right then and there."

Becca's body stiffens and she looks up at the ceiling.

"And Emma isn't going to stop there," I say. "She's going to report the assault to the police this afternoon."

Becca lets out a snort and cracks her knuckles at the same time. "They won't do anything," she says. "They won't believe her."

"Probably not," Julia says.

"That's why she's going to talk to a lawyer first," I say.

"Karen Roberts," Julia adds. "She's with a law firm in Monrow City. She would have taken my sister's case if she thought we could win."

What a strong and wise young woman Emma is, I think. She hasn't told J. B. about what happened yet, but I know she will. One step at a time.

"I have no doubt," I say, "that there are other women. Emma's already thinking that at least one of them may press charges against Jordane with her. Julia and I are going to help her find others."

"And when it's time," Julia says, "Sylvia and I will come out in the press with our stories, too. Show the world who he is."

Becca squints at me. She purses her lips. I know this has been a lot for her to absorb. It's still too much, even for me, and I was awake most of last night thinking about it.

"Don't expect me to be part of this!" Becca's voice is filled with both the assurance of an adolescent and the mature resolve of an octogenarian. But those are tears of dismay and fear I see in her eyes right now, not determination.

"No, Becca, no, no," I say. "We don't expect you to do anything."

"Of course not," Julia quickly says. "We're just interested in finding other women that Jordane assaulted."

Becca tucks her head into her neck like a turtle, like a victim. I reach for her hand and squeeze it reassuringly. *Your secret is safe with me,* I say but not out loud. She raises her head and looks at me.

"Then why am I here, Sylvia?" She scrunches her eyebrows together.

"It's about Will." I look directly into her eyes. This is it. The moment I've been waiting for.

Her eyes widen. She knows what I'm asking. She doesn't want to answer. But she knows what happened. I can hear her guilt buzzing around the kitchen like a trapped fly.

"Jordane killed Will." I say it slow and careful. I'm walking on eggshells but I'm not wavering in my resolve. This is my chance. I'm not going to blow it again, not this time. "If you think I'm wrong, Becca, tell me. If you think I'm crazy, tell me. J. B. thinks I am. Maybe he's right."

I tighten my grip on her hand and wait. My fingers start to go numb. Finally, she pulls her hand away and slumps forward, defeated. She rests her elbows on the table and holds her chin in her hands. I feel it, I can see it, a cloud of crushing misery hanging over her head.

"You're not crazy, Sylvia."

Finally! I knew it. I knew Jordane murdered Will, and now I am finally going to find out exactly *how*. My insides jump up and down, but I force myself to hold my body perfectly still. *Don't push her. Don't rush it.*

"Can you tell me what you know, Becca?" I keep my voice calm. "Please?"

"It can't leave this room." Becca glances at Julia, who right away nods. Then she turns back to me, looking for the same assurance.

I cross my fingers under the table. *Please don't ask me to promise not to tell anyone,* I beg her silently. My breathing starts coming in short spurts as if something's blocking the air so it can't reach the bottom of my lungs. Becca will shut up like a clam if I tell her I plan to get Jordane charged and convicted of murder.

"I just need to know the truth." I smile encouragingly, but that's all I say.

Becca lets out a long sigh. She shakes her head. My heart sinks.

"My brother Ray was there." Becca chokes on a sob, then takes a sharp intake of breath and covers her mouth with her hand like she's afraid she's already said too much.

I nod and stay calm, start breathing normally again, wait for her to recover and go on.

"But Tony threatened that he would tell the authorities that my brother killed Will," Becca finally says. "If Ray ever breathed a word to anyone about what he saw."

Right now, so many questions are twisting through my head like a tornado. But I hold my tongue. Wait for her to come to me. Wait for her to say more.

But she doesn't. She's not going to tell me anything else.

"How horrible for you," I say. "How hard it must have been to know how Jordane killed Will and to have to carry the guilt of keeping it a secret all these years."

"But I don't know." Becca shakes her head sharply. "I never asked my brother what he saw. I didn't dare. I was terrified that, if he told me, he would go to prison for something he didn't do. I couldn't let that happen."

My jaw drops and I lean back in the chair. Am I never to know what happened? Has this all been for nothing?

Julia leans forward. "Becca, do you think maybe your brother watched them lynch Will?"

"Oh my God! Is that what happened? Is that what Ray saw?"

"J. B. talked to a man," Julia says, "whose father was one of the men who dragged Will into the woods, forced him up a ladder, and hung him by a noose from a tree."

Julia looks at me sideways, apologetic-like, and my hands fly up in the air like they have a mind of their own and bang down on the table, so hard I cry out in pain. "No! No, no, no! Something is off about this! This isn't making sense!"

Becca and Julia stare at me, their mouths open. Like they think I've lost my mind.

"Listen," I say, "if a group of men lynched Will, then what reason would Jordane have had to threaten your brother? Unless, of course, Tony was the ringleader. Or if his father was involved, and he was protecting him. But the question still is: Why was Ray there in the first place?"

"My brother wouldn't . . . Ray *was not* involved in any lynching!"

I look into her face, beet red with rage, and it's like a door flings open in my brain. I remember something Becca said when we were in high school, that even though her brother Ray hung out with Tony sometimes, he didn't much like or respect him. That had to mean Ray didn't trust Tony either. That gives me an idea.

I reach for Becca's hand again. "All the guys looked up to Tony," I say, "but your brother didn't, did he?"

"Are you kidding me? Ray warned me to stay away from him, and after, well, you know, my brother didn't want to have anything to do with him. He didn't see him at all for four years, but then he ran into him during the Christmas holidays, when everybody was bar-hopping downtown. He told me that Tony was drunk on his ass, bragging about all his conquests, all the pussy he'd had, the youngest one being only fourteen . . ." Becca's eyes get real wide and she looks at Julia with her mouth open.

"My sister," Julia whispers.

Becca lifts her head up, then drops it down.

"He *bragged* about raping a child." I spit out the words. "*Bragged* about it." *If only, if only, if only,* I think. If only Becca's brother hadn't died, if only he were still here to testify against Jordane.

"Ray told me that Tony bragged about you, too," Becca says. "He said he fooled everyone into thinking that he'd done it with Miss Goody Two-shoes—that's what he called you, Sylvia—and he would have made you do it with him if only that bastard Will hadn't come along at the wrong time . . . oh, *Will . . . That's* why you think Tony killed Will."

"That's exactly what I think," I say. "It sounds like Tony told your brother a lot, Becca. Maybe too much. Now, you and I both know that Ray was smart. He would have figured out some way to protect himself, in case Tony decided to carry out his threat or hurt him in some other way."

"Well, he can't hurt Ray now."

I lean forward. An argument is forming in my head even as I'm saying it out loud. "But think about this, Becca. Now that Jordane is running for public office, he's under a lot of scrutiny. People want to know who he is, where he comes from. If the story ever got out that in 1960, a boy may have been lynched in the small midwestern hometown that he grew up in, *and* that he may have been involved, just imagine what he would do. Think about all the lies he would tell. How quick he'd be to point the finger at your brother. You and I both know he would do anything and everything to exonerate himself no matter who it hurt."

Becca clenches her teeth. "But . . . but . . . a story like that would never come out . . . It wouldn't, would it?"

"I don't know, but I think we should be prepared to prove your brother's innocence," I say. "Maybe he kept a journal about what he saw that night. Or maybe there's something else we could use. I mean, if we had to."

Becca shakes her head. "I cleaned out his apartment after he died. I sold some of his stuff and gave the rest away. All his things are gone now."

She moans and looks beaten down, her body hunched over. I feel bad for her, but my insides are screaming at me to keep pushing. I can't let up, not for a minute, not until Jordane is locked in a prison cell and left there to rot for the rest of his damn life.

"Maybe Ray hid some kind of evidence, a journal or something? Maybe in your house? He was still living at home when Will was killed, right?"

Becca looks startled, like something just occurred to her. I raise my eyebrows encouragingly.

"It's probably nothing," she says, "but when I closed Ray's checking account at the credit union, they mentioned that his safe deposit box was paid up through the end of the year."

I try to suppress my excitement. "Do you know what he might have kept in the safe deposit box?" I'm sweating. It feels cold and wet on my skin.

"No." She cringes and covers her head with her hands. "And now I don't think I want to know. I have to live in Bigger. I want to die in peace there. I can't be part of this. *Any* of this."

I hear the steely tone in her voice, and I know that underneath it there's a real fear. Survival-level fear.

I have to control my disappointment, try not to scream at her. But her whining is irritating as hell. I do try to sympathize. Her life is pathetic, and who am I to judge her for wanting to protect the little she has left? I take a few deep breaths in, then long breaths out. I hear J. B.'s voice in my head, something I've heard him say so many times—*Without evidence, it's only hearsay; protect your sources and you will find what you need.*

Now I know what to do. And I'm ready to do it.

But first, I need to send a text to Emma and to Karen Roberts, the lawyer. *I just found out that Anthony Jordane bragged to someone about having sex with a fourteen-year-old girl.*

Within seconds I get a reply from Emma: *Karen Roberts went with me to the police. I filed a report. Keep digging. See what else you can find. Something that will convince Karen to take my case.*

Chapter Twenty-Two

"Wait here. I'll go find out how to get into my brother's safe deposit box."

I sit down on a bench by the window and watch Becca approach a teller at one of the windows, a pleasant-looking young man, maybe in his late twenties or early thirties. I'm guessing, based on his half-green, half-red hair, that he's a university student working at the credit union to pay his tuition. Becca shows him some ID, then points at two small keys on her key ring. He smiles, a good sign. She points at me, and he looks apologetic and shakes his head. Not good. He's on the phone now. She's coming back here. Something's wrong.

I stand up. "What?"

"It's all right, Sylvia. Everything's okay. He's getting someone with the master keys to come and escort me downstairs. You aren't allowed in the vault, but I can bring the container up here to a private office where you can examine what's in it."

A middle-aged woman with a badge on her blouse that says *Welcome, I'm Nora* walks up to us. Becca leaves with her. I sit down, my back rigid, my imagination running wild. What if Becca's key doesn't work? What if it does, but there's nothing about Jordane in the safe deposit box? What if there is something about Jordane in the box and, for some reason, I'm legally required to tell Becca about it or involve her in some way? What about my promise? She only agreed to do this in the first place if I promised to leave her out of it, not even tell her anything about what I find. *If* I find anything.

From the bench where I'm sitting, I have a clear view of the credit union lobby, ideal for people-watching, which, if I were in the mood for it, which I'm not, would help me relax. I turn around and look out the window at Julia, who's waiting out front, her car parked right next to Becca's. She waves and smiles encouragingly, gives me a thumbs-up.

Fifteen more minutes of fidgeting go by. Finally! Here comes Becca. She's carrying a long, gray metal container, about fourteen inches long and eight inches wide. I stand up and follow her and Nora the escort to a tiny room off to the side of the tellers' counter. Nora leaves, closes the door behind her.

Becca places the container on a small round table and hands me her key ring. "It's this small one," she says. Then she places a chair close to and facing the door and sits down with her arms crossed. "Don't tell me," she says.

There's a lock on top of the long metal container. My fingers are shaking, but by some miracle I manage to insert the key. It works! This is it. I lift the long metal lid up and look inside.

This is not what I'd hoped to see.

"Not much in here," I tell Becca with a long sigh. "A few papers. They look like financial records. Do you want them?" She nods but doesn't turn around, just raises her hand for me to place the papers in her palm. "The only other thing in here is a black metal box," I say to her back. "It looks like one of those cash boxes. It's locked. Is it okay if I try to open it with that other small key?"

"Wow!" I guess she didn't hear me. "There's a CD in here for five hundred dollars! I'm the beneficiary. Wow!"

"Maybe your brother left some cash in this black box, too," I say. At least some good might come of all this. I think she's probably living on a small social security check, and anything extra will be a big deal for her. "Is it okay if I unlock it?"

She nods, so I take the small black metal box out of the container and place it on the table. It's not heavy at all, and the smaller key turns easily in the lock. There's a money tray on top but no money in it, just a three-by-five index card. I pick it up and turn it over. In thick, bold letters, written with black marker, it says: *5 JUNE 1960.*

I gasp and cover my mouth to hide it from Becca. June 5, 1960. The day Will was killed. My stomach churns with something, but I don't know what it is—not terror, not excitement, not fear, not suspicion. Not anything I've ever experienced before. Careful not to make a sound, I lift up one side of the tray and peek under it.

I let out a breath I didn't even know I was holding in and drop the tray back into place, quick shut the lid. Something in my throat is trying to choke me. I try to swallow, try again. I cough. Cough again. Finally, my throat clears.

"I'll take this black metal box with me, Becca, and look at it later." I keep my voice as normal as I can, careful not to alarm her. "Sorry, there's no money in it."

My hand shakes so hard I don't know how I do it, but I manage to lock the box. I dig into my purse and pull out one of the cloth tote bags I always carry with me, unfold it, and place the black box in it. Then, with the straps of the tote bag over one shoulder and the straps of my purse over the other, I walk over to Becca. She is standing by the door now. I hand the key ring back to her.

"Oh, dear," I say, all of a sudden remembering. "I'm afraid I locked it again. Habit." I shrug.

Becca removes the smallest key from the ring and hands it to me. Then she pushes the chair away from the door with her foot and glances at my tote bag. "I can't know what's in there," she says.

She opens the door for me then, and after a short, heavy silence, I walk out, not knowing if I will ever see her again. I walk as fast as I can, without drawing attention to myself, through the lobby and out to the parking lot. Out of breath, I slide into the passenger side of Julia's car and set the tote bag on the seat between us. I lean forward to get a closer look at the dashboard, see that Julia's car only has a radio and a CD player.

"I should have known." I shake my head. "There are two cassette tapes in Ray's safe deposit box, and we don't have any way to listen to them."

Julia breaks out in a big smile. "Oh, but we do. I have one of those complete stereo systems that plays cassettes, records, and CDs. It even has a radio."

We can't get to her house fast enough for me. I clench my jaw all the way, wishing she would drive faster. She pulls into the driveway next to her house, and I grab my tote bag, jump out of the car before she even has a chance to take the key out of the ignition, and then rock back and forth on my feet by her front door, waiting for her to unlock it.

"We should eat something," she says, "while we listen to the tapes."

I shake my head *no*. I've already pulled the black metal box from the bag and it's on the coffee table before she even closes the door behind us. I unlock the box and take out the money tray, careful to remove the two cassette tapes without disturbing the drab white washcloth underneath. On one cassette, in tiny letters, it says, *First recorded 6/8/1960 on reel-to-reel, transferred to cassette, 1965.* On the second cassette, in the same tiny handwriting, are the words *December 1964.* I give Julia the tape that was recorded three days after Will died. "This one first. Where's your stereo? How do we do this?"

Julia raises her eyebrows. She's irritatingly slow and calm as she takes the cassette from me. I sit down on the couch and grab a pillow, clutch it on my lap like a security blanket, as she stands by the bookcase next to the fireplace inserting the tape into her stereo system. She comes and sits down next to me, then presses the Play button on the remote control.

> *My name is Ray Milley. Today is June 8, 1960. This recording is an honest and accurate account of what I saw three nights ago. I swear on my life that everything I am about to say is true and anyone who claims otherwise is lying.*

I bring the pillow up to my chest and squeeze it tight, then close my eyes. "This is it," I whisper. "The truth. Finally. Please. Let this be the truth."

Julia puts her arm around me. Her hand is resting lightly on my shoulder.

> *On Monday morning, June 6, the body of William James was discovered in the woods outside Bigger. I don't know who found him, but I do know when he died and how he died because I was there. I saw what happened. It was Sunday night, June 5, 1960. Tony Jordane and I were hanging out at the Texaco station on Main Street like we often did, only he kept looking at his watch like he was nervous about*

something. At nine o'clock he said, "Okay, let's go." When I asked him "Where to?" he said something was going to happen at City Hall and he wanted to watch it "go down." I asked him what, and he said I should come and see for myself. I was curious, so I went with him. I am so sorry I did. I will regret it for the rest of my life.

The tape goes silent, except for the sound of sniffing, then Ray blowing his nose. I am beside myself, so agitated I feel like jumping off the couch or screaming or who knows what. Finally, after a few long, long seconds, Ray's voice comes back on.

So . . . I went with Tony to City Hall. He put his finger on his lips for me to be quiet, and we peeked around the back corner of the building. I saw five maybe six men standing by the back door. We stayed out of sight, and it was dark, so they didn't see us. But there was a light over the back door, so I saw some of their faces. Just a minute. I'll write down the names of the ones I recognized and keep the list with this recording.

There's a *whoosh* sound on the tape. Maybe it was Ray sucking in his breath? Then there's a click, the recorder turned off. My eyes slide to the coffee table where the metal box sits, still open. I don't see any list with the names of the men Ray just said he recognized that night. Maybe it's under the washcloth. I'm about to reach for it when Ray comes back on the tape—his voice, for some reason, echoes through the room louder than before.

Okay, the list is done. Tony and I stayed out of sight and waited. After a few minutes, the back door of City Hall swung open, and Will came out. I knew, well, everyone in town knew, that he was in jail for raping a girl at the senior kegger. At first, I thought maybe he'd been released on bail or something, but then three of the men grabbed hold of him and tied a scarf or something over his mouth so he couldn't scream. Okay, just hold on a minute while I put a star in front of those three men's names on the list. Okay. They start dragging Will down the alley and Tony whispers "Come on, let's follow them," but I said no, we should go tell the deputy in the jail what was going on. But Tony laughed and said his dad already knew. I was confused. I didn't know what to think. I wasn't thinking. I just followed along. How could I have been so stupid?

There's a long silence on the tape. I try to move but it's as if my body is frozen. I can't breathe. I can't think. Ray blows his nose again. Julia mumbles under her breath, "I don't know if I can stand this." I'm biting my thumbnail.

Tony and I followed as they dragged Will out of town. When we got to the woods, I saw a light come on. It was a flashlight, and it was pointed at a tree that had a ladder under it. Tony and me, we crouched down behind some bushes. I saw the men trying to push Will up the steps. He was trying to fight back. The light went out and one of the men swore. Then I heard the sound of feet shuffling in the dirt. I jumped up and whispered to Tony, "We have to help Will!" But he grabbed my arm and pulled me back down. "Are you crazy? You want them to hang you, too?" He had such a tight grip on my arm, I couldn't move, and I was scared about what he said the men might do to me if I interfered.

The light came on again, and I saw Will standing on the top of the ladder with a noose around his neck. He was crying and shaking. I jumped up and Tony pulled me down again. One of the men said, "We're leaving now, boy, and when we come back, you better be gone from here. You go get that whore mom of yours and leave Bigger for good, you hear? You're lucky, boy. We're giving you a warning. But understand this, it's the only one you're going to get." Then they all ran off, laughing.

I was so relieved! I waited until I couldn't hear them anymore. Then I told Tony I was going to go get Will down.

Only he didn't say anything, and I realized he wasn't next to me anymore. I thought maybe he ran off with the men. I started to run toward the tree to help Will, but it was dark and I tripped on something and fell. When I got up, I could hear Will crying, saying "No, please, I'll leave. I'll never come back. I promise." I ran toward the sound of his voice, but . . .

Sounds of Ray sobbing, moaning, even wailing, ring in my ears. My eyes sting and tears run down my cheeks. Julia and I hold onto each other. She's crying, too.

I'm sorry. Okay, I'm back. I heard Will crying and begging and I didn't know what was going on. I ran toward the tree. I was in a panic. That must be why I stumbled and fell again. Oh God, Oh God. By the time I got there, it was too late. Will was dead. I'm sorry.

Ray stops to blow his nose again. Julia and I both blow our noses, too.

Okay. When I got there, the ladder was on its side and Will was lying on the ground next to it. Tony was standing over him, a flashlight in one hand pointing down at his body, a pocketknife in his other hand, dripping blood onto the ground. I grabbed his shoulders and screamed, "What did you do, Tony? What the hell did you do?" He gritted his teeth and said, "I did what they didn't have the guts to do." He pointed his flashlight at a hollow in the tree and threw his pocketknife into it. Then he yelled, "Come on, let's get out of here."

I was in shock. I ran and ran and ran. When we got to town and I saw the blood on his hands and shirt I started shaking and crying, shaking and crying. He grabbed my arm and pulled me into a dark alley, pushed the back of my head up against a telephone pole. "Don't you dare breathe a word to anyone." He was hissing. Not just talking or whispering. He was hissing in my ear. I can still hear him. I'll never forget what he said. "You keep your mouth shut or I tell the police you killed Will and that I tried to stop you. And you know, Ray, you know full well, that everyone will believe me, and no one will believe you." He kept pushing my head, hard, against the pole until I promised I wouldn't tell anyone what I saw. Then he let me go.

I ran home, crying, stumbling. I hid in my room, terrified that when Tony got home his dad was going to see his bloody shirt and start asking questions. I waited all night for the police chief to come to our house and arrest me for killing Will. But nothing happened that night, and no one knew Will was dead until the next day. I know there will be an investigation. And if there is and Tony points the finger at me, I have to be able to prove that he's lying. That's why I went back to the tree yesterday. To look for evidence. The ladder was gone. So was the noose. There were no traces of blood on the ground. But when I looked inside the knothole in the tree, I saw the shiny blade of Tony's pocketknife. I used a rag to grab it and pull it out. It's in a plastic bag now, and I was careful not to touch it with my fingers. I'm keeping Tony's pocketknife with this tape. Along with the list of those men's names. Oh, and I'll draw a map, too, best as I can, to show how to get from City Hall to the tree. Then I'm going to hide all this evidence. After that I don't know what. I'm too scared to think straight right now. So, this is it for now.

My heart is thumping in my ears, beating fast, much too fast. Like a robot, I reach for the black metal box and put it on my lap. I pick up the washcloth, and there's Jordane's pocketknife, still bloody, in a plastic bag. Plus, a roughly drawn map in pencil: the alleyway leading from City Hall to the edge of town, a squiggly path into the woods, a shaky drawing of a skull and crossbones on an oversized tree. It's all here. Everything needed to get a conviction. An eyewitness account. Forensic evidence. Even the scene of the crime mapped out.

I pick up the second cassette tape, that says *December 1964.* Julia removes the first tape and inserts this one, pushes the Play button again.

There's a lot of background noise. Voices talking over each other. Loud music. Clinking glasses. Then a male voice, but only bits and pieces of conversation break through. *Any bitch . . . whoever I want . . . youngest . . . fourteen . . .*

"That's Tony's voice," I say. "It's him bragging about his conquests to Ray that night in the bar."

"Disgusting," Julia says. "Vile!"

I can't make out many of the words. It's too noisy. But then Ray's voice comes through loud and clear like he's speaking right into the recorder.

"Why did you stab Will that night, Tony? You never told me. What was that about anyway?"

I lean forward, strain to listen to what Jordane says, but his voice is garbled. The only words I can make out are "he knew."

He knew. Only two words. But they are enough. I was right. Tony killed Will because *he knew* the truth.

So that's it. I reach down to close the metal box. But wait. There's another three-by-five card in the bottom. The list of men who had threatened to lynch Will. I pick it up. The names are numbered. Six of them. Ray's tiny and shaky handwriting is almost indecipherable, but one of the names, number four, jumps out and shoots a bolt of electricity through me. My head whirs like the revving of an engine. I wrap my arms around myself.

I have found the truth at last, and it is worse by far than anything I had imagined.

Chapter Twenty-Three

Julia's hand brushes against my arm. I shriek. My hands fly up in self-defense.

The black metal box is open on my lap. I slam it shut, press my palms on the lid, rock back and forth on the couch.

"It's just me, Sylvia. I'm picking up the index card. You dropped it on the floor. Okay?" Julia's voice is soft and soothing. She sits up, hands me the card. My fingers are shaking.

"I must have read it wrong," I say. "My mind is playing tricks on me. I'll look at the list again."

I'm sure I made a mistake. It's because of my cardiac arrest. But then I look at the card, and there it is, number four, with a star in front of it: *Harlan Jensen Jr.*

My body goes numb. I cover my face with my hands. *You, too, Daddy? You, too?* No, please, no. Not my daddy.

Julia takes the card from my hand. In slow motion, she opens the black metal box, drops the card in. Without making a sound, she closes the lid, then takes the box from my lap and puts it back on the coffee table. I reach for it. To do what? Smash it to smithereens? She grabs hold of my arm and pulls me back on the couch. She holds my hand in hers. I lay my head on her shoulder. For a long time. I have no idea how long. Until I have an urge to move. To get up. Go somewhere. Do something.

I push up from the couch. I take a step. My legs are wobbly. Julia takes my arm and leads me through the dining room and out to the kitchen.

"Sit." She pulls out a chair. "I'll make turkey and cheese sandwiches." She places an open bamboo box on the table in front of me. "There are eight different herbal teas here. Choose the one you want while I put the kettle on."

I sit back and watch. She opens the refrigerator. Takes out some turkey and cheese, a tomato, an onion, a small jar of mayonnaise. Kicks the refrigerator door closed with the back of her foot. Slices the tomato and onion. Spreads mayonnaise on slices of bread. Places the sandwich in front of me. I push the plate away. She sits down. Pushes the plate back at me. I stare at the sandwich.

"I can't believe it. I don't want to believe it." I take in a deep breath. "Not my *father*. Ray could have got the name wrong. He could have meant Harlan Jensen Sr., not Jr.."

"Anything's possible." Julia says that in way that makes me think she's humoring me to get me to calm down.

"My grandfather was the rigid and judgmental and self-righteous one. But I can't imagine, horrible as his talk was sometimes, that even he would do something so cruel. But my father? Daddy? No, not my daddy. Why would he do that to Will? To anyone?"

Julia reaches for my hands and squeezes them. Was my daddy afraid that Will and I might have been more than just friends, I wonder? I never told my parents about Will wanting to ask me to the senior prom, but maybe, when Will was in jail and I defended him and begged my parents to help him, well, maybe then Daddy could have thought that I was in love with him. But what would have been so bad about that? Will was the nicest boy in town!

I jerk my hands back from Julia. "You know what I think? I think my father wasn't who I wanted to think he was. He was just like my grandfather. He just hid it better. That's what I think."

"Try to eat. Just a bite." Julia picks up the sandwich. I ignore her.

"Do you think any of this is real, Julia? I mean, think about it. Where did Ray hide that evidence at first? Did he have his own reel-to-reel tape recorder? He was still living at home when Will was killed. We should ask Becca about that. And if he hid it at home, then when and why did he move it and hide it somewhere else? Becca said he opened a safe deposit box when he was diagnosed with cancer. But where did he hide the evidence before that? And why didn't he tell anyone? I know he was afraid the police would come for him that night. Probably for a while after that, too. But later? Years later? Why did he keep it a secret all his life? You know, the more I think about it, the more I seriously wonder if any of this is real."

Julia looks at me over the rim of her mug, then puts the mug down on the table with a thud.

"It is real, Sylvia." She leans toward me, looks me straight in the eye. I don't think I've ever seen her look this determined. "And we are going to *nail* Anthony Jordane. We have all the evidence we need. My sister's diary, proof in writing that Jordane raped her. Jordane's voice on a tape, *bragging* about it. Ray's eyewitness account, recorded on tape. The murder weapon. Names of the men who threatened to lynch Will. And then there's everything J. B. learned when he went to Bigger. It's all there. Everything we need to get a conviction for both rape and murder." She takes in a deep breath and lets it out, her eyes still fixed on me. "Don't you see, Sylvia? We've got him now."

I hear her. But I'm tired. I want to lie down. It's too late.

"Who is going to want to hear any of this now," I say. "Especially when Jordane is moving ahead in the polls. They'll say it's a conspiracy theory. They'll say it's election interference. They'll say Ray made it all up, that he recorded a story about Jordane just to get revenge on him for what he did to Becca."

Julia looks at me with her lips curled up. "You know, Sylvia, when J. B. told me that Will was lynched for raping my sister, I made a vow that I would get Jordane, and that I would make sure that J. B. helped me."

I clench my fists. "J. B. doesn't believe me. He never did. He'll still think Will was lynched."

Julia reaches for her phone. "Well, let's find out." She glances at the clock on the wall. "It's later in New York. He should be home from work by now."

"Put him on FaceTime," I say with a growl. "I want to see his face."

The phone rings several times, and finally J. B. answers with his mouth full. "Hey, Julia! Mentayer and I were just having dinner. We've been wondering how you and Sylvia are doing. Anything new?"

Why does he sound so upbeat, so damn confident, so normal? My blood is boiling. I grab the phone from Julia and bring it close to my face. "Jordane killed Will. He stabbed him with his pocketknife! We have the knife." My neck and cheeks are burning up. "Didn't I tell you? Well, didn't I? And you know he hasn't changed. Not one bit." I know I'm out of control, but I can't stop myself, don't want to if I could. "I'm not delusional. I never was. I always knew."

Julia takes the phone from my hand. "Why don't you fix yourself a cup of tea, Sylvia, while I tell them the story."

I stand up, shove my chair back. She's right. I need to calm down. Only the rage and fury I feel inside is relentless. "What about Emma? Do you believe her, J. B.?"

Sweat drips into my eyes, runs down my cheeks and onto my neck. Julia takes my arm and steers me over to the stove, then goes back to sit at the table. I stand there listening while she tells J. B. and Mentayer about the safe deposit box and Ray's recording. I hear her say, "So now we've got him," and rush back to the table. I want to see their faces.

"That bastard!" J. B. says. "That fucking bastard!"

His anger sets me off again. I don't think about what I'm saying, I'm just jabbing at everyone and everything. Punching at Bigger and all the people there who didn't listen to me. Taking a one-two punch at Ray, for hanging out with Tony in the first place, then for being a cowardly bystander instead of saving Will—okay, so maybe it was too big a risk with it being half a dozen men against one, but then why did he keep it a secret forever and let Jordane get away with it? I punch at Becca for allowing Jordane to ruin her life, protecting him all these years, keeping her brother's secret, not believing me. I punch, hard, hard, at Daddy, slam him and his damn church, so pure and righteous, preaching love but creating guilt and shame. If he knew what Jordane did to me, I'm sure he'd only think about what *I* did wrong, not what *Jordane* did, but what *I* did. Just like everyone was going to do to Emma, talk about what *she* did to lead Jordane on, not about what he did. My heart is pounding hard. Too hard. I grab my chest. Julia, J. B., and Mentayer are all shouting: "Stop! Calm down! Enough!" But words keep spewing out of my mouth.

"I only have myself to blame," I say, "I should have stayed in Bigger. I shouldn't have run away. Why did I think I could leave without ever looking back? Why did I shove it all to the back of my mind? Why the hell did I wipe it from my memory?"

I'm out of breath and my heart feels tight, constricted. It hurts. I lean forward. Bend over. Moan. Groan.

"Sylvia! Are you okay?" Julia jumps up from her chair. Her hands are on my back, massaging my shoulders, my neck. She whispers in my ear, "Shh, just relax, let it go, everything's going to be okay, everything's okay now."

"Call 911!" Mentayer shouts through the phone.

"No, no!" I sit up, raise my hands. "Stop it, everyone! I'm okay. I got worked up, that's all. Just give me a minute."

I close my eyes, and after a while I'm breathing normally again. My heart slows, stops pounding in my chest. The pain is gone. I tell them I'm okay. I'm embarrassed for going off like that, for scaring them.

"I'm the one who needs to apologize." J. B. is holding the phone close to his face. All I can see are his lips. Turned down. Sad. Filled with remorse. "Even when you kept insisting that Jordane killed Will, I refused to believe you. I should have known better, Sylvia. I'm sorry. And even when you and Julia were practically begging me to expose Jordane's sexual exploits, I wasn't there for you. I'm sorry. I should have been there for you. I was wrong to hold back. I should have helped. I talked to Emma. She told me what happened. I believe her. And I believe you, Sylvia. I believe everything you told me."

"I always believed you," Mentayer calls out in the background.

J. B. holds the phone back. He's smiling but his eyes are moist. "This has been too much for you. And you've had to carry it all alone. But I'm here now, Sylvia. I'm here."

Mentayer's face is on the phone screen now. "You need to take care of yourself, Sylvia. See a doctor if you still don't feel well. Make sure you're okay before you take the bus back home."

"You can stay here and rest," Julia says. "I'll bring the evidence to the sheriff's office and ask them to reopen the case."

My heart speeds up again. "And what makes you think they won't cover it up, like the Bigger police did? They even got the coroner to lie. The whole town lied. No one is going to want any of this to come out. I mean, a lynching in their friendly little town, a murder committed by the son of the police chief?"

"Well, there's good news in that regard," Julia says in a calm, low voice. "Bigger doesn't have a police department anymore. After the mine closed, the county sheriff's office took over."

"So, what makes you think the county sheriff is any different?" I hear the high pitch in my voice. I think my blood pressure may be spiking because I have a terrible headache. "You think they want to file a murder charge against a man running for the U.S. Senate? What if he wins the election and there are charges pending against him? What if they lose the case?" My breath is coming in short spurts now, my head chasing a string of anxious thoughts, one after the other, from the authorities refusing to press charges to Becca being run out of town if they do.

"Sylvia." J. B.'s hand fills the phone screen, his palm facing me like a stop sign. "Let me do this now."

"I'm sorry."

"No need to be sorry. What you *do* need to do is take care of yourself. You've done your part. I will take it from here." J. B. says that with a firmness that stops any further discussion.

I *do* want to take care of myself. I want to live to see Jordane in handcuffs. When I die, I want to die knowing he is in prison. And if anyone knows how to make that happen and what to do next, it would be J. B., wouldn't it? During our history together, with all its ups and downs, haven't we always landed on our feet?

I smile at Julia, then at J. B. and Mentayer. I think about Emma and Karen Roberts. About all the women I know but don't know. They're talking, calmly, confidently, as if we are in the same room as opposed to being in my head. But when I open my mouth to speak to them, they are gone.

Part Four

Together We Rise

Chapter Twenty-Four

It's the morning of October 20, only two weeks before Election Day, and the media event in downtown Monrow City is about to get under way. A week ago, when J. B. suggested a press conference, Anthony Jordane jumped at the chance to promote himself as a caring humanitarian. It was his idea to stage the event here, outside the Federal Building where the U.S. senators' local offices are housed, no doubt thinking it would increase his chances of winning the election.

J. B., feeling both professional and comfortable in his signature gray three-piece Havana suit, stands with his interns on a slight incline with a straight-on view of Jordane, who is busy glad-handing and schmoozing with political pundits, reporters, camera crews from the local TV affiliates, broadcasters from local radio stations and National Public Radio, journalists from major national and local newspapers as well as alternative papers like the weekly *Observer* and three or four small neighborhood and ethnic newspapers, the editor of the *Anishinaabe News*, and an assortment of online bloggers. With election fever at its pitch, and with this being a critical Senate race with two new and relatively unknown candidates virtually tied in the polls, the turnout is even larger than they had hoped it would be.

"We couldn't have asked for a better setup," J. B. says, with a sweep of his hand as if painting a picture in one fell swoop of the ten-story historic Federal Building that covers an entire downtown city block.

"Just look at him . . ." Rory points at Jordane. "That man is clueless."

"He's acting like this is a pre-victory celebration or something," Emma says, her eyes sparkling with confidence and excitement.

Emma looks more like J. B.'s professional peer than his intern today, in a bright red three-piece woolen suit with a single-breasted jacket shaped in at the waist and slim-fit ankle-length slacks. Rory, on the other hand, looks more like a hippie than a *New York Times* intern as he runs his fingers through his shoulder-length dirty-blond hair and bounces on the balls of his feet, shivering inside a T-shirt and threadbare jeans that are no match for the biting coolness of fall mornings in the Midwest.

"Peter texted me. He's ready whenever we are." J. B. nods at the bank of microphones set up in front of the main entrance to the building. "You two can join them as soon as I give you the signal," he says. "Probably in ten minutes or so."

Rory's eyes flit back and forth from J. B. to Jordane and the slightest sound makes him jump as if he's just heard a gunshot or a car backfiring.

"Sorry," he says, "I don't want to be the one to screw things up."

"You won't." J. B. gives him a reassuring smile. Knowing that the responsibility for ushering more than a hundred people into the plaza at just the right time to catch the media's full attention has weighed heavily on Rory, he adds, "Don't forget, you were the one who discovered that Jordane's divested from his casino resort development ventures and is now investing in uranium mining instead."

"That was huge," Emma adds.

Rory smiles. "Not as huge as what you did, Emma," he says.

Rory and Emma stand next to each other with an easy camaraderie despite their differing dispositions, and with their eyes on J. B. as he makes his way down the hill to shake hands with Jordane. And when the reporters, journalists, and TV cameras surge toward Jordane and J. B. glances at his interns one last time with his forefinger raised, they make a beeline for the sidewalk, both talking on their iPhones as they run from the plaza.

J. B. stands next to Jordane, facing the microphones and multitude of smartphones and listening to the soft whirring sound of the TV cameras. He knows exactly how things will go. Two days ago, he sent a briefing paper—the findings of his investigation—to his network of journalists so they will be ready with questions that Jordane isn't prepared for and certainly doesn't want to answer. And yesterday, Peter Minter told him what *he* planned to do today and assured him everyone was ready. Now all J. B. has to do is get things started. The rest will take care of itself.

"Good morning! My name is J. B. Harrell," he says into the microphones.

"I'm with the *New York Times*, but I got my start in journalism right here, as a reporter for the *Monrow City Tribune*." He pauses, returns a thumbs-up to some of his former colleagues. "Thank you, Anthony Jordane, for agreeing to come today to answer some questions that have come up about your campaign platform. Would you like to make a statement first?"

Jordane eagerly leans into the microphones and, with his muscular arms open and a sparkle in his eyes, proceeds with his usual stump speech about how he is going to improve the economy, education, and life circumstances for everyone. J. B. stands back and lets him ramble on for several minutes before stepping in.

"Thank you, Mr. Jordane. And now, I presume, you are ready to take questions?"

"Of course." Jordane smiles as if he isn't at all bothered about being interrupted, but his eyes betray him.

Here we go, J. B. tells himself. He takes in a deep breath and, remembering Jordane's angry reaction when he first realized he was being extorted, braces himself for whatever his reaction will be now. Then he asks the first question to get things started.

"When you began your candidacy, Mr. Jordane, there was a considerable amount of excitement and support for your platform. I think it included five, or was it six, promises, is that right?" J. B. lowers his chin and raises his eyes at Jordane, waits for him to nod before going on. "Please remind us now, if you will, what those promises were, and tell us how you plan to keep them."

Jordane smiles like he thinks he's a savvy politician, and even as his eyes shoot daggers at J. B., he doesn't miss a beat. "The reason the latest poll shows that I am ahead," he says, "is because the people of this state know me as someone who keeps his word. They trust me to follow through on all the commitments I have made."

J. B. wants, with every fiber of his being, to jump in and expose Jordane right then and there, call him out for spouting bullshit as if it were fact, dispute every single outrageous claim he just tried to make. But he holds back, trusting the other reporters to do that, his impatient fingers tapping the lining of his jacket pocket as he waits for things to unfold.

Fortunately, he doesn't have to wait long. From half a block away he hears the rhythmic heartbeat of Anishinaabe drumming and the sound of Indigenous singing. The music gets closer and louder, then echoes through the plaza, drowning out Jordane's voice and diverting the attention of the microphones and cameras away from him. J. B. crosses his arms and smiles as he takes in the beautiful sight: Peter Minter, leading close to two hundred people into the plaza, some dancing and wearing traditional clothing, some carrying signs.

Indigenous Lives Matter!

Ban Uranium Mining on Indian Land!

It's All Indian Land!

Looking physically diminutive and wizened inside the rabbit-skin blanket that warms him, and walking with slow, deliberate steps, Peter makes his way toward Jordane. He turns to face the reporters. The drumming and singing stop. The plaza is silent as everyone falls under the spell of the Indigenous elder now standing before them, a giant of spirit, dignity, and wisdom.

Rory scurries to place a stool behind the microphones, high enough for Peter to be seen and heard without him having to stand, and then moves inconspicuously into the background, his job successfully finished. Jordane, barely able to hide his irritation with a flick of his shoulder, steps away from the microphones to make room for Peter to sit down. Peter raises his hand in a gesture that puts him in charge. All the cameras turn toward him.

"My name is Peter Minter. I am Anishinaabe."

Jordane moves in fast, stands next to and towers over Peter with a full-of-himself smile. "It is good to see you, my friend. Thank you for coming."

With no visible expression on his face, Peter turns his upper body ever so slightly toward Jordane. "We have questions." He pauses like a pro, waiting for the microphones and cameras to zoom in on them, and then, with one simple word that says it all, asks, "Why?"

"I'm afraid I don't understand what you mean," Jordane says. "Why what?"

"Why don't you answer my calls?"

"Oh my, I do sincerely apologize if that is true. My staff has been very busy. As have I, of course, with all the demands of campaigning, but trust me, that will change once I am elected, and things settle down. I'm sure you understand."

Peter looks up as if contemplating the sky before saying, "What I understand, Mr. Jordane, is that it takes much energy when you are pursued by larger animals."

"That is just so true, isn't it," Jordane says, oblivious to the smiles appearing on people's faces or the sounds of chuckling.

"I am sure it has been very time-consuming," Peter says, "for you to take so many calls and meetings and contributions from so many nuclear power and uranium mining interests."

A tinge of pink travels up Jordane's neck and settles on his cheeks. "I'm not sure where that information is coming from," he stammers.

"Perhaps you want to check your financial records?"

Jordane touches Peter's shoulder, then quickly withdraws his hand when Peter winces. "The thing about politics is this," Jordane says. He bites his bottom lip and examines his right hand as if looking for the next lie in his palm. "Well, you know, much as we may not like it, the more money you raise, the more people you talk to, the better chance you have of winning. And the reality is that before I can help your people, I must first get elected. I am on your side, Peter, and I do so appreciate your coming and asking me such hard questions so I can set the record straight." He raises his arms, palms out, in a gesture more dismissive of Peter than expressive of gratitude.

Everyone stands in silence as if waiting for a signal from Peter, whose face speaks volumes that his people understand only too well and about which, they know, Jordane is clueless. The reporters, anticipating an altercation, move in closer while J. B. stands back and relishes the scene from a distance.

"Why?" Peter raises his hand again. "Why have you stopped financing the development of casino resorts? Why have you invested in uranium mining instead?" His voice, until now rising like a symphonic crescendo, strong and loud, crashes to a stop. "It's okay, Mr. Jordane. We already know the answer." He turns his head from side to side, rests his eyes one by one on the reporters, then looks into the TV cameras. "What we want is for the American people to hear us. And believe us."

Peter stands up from the stool, turns away from Jordane, and walks away. The drumming and singing resume, along with chanting. *White man lies but we won't die . . . He always lies. We never die. Gichi-mookomaan giiwanìmo. He always lies.* The reporters chase after Peter with their arms outstretched, shoving microphones in his face. He swats them with the back of his hand.

Anthony Jordane is beside himself now, stuttering and glaring at J. B., holding his hands up, near his face, in a fighting stance. "Did you know they were coming? Did you?"

J. B. suppresses a grin and says, "I can see why you're upset. Just let it play out. Wait for your chance to respond."

The protesters encircle Peter, hiding him so well that he seems to have disappeared. The drumming and chanting stop. With nothing to see or hear, the reporters turn away, shift their attention back to red-faced Jordane. They shout out questions: *Mr. Jordane, are those allegations true? Mr. Jordane, are you really supporting the mining industry now? Mr. Jordane, what happened to your platform?*

Jordane, with an ingratiating smile, raises both hands for silence, and then makes an eloquent attempt to repair the damage. "I want to thank my dear friend Peter Minter, and all you beautiful original peoples, for coming out today," he says. "I sincerely apologize for this unfortunate misunderstanding. Let me assure you, winning this election is critical to our success together. That is what my campaign is about. Winning. For *you*, dear friends." He brings the palms of his hands together as if saying a prayer or conferring a blessing on the protesters. "And now, I think we have a few more minutes if there are any other questions?"

The silence that follows sends a clear message that no one is buying Jordane's bullshit and no one wants to hear any more of it. There's no need for the reporters to ask any more questions. No point in challenging him only to hear more lies.

"Mr. Harrell?" Jordane steps back from the microphones with a look of angry desperation on his face, clearly thinking the ordeal is over.

J. B. smiles and places his hand on the man's shoulder. "You might want to stick around a little longer, Mr. Jordane."

Chapter Twenty-Five

"Are you ready for this, Mr. Harrell?" Karen Roberts rubs her hands together.

J. B. recognizes Karen's deep voice before he sees that she's standing next to him with her feet apart in a combative stance. He has never seen her in person, only on Zoom, and he is struck by how short she is for someone with such outsize confidence.

"Sylvia said you'd be here," he says.

"I wouldn't miss it for the world."

Karen Roberts, after a quick up-and-down attorney examination, nods her approval. "You're taller than I expected, Mr. Harrell."

And you're shorter than I expected, he says, but not out loud. Just then the Indigenous drummers, singers, and dancers move off to the side, and the reporters and TV camera people focus on the pathway they've created down the middle of the plaza. For a few seconds, the only sounds are the chirping birds in the trees and, intermittently, the cars driving by on Sixth Avenue.

Then, here they come, a silent river of red moving along the sidewalk in front of the Federal Building then flowing down the path into the middle of the plaza. Jaws drop. Cameras click and whir as they capture the breathtaking image of thirty-six women—in twelve rows, three women in each row—marching toward the entrance to the Federal Building with their chins raised in defiance. Young women in their twenties and thirties. Older women in their seventies and eighties. Women of all ages in between. Women of different sizes, shapes, skin tones. All dressed in red. Ankle-length dresses or skirts. Thigh-length miniskirts. Pantsuits. Coats, jackets, shawls. Bright, penetrating red. Blood red.

J. B. nudges Karen Roberts's shoulder. Sylvia is at the front of the line, walking with a surprisingly steady gait, pointing at Jordane with her cane.

"She'll be on the front page of every newspaper tomorrow," he says, "and on every TV news station tonight."

"She's an incredible woman," Karen says, "but I guess you've known that for a long time."

"All my life," he says with a proud smile.

The line of women is getting closer. *Damn,* J. B. says to himself as he takes in the new, and clearly expensive, clothes Sylvia is wearing: the bright red ankle-length wool dress, red felt boots, and red faux-fur knee-length coat topped by a stylish wool beanie hat with a big floppy red bow. She looks even more stunning to him than Julia, who flanks her on one side in an attractive red double-breasted wool coat, or Emma, on the other side, in her stylish red pantsuit.

Emma sees them watching and gives Karen Roberts a little wave. It's an *I am so grateful that you are my attorney* kind of wave. Karen nods at her, a *You're the best client ever* kind of nod. Then Emma winks at J. B. It's a *Didn't I tell you?* kind of wink. He salutes her, a *Bravo for you, you proved me wrong* kind of salute.

"I was skeptical about her plan," he says to Karen, "to use social media platforms—all of them! Facebook, YouTube, Instagram, TikTok, Pinterest, even more—so they could reach women from a broad range of ages and demographics. I was surprised when she got six hundred hits, but I thought most of them would turn out to be illegitimate."

"I guess she's proved she can deliver what she promises," Karen says.

He laughs. "At first she stuck out her tongue ever so slightly and bit the tip of it, like this."

"Like a dog with a bone," Karen says with a knowing smile. "Once Emma's teeth are in something, she won't let go. I'm like that, too."

J. B. realizes now what a herculean effort it must have been for Emma, Sylvia, and Julia to track down every last one of those social media hits. Interviewing every woman who as much as mentioned Jordane's name. Spending hours and hours on the phone or on Zoom. Traveling to meet with some of the women in person. All that listening, sympathizing, sharing, reassuring, persuading. All that money raised to cover some of the women's travel expenses for today.

And now here they come, thirty-six women walking tall, moving as one body with no shame, victims no longer. Jordane watches them with a smile on his face.

He leans down, his hand over the side of his mouth. "Do you think he's flattered to have so many women approaching him?"

Karen Roberts looks up at Jordane, and chuckles. "Hah! He doesn't know what's happening."

But when the women form a tight shoulder-to-shoulder circle around him, Jordane's smile quickly evaporates. He turns his head from side to side, takes a step to the left and then to the right in search of an escape. There is none. The women have him surrounded, and in their eagerness to capture the scene for posterity, scores of reporters with microphones and cameras jockey for position outside the circle.

With their arms linked and their feet taking one sideways step at a time, the circle of women slowly revolves around Jordane in silent judgment, a singular moment of reckoning.

After one revolution, the circle stops, and Emma steps forward. She reaches into her jacket pocket, pulls out a piece of paper, and slowly unfolds it to its full eleven-by-seventeen-inch size. She holds it up in front of Jordane, a mere six inches from his face. He shakes his head. Flashes a smile of fake sympathy. Reaches his hand out to her. She shakes the sign at him. It brushes his cheek. He recoils. She turns around and holds the sign high. Makes sure all the media can read what it says:

> *Last month, Anthony Jordane sexually assaulted me in his campaign office. I was a volunteer.*

TV cameras whir. Smartphone cameras click. Emma lays the sign on the ground, face up, and rejoins the other women. Arm in arm, the circle moves again, the women chanting: *We're survivors, we're united, we will never be divided.*

One more revolution and the circle stops again. This time Julia steps forward and, like Emma, unfolds a piece of paper and holds it in front of Jordane's face, then turns around and shows it to the media.

Anthony Jordane raped my sister. She was only fourteen.

After placing her sign at his feet, Julia rejoins the circle. The women chant as they make one more revolution around Jordane. Then they stop and, one by one, each woman holds her sign up to Jordane, then turns and shows it to the media.

Anthony Jordane grabbed my breasts and forced me to kiss him.

Anthony Jordane sexually assaulted me at the office holiday party.

Anthony Jordane raped me and said it was consensual.

Anthony Jordane threatened me.

After each woman has had a turn to make her indictment public, the circle moves around Jordane again, this time with the women chanting louder and more defiant than before: *Hey hey, ho ho, Anthony Jordane has got to go! Hey hey, we say no, sexual assault has got to go!*

Jordane claps his hands. He raises his arms high and waves his hands in the air. He brings his fingers to his mouth and whistles. Whistles again. He grabs a microphone from a baffled-looking young reporter and brings it close to his lips. The mic makes a screeching sound that is deafening. Even the women hear it and stop chanting.

"Oh, ladies! Ladies!" Jordane shakes his head and speaks into the mic in a sugary-sounding sympathetic voice. "I am sorry that you have been hurt. It is nothing short of criminal the way my opponents have exploited your pain in this way." He turns to look directly into the cameras, purses his lips. "I am innocent of these charges," he says. "And while they are categorically false and invented solely for political purposes, the pain these women are feeling is real. That is why I am listening to them. That is why all of us must listen to them. The way they are marginalized is nothing short of criminal."

He turns to face the now open-mouthed women and says, "Ladies, you have my word. As your senator, I will stand up for you. It is way past time for an equal rights amendment, and I promise you, I will fight to get it passed."

Jordane's brazen show of arrogance is astounding even to J. B., who looks on in disbelief. Is there no end to what that man thinks he can get away with? Is there no end to what he really *will* get away with?

"Where are they, anyway?" Karen Roberts stands on her toes and tries to see over all the cameras, reporters, and protesters. "They should be here by now." She reaches into her jacket pocket and pulls out her phone.

Just then pandemonium breaks out. Sylvia is shouting at Jordane. "Shut up, shut up, shut up!" she screams. She waves her cane at him with one hand, and with her other hand reaches for a microphone offered by a sympathetic young woman reporter. She stands in front of Jordane, her face flushed as she looks him in the eye.

Karen elbows J. B. and looks up at him. "Amazing," she says. "She looks more than twenty years younger than she really is, don't you think?"

He shakes his head and crosses his arms over his chest. Yes, Sylvia looks good, standing ramrod straight like she has no arthritis. But J. B. knows her. Only too well. He's alert and ready. Just in case.

"Remember me, Tony." Sylvia uses the mic as she talks to Jordane so the media doesn't miss a word. "You tried to rape me. I was seventeen."

"I'm sorry, but who are you?" Jordane curls his lip up on one side.

"You know damn well who I am, Tony. You tried to force me into your car, only I got away thanks to my friend Will, remember? And that pissed you off so bad that you beat him up, didn't you? Then you found someone else to rape, a very young girl, only fourteen, who was even more naive than me. Did you know she committed suicide, Tony?"

"This woman seems to be having a mental breakdown!" Jordane calls out. "Could someone please help her?"

"But Will knew what you did, and that's why you killed him, isn't it, Tony?"

Jordane grabs Sylvia's cane and raises it up in the air. J. B., chilled to the bone when he sees the icy look on the man's face, tries to push his way through the media maze to get to them. But Sylvia, in what would be considered an amazing show of strength for any octogenarian, much less one who only recently was in the hospital for a cardiac arrest, uses both of her hands to grab her cane back from Jordane and strikes him with the end of it, right in his lying mouth.

"Security! Someone! Call security!" Jordane cries out.

Just then three uniformed police officers push their way through the chaos. One stands directly in front of Jordane and the other two stand next to him, one on each side.

"Thank God you're here," Jordane says to the officers. He touches his bottom lip, looks at the blood on his fingers, and escalates his performance. "She assaulted me! That woman right there! The crazy one! The one in red!"

Sylvia stares at the officers, her body shaking and her hand covering her mouth like she trying to hide that she's laughing. The other women look at her with worried expressions on their faces. "Oh God, Sylvia," one of them moans. "Did you have to go and get yourself arrested?"

"If they arrest one of us," Sylvia says with a defiant smile, "they'll have to arrest all of us." She hands the microphone back to the reporter and lowers herself down onto the hard concrete, her legs out in front of her and her hands holding her back straight.

That does it. One by one the other women also sit down, and soon all thirty-six of them are on the ground with their arms linked.

"Just wait," Sylvia tells them, barely able to suppress a giggle.

"You are *not* going to believe this," Julia adds with a smile.

"All's well that ends well," Emma tells them. "You'll see."

Karen Roberts pumps her raised fist up and down with unbridled exuberance.

J. B. scrunches up his face, at first confused. But then he sees the patches on the officers' uniforms.

"You knew? This is who you were waiting for?" he exclaims.

"I was hoping," Karen says with contagious excitement.

They stand side by side and watch, knowing that on TV, computer, and smartphone screens all across the country, untold numbers of people will also be bearing witness to this same unfolding scene.

"Are you Mr. Anthony Jordane?"

"Yes, I am. And I will soon be Senator Jordane!"

"We are officers with the Altos County Sheriff's Department, sir."

"Okay, okay, I don't care what department you're from. Just arrest that woman. Do it!"

"Mr. Jordane, we have come to take *you* into custody."

"What? You're kidding me, right?!"

"No sir, we have a warrant here for your arrest."

"For what? Come on, is this a media stunt? Who's behind this?"

One of the sheriff's deputies holds out a pair of handcuffs, another one puts his hand on Jordane's shoulder and turns him around. "Anthony Jordane, you are under arrest for the murder of William James. You have the right to remain silent. Anything you say can and will be used against you in a court of law. You have a right to an attorney. If you cannot afford an attorney, one will be appointed for you."

The whir and click of cameras drowns out the songs of birds and the engines of cars as, in shocked silence, people in the plaza step aside and make way for three deputy sheriffs to escort an angry and shaken Anthony Jordane to a black-and-white car parked on the street. People crane their necks, eager to watch him put into the back seat by an officer, who places his hand on the top of Jordane's head. They scramble to capture images of the car, the gold letters *Sheriff Altos County* on its side, and Jordane's profile in the back window. And as the car slowly pulls away from the curb, J. B. turns to Karen Roberts with his hands outstretched and asks, "How the hell did you pull that off?"

Chapter Twenty-Six

Two Months Later

J. B. and Mentayer snuggle together on the couch. The late-afternoon sun casts shadows over the exotic pink wall in their high-ceilinged living room, and the old radiator in the corner wards off the winter chill with a loud clanking noise. Sylvia sinks into the faded brown chair in the corner, her frail body swallowed up by cushions worn over the years into the shape of Mentayer's grandmother, her small hands resting on frayed armrests saturated with precious memories. There's no need for the lightweight throw blanket folded neatly on the footstool in front of her. She is plenty warm in the new purple hoodie and matching pants she bought at the after-Christmas sale that Mentayer took her to yesterday. She'd never been to Saks Fifth Avenue before. Never witnessed such extravagance. Hadn't known what Mongolian organic cashmere was. Had never before experienced the pleasure of such luxurious softness on her thin, aging skin.

"It's almost time." J. B. reaches for the remote control on the coffee table in front of the couch. He presses the button and the large TV mounted on the wall comes to life with the news anchor on the screen. The anticipation in the room is palpable.

> *Our next news segment is an object lesson in how to lose an election. Stay tuned to learn some of the ways a recent candidate for a U.S. Senate seat doomed his own campaign. Our coverage begins in sixty seconds.*

J. B. mutes the commercials and leans back on the couch. Mentayer pats his knee, then smiles and winks at Sylvia. "Do you remember," she says, "how worried he was that your allegations against Jordane were going to be leaked to the press?"

"Be fair," J. B. says with a defensive shrug. "I was worried about the tabloids, not mainstream news like this. And that was before we had evidence to support the charges against him."

Mentayer raises her eyebrows, not about to let her husband off the hook. He knows she's right. He knows she loves him. They both love him. He looks at Sylvia with a sheepish grin and says, "And that was back when I still didn't believe you."

Sylvia shrugs to let him know that's all water under the bridge, then looks him up and down with a twinkle in her eyes. "Oh, you mean back when you used to iron your clothes."

J. B. studies the wrinkles on his long-sleeved red and white striped shirt in mock horror, then points at Sylvia with a mischievous smile. "And when you used to buy all your clothes at the Salvation Army and Goodwill."

"And you styled your hair." She giggles. "Or at least combed it."

J. B. runs his fingers through his hair and leans forward, ready for his turn.

"Enough, you two," Mentayer says. "It's starting." She grabs the remote from J. B.'s hand and unmutes the TV, turns up the volume.

> *Two months ago, Anthony Jordane, a candidate for the U.S. Senate, was ahead in the polls and expected to win. But then he held an ill-fated press conference at the Federal Building in the capital city of his home state. This is what happened.*

A video clip appears on the screen of the Anishinaabe drummers, dancers, and singers making their grand entry into the plaza. It is followed by a news clip of an interview with Peter Minter, but before they watch it, Mentayer pauses the TV.

"I didn't realize he was that small," she says.

Sylvia nods, thinks about how Peter looked like a miniature person with that rabbit-skin blanket billowing out like a curtain from his slight frame. "But whenever he speaks," she tells Mentayer. "I tell you, he turns into a giant among men. Turn it back on, you'll see for yourself."

The camera zooms in on Peter's face, so he does indeed look like a giant among men on the screen. And with the microphone held close to his lips, his voice is loud and clear when he pronounces Anthony Jordane a liar and a charlatan, having made promises to defend sovereign rights and protect his people and their land from uranium mining that were bogus. A graphic illustration of Jordane's six-point campaign platform is shown while Peter describes all the ways that Jordane violated it. Then the camera focuses back on Peter.

"Does this mean, Mr. Minter," the reporter asks, "that you're giving up on the uranium mining issue?"

"Oh no, not at all," Peter says. "The fight continues, with inspiration from people like Leonard Peltier, an old AIM friend of mine, who reminds us that our strength is in the power of our people, and that nothing is over until it's over."

Sylvia asks them to pause the TV for a minute. "I still find it hard to believe," she says, "that you and Peter were willing to give Jordane the benefit of the doubt."

"You say that like it's a bad thing," J. B. says with a chuckle.

"And what makes you think it isn't?" She gives him a look that says she's half-teasing and half-serious.

"Aww, so glad you asked," J. B. says with a wide grin. "It isn't a bad thing when good comes out of it." He points at the image frozen on the TV screen, the one that lists all the dangerous health risks of uranium mining. "Getting national coverage like this, for example, is a really good thing."

"You're right," Sylvia says.

"As always." He grins.

"I do believe," she says, falling right into it, "that you are referring to me, not yourself."

J. B. picks up one of the colorful pillows on the couch, the bright yellow one, and tosses it to Sylvia. She tosses it back. "The red one, please. It goes better with purple." He blows her a kiss and tosses the red pillow to her. They watch the rest of the news clip with Peter Minter, and when there's a commercial break, Mentayer goes into the kitchen for more tea and cookies.

"Thank you again, Sylvia, for reading the draft of the exposé I wrote about Jordane for the *New York Times Magazine*," J. B. says with a smile. "It's going to be published next Sunday. Are you sure you're okay with how I portrayed you and your family?"

"The truth is the truth," she says, "no matter how ugly and no matter how close to home. The religious PAC that contributed to Jordane's campaign is affiliated with the evangelical church that my grandfather, Harlan Jensen Sr., founded. My father, Harlan Jensen Jr., was a member of the lynch mob that threatened Will. I like to think my mother didn't know about that, and I'm glad she's not here to read about it now. But you had to write the truth, all of it. You had to make all the connections. And your piece is brilliant. Are you really sure you want to retire, J. B.?"

"A year from now," he says. "I want to research my family, too. Get to know my siblings. Thanks to my birth parents, I'm officially enrolled as a member of the tribe, and Peter's already helping me explore my roots. I'm thinking about writing a memoir."

Sylvia hugs the red throw pillow to her chest and rests her head on the back of the chair, thinks about what a struggle it had been for J. B. to make a decision about what to do about Jordane, and about all the good that came out of that struggle.

A short teaser appears on the TV screen—another video clip from the media event, this time showing the sea of women in red streaming into the plaza—just as Mentayer returns with the tea tray.

After one more commercial, the full video clip comes on the screen: the women marching toward Jordane, getting closer and closer to him. Sylvia shudders, remembers when she first found herself face-to-face with Jordane, the sudden and inexplicable fear she felt in that moment.

"Hey! Look! That's you!" Mentayer points to another news clip that is now on the screen. A Monrow City reporter, an enthusiastic woman in her late twenties or early thirties, is interviewing some of the women as they left the plaza that day.

"Can you tell us, ma'am," the reporter asks, "why you came today?"

The hard-edged fury in Sylvia's eyes blazes out through the TV screen. "I am here because Anthony Jordane is a rapist and a murderer," she says. "I am here because he belongs in prison, not the U.S. Senate."

J. B. grins and leans back on the couch, his hands clasped behind his neck. Mentayer whoops, claps, and bounces up and down on the couch. Sylvia covers her mouth, wonders if that floppy bow on top of her red beanie looks classy or just plain gaudy.

But it doesn't matter one way or the other. What matters is that all those women, especially the younger ones, when they think back to that day, they will always remember how they spoke out and said they weren't going to take it anymore.

> *And now we are joined live in our New York studio by Karen Roberts, the attorney for some of the women you just saw in that video and in those interviews. Thank you, Ms. Roberts, for coming today. I understand you are representing a New York Times intern who has accused Anthony Jordane of sexually assaulting her while she was a volunteer at his campaign headquarters, is that right?*

Mentayer moves to the edge of the couch, her hands clapping. "I can't wait for tomorrow! Where are we meeting her again?"

"Shh," Sylvia says with a flap of her hand.

J. B. is mesmerized by the no-nonsense image Karen Roberts projects on TV in a plain and inexpensive-looking black jacket and black blouse, no jewelry or makeup, her short blondish hair parted on the side, nothing stylish about the woman. It strikes him that she reminds him of Sylvia, twenty years ago. How is it that he never noticed that before, he wonders?

> *Yes, that's right. Thank you for inviting me. It's an honor to be here.*
>
> *Ms. Roberts, what can you tell us about the sexual assault case against Anthony Jordane at this point?*

Sylvia, J. B., and Mentayer watch, all three of them spellbound by the way Karen Roberts responds to the anchor's questions with both the combative instincts of a street fighter and the shrewd cunning of a seasoned diplomat.

> *I recently deposed Mr. Jordane, who is charged with*

second-degree sexual assault in the case you're referring to. Just last week in fact . . . The trial isn't scheduled yet . . . Three more women have filed sexual assault charges against him . . . so far . . . There may be more . . . Living through what these women have lived through is extremely hard. Yet they have endured. And they didn't just survive, they stood up. I'm very proud of them, not just the ones who are willing or able to file charges against Jordane, but all those women who have stood up to other men like him . . . The women in the video clips are just a tiny sample of innumerable other women who have been assaulted by men . . . I can't tell you much more about this particular case at this point. Murder cases take precedence, so it's likely that our case will be slow-tracked pending the murder charges against Jordane.

I want to ask you more about those charges as well, Ms. Roberts. But first I want to show this next video clip.

Another video clip from the media event appears on the TV screen, this one of the sheriff's deputies approaching Anthony Jordane. Handcuffing and arresting him for the murder of William James. Mirandizing him. Leading him through the plaza and out to the street. Putting him in the back seat of the Altos County Sheriff's car.

Mentayer pauses the TV. "Sweet, sweet revenge," she says. "This must feel soooo good."

Sylvia has to think about that for a minute. "It was never about revenge," she says. "It was more about spending my life making amends to Will for not saving him, and now, finally, getting justice for him. No, it's not about revenge. But watching this sure does feel good." She laughs, something she does often these days.

"I didn't know the deputies were coming," J. B. says. "I still don't know how Karen Roberts orchestrated his arrest—in public, no less." He sighs and then says, "I tried every trick in the book, and still couldn't get the sheriff to reopen the case."

"He was facing a tough re-election campaign," Sylvia says. "He wasn't about to do anything controversial or upsetting to the voters."

"I tried to convince him that reopening the case would advance his career, not hurt it," J. B. says with a faux grumble. "I should have known better."

"It's easy to forget what it's like in small-town white America," Sylvia says. "Especially when you've lived in the big city for such a long time."

"See, there you go," J. B. says with a wry smile. "You forget about your past, and it's only a matter of time before it turns around and bites you in the ass."

"And we all know what that's like," Mentayer says.

"Well," J. B. says with a long sigh, "whatever Karen did or said to the sheriff worked."

"She didn't do anything," Sylvia says. "She went around him. Went to a judge instead. Got him to issue an order to reopen the case and authorize a full forensic investigation of the new evidence to determine if there was a compelling reason to pursue charges against Jordane. And that was that."

"I talked to a guy I know who's in the FBI," J. B. says. "He says convicting Jordane of murder will be a slam-dunk. The evidence is damning. His fingerprints and William James's blood on the pocketknife. The tape-recorded testimony of someone who was there. Plus, a tape-recorded confession."

"And," Sylvia adds, "Becca's now willing to testify, too, if they need her."

"Instead of being a U.S. senator for six years, Anthony Jordane is going to be a prisoner for the rest of his life." Mentayer claps her hands and then unpauses the TV.

> *One more question, Ms. Roberts. What do you know about the murder case against Jordane?*
>
> *I don't know much. I do know that Jordane has been charged with murder and released on bail pending trial. I don't know anything else at this point, only, as I said before, that the murder case will likely take precedence over the sexual assault case. There is, however, an overlap between the two cases, since Jordane's sexual assault of two women is part of causation in the murder case. One of those women is dead, but it's likely the other one will be called as witness. Women's*

voices will be heard. In both cases. As for the sexual assault case, I am confident that we will win that one, too. Mr. Jordane is a bully. And these women eat bullies for breakfast. And lunch. And dinner.

Sylvia throws herself back in the chair, laughing. J. B. and Mentayer join in, although neither of them seems to be completely comfortable with what Karen Roberts just said on national TV.

"That Karen," Sylvia says once she's collected herself. "She says whatever she's thinking sometimes. And she can talk anyone's arm off. Did I tell you about the time she was at my place? Emma was there, too, and we had work to do, but Karen just kept talking, talking, talking about this, about that. Finally, Emma asked her if she could stop talking for a minute, and you know what she said? She said, 'No, Emma, I can't. I honestly can't. I was born talking, and I haven't been able to stop since.'"

Sylvia starts laughing again, short, sharp, guffawing sounds that expand into a full-out belly laugh. Tears stream down her cheeks. Her laughing is contagious, too, and soon Mentayer is doubled over. J. B. is holding his stomach. He says something indecipherable, and that sets them off again. They don't stop until they collapse with exhaustion.

"You and Karen are cut from the same cloth," Mentayer says as she wipes the tears from her eyes.

"I can't wait to see what the two of you will tackle next," J. B. says. "I bet you're already plotting something."

What an odd thing to say, Sylvia thinks. *He knows how old I am. And aren't he and Mentayer always saying that I should slow down, that I've done more than enough in my life already?* She looks out the window at the night sky and the reflections of the city lights. It's her bedtime.

"I'm old, I'm tired, and I am done," she says in the end. She tries to stand up but flops back down with a sigh. She's a bit out of breath. She moves to the edge of the chair, her hands on the armrests, tries again.

J. B.'s eyes mist over as he rushes to help her. "I wish you'd reconsider coming to live with us," he says.

She shakes her head and pats his hand. She looks forward to tomorrow. Having lunch with Karen Roberts at the rink at Rockefeller Center, always lovely over the holidays, then packing for an early-morning flight the next day. This will be her last trip to New York.

"I've loved every minute being here with you," she says, "but now it's time to go home."

She sees J. B. and Mentayer exchange worried looks. They know she lives in the only building still standing after years of gentrification consuming her neighborhood, and that it's only a matter of time before it, too, will be demolished. But even though her apartment is shabby, and the building is in disrepair, it's her home. It's where she intends to live.

"Would you at least consider extending your visit," Mentayer says. "Maybe another week? We could spend a day in the Bronx."

Sylvia shakes her head. "I want to remember the Bronx the way it was. Not like Bigger. I didn't *want* to remember my hometown the way it was, or even remember it at all. Maybe I was afraid to. I mean, if I remembered that everyone thought something was wrong with me, then maybe *I* would think that, too. Maybe forgetting was my way of protecting myself. Anyway, I guess it worked, because most of my life I didn't think I had a problem. And I for sure know that now. You know it, too, don't you?"

J. B. squeezes her shoulder. "Do you really want me to answer that?"

She laughs and slaps his hand. Then she hugs them both, says good-night and goes into the guest room, closing the door behind her. She lies down in bed to the quiet of snowflakes dancing in the air outside the window, carried by a gentle night breeze. With an extra quilt keeping her toasty warm and J. B.'s playful banter putting a smile on her face, she decides to buy a new coffee pot, one of those nice espresso makers, when she gets home. Then she drifts off to sleep.

Notes

1. “In the power of our people, we find strength” From Leonard Peltier: “I remain undestroyed,” *Workers World*, June 26, 2024, https://www.workers.org/2024/07/79600/. Leonard Peltier, once an American Indian Movement (AIM) activist, spent nearly fifty years in prison for murder, after a trial whose fairness has been questioned ever since. On January 20, 2025, Leonard Peltier’s sentence was commuted by President Joe Biden so that he can live the remainder of his life at home.
2. United Nations Declaration on the Rights of Indigenous Peoples Adopted by the UN General Assembly in 2007, UNDRIP is the most comprehensive international instrument on the rights of Indigenous peoples. It establishes a universal framework of minimum standards for the survival, dignity, and well-being of the Indigenous peoples of the world and elaborates on existing human rights standards and fundamental freedoms as they apply to the specific situation of Indigenous peoples. https://www.un.org/development/desa/indigenouspeoples/wp-content/uploads/sites/19/2018/11/UNDRIP_E_web.pdf
3. United States Radiation Exposure Compensation Act Enacted in 1990, RECA was intended to provide one-time payments to uranium workers who worked in the uranium industry from 1942 to 1971 and later developed specific diseases after being exposed to radiation from uranium mining. RECA expired in June 2024. S.3853, the Radiation Exposure Compensation Reauthorization Act, which passed the Senate

on March 7, 2024, with a vote of 69-30, would extend this act for six years. As of February 2025, this bill has yet to be considered or voted on in the House. https://armscontrolcenter.org/fact-sheet-radiation-exposure-compensation-act-reca/

4. Uranium is required for nuclear power
The nuclear power industry is currently making a comeback as a solution to the climate crisis based on a false belief that nuclear power is clean energy. The reality is that nuclear power plants produce nuclear waste in a process that begins with uranium mining. The mining of uranium is an extremely dirty process that isn't immediately apparent to consumers. A lot of fossil fuels are required to extract uranium and process it. In addition, for every pound of "enriched" uranium that goes into a nuclear reactor, an average of over 5,000 pounds of radioactive waste is produced. Most of this waste is in the form of rocks, dust, and uranium mill tailings that are primarily dumped on the ground or in ponds located at or near mines and mills. In the United States and in most other parts of the world, uranium mines, mills, and enrichment plants are disproportionately located in Indigenous peoples' territories and in communities of color. Many of these communities now suffer from birth defects, cancer, immune deficiencies, and other diseases as a result of contamination from uranium and its byproducts. See https://www.nirs.org/one-small-step-for-nuclear-fusion-no-giant-leap-for-climate-action/ and https://clamshellalliance.com

5. For more information:
    - The Anti-Uranium Mapping Project: https://www.antiuraniummappingproject.com
    - *Wastelanding: Legacies of Uranium Mining in Navajo Country (2015)* by Traci Brynne Voyles, University of Minnesota Press

Until It's Over: A Book Club and Readers' Guide

Questions and Topics

1. What is the significance of the novel's title, *Until It's Over*? Discuss possible meanings and why you think the author selected the title.
2. In *Until It's Over*, the two main protagonists (Sylvia Jensen and J.B. Harrell) must face the past traumas they experienced related to the social issues that impacted them personally (sexual abuse and childhood separation and loss). How was Sylvia's life impacted by the trauma she experienced as an adolescent, both in positive and negative ways? Similarly, how was J.B.'s life impacted by the trauma of childhood loss?
3. Both Sylvia and J.B. heal from their childhood traumas while in the process of addressing a social issue (uranium mining on indigenous land). When and how did you first become aware of issues related to uranium mining? Discuss the concerns that were raised for you about uranium mining in the story. What more do you want to learn about the issue?
4. Both J.B. Harrell and tribal elder Peter Minter in *Until It's Over* face ethical dilemmas about whether or not to support a clearly flawed candidate for the U.S. Senate. How do they resolve those dilemmas? What were their reasons for taking the stances they took? Did your notion about what was the best or right decision shift as you read? Discuss your thoughts and questions about the ethical implications embedded in the story.
5. *Until It's Over* is a story about healing from childhood trauma. What made it possible for Sylvia Jensen and J.B. Harrell to heal? Discuss how each of them changed at different points in the story

and why. What evidence is there that healing was occurring and/or had occurred?

1. What did you think about how the book ended? Was it satisfying? If so, why? If not, why not? How would you change it?

Further Resources About Uranium Mining

Anti-Uranium Mapping Project
https://www.antiuraniummappingproject.com/

Developed by Shayla Blatchford, this is a vital historical documentation of the uranium mining era from a Native perspective, an immersive learning experience that weaves together personal stories and environmental concerns.

Wastelanding: Legacies of Uranium Mining in Navajo Country. Voyles, T.B. (2015). University of Minnesota Press.

Websites providing information about Uranium mining and the current push to advance nuclear Power:

1. Nuclear Information and Resource Service (NIRS) https://www.nirs.org/one-small-step-for-nuclear-fusion-no-giant-leap-for-climate-action/
2. Clamshell Alliance https://clamshellalliance.com

ACKNOWLEDGMENTS

My deepest gratitude and respect go to all the survivors of sexual assault and abuse and to all the people impacted by uranium mining on indigenous land whose stories inspired, infuriated, and informed me while writing *Until It's Over*. A special thank you to those who helped me ground the novel in real people and historical events: to April Obi (Quinault) for sharing her personal story of how her life trajectory, like that of J.B. Harrell, was shaped by the Indian Child Welfare System; to Fran Danis for compiling the transformative stories of sexual abuse survivors and change agents in *Origin Stories from the Movements to End Domestic Violence*; to Shayla Blatchford (Diné) for creating the Anti-Uranium Mapping Project https://www.antiuraniummappingproject.com/; to Traci Brynne Voyles for writing *Wastelanding: Legacies of Uranium Mining in Navajo Country*. While *Until It's Over* is a work of fiction and all persons, geographic locations, agencies, and community organizations are entirely the creation of my imagination, the too often ignored and invisible injustices inflicted on survivors of sexual abuse, uranium mining, and a flawed child welfare system are imbued in every character developed and every storyline plotted.

Writing this book was, as always, a team effort. I continue to be indebted to two outstanding writers, editors, and teachers who have been critical to my development as a novelist. Hal Zina Bennett coached me through those first fledgling steps many years ago, and the wizardry of Max Regan helped transform *Until It's Over* (and all my other novels) into the mystery you now hold in your hands. Thank you to my writing group members, Mary Kabrich, Roger Roffman, Cedar Monroe, and Milla McLachlan for their always wise feedback. For the Boulder writers' group for their support and feedback, Beverly Kimmons and Melanie Miller. For the final stages of production, I am grateful to Kyra Freestar for her outstanding copyediting. With deep admiration and appreciation, I thank my step granddaughter Kai Conrath for designing the cover. A special shout out and deep gratitude, as always, to Kevin Atticks and the entire Apprentice House publishing team. As always, I am indebted to my wife, Susan, whose unwavering support makes everything in life possible.

ABOUT THE AUTHOR

Dorothy Van Soest is a professor emerita and former university dean with four previous novels published by Apprentice House Press—*Nuclear Option* (2021 winner of Reader Views and IPPY awards), *Death, Unchartered* (2018 winner of an American Fiction Award), *At the Center* (2015) and *Just Mercy* (2014)—in addition to eight nonfiction books and over fifty journal articles, essays, and book chapters. Van Soest and her wife live in Seattle. www.dorothyvansoest.com

Apprentice House is the country's only campus-based, student-staffed book publishing company. Directed by professors and industry professionals, it is a nonprofit activity of the Communication Department at Loyola University Maryland.

Using state-of-the-art technology and an experiential learning model of education, Apprentice House publishes books in untraditional ways. This dual responsibility as publishers and educators creates an unprecedented collaborative environment among faculty and students, while teaching tomorrow's editors, designers, and marketers.

Outside of class, progress on book projects is carried forth by the AH Book Publishing Club, a co-curricular campus organization supported by Loyola University Maryland's Office of Student Activities.

Eclectic and provocative, Apprentice House titles intend to entertain as well as spark dialogue on a variety of topics. Financial contributions to sustain the press's work are welcomed. Contributions are tax deductible to the fullest extent allowed by the IRS.

To learn more about Apprentice House books or to obtain submission guidelines, please visit www.apprenticehouse.com.

Apprentice House Press
Communication Department
Loyola University Maryland
4501 N. Charles Street
Baltimore, MD 21210
Ph: 410-617-5265
info@apprenticehouse.com • www.apprenticehouse.com

www.ingramcontent.com/pod-product-compliance
Lightning Source LLC
LaVergne TN
LVHW010611100826
845148LV00014B/2915

* 9 7 8 1 6 2 7 2 0 6 7 8 5 *